Highland Wedding

Pink

For Freddie, my wee star

First published 2019
PRINT ISBN: 978-1-9997738-5-4
Copyright © Emma Baird 2019
The right of Emma Baird to be identified as the author of this work has been identified by her in accordance with the Copyright, Patents and Designs Act 1988.

All rights reserved. No part of this book may be reproduced or used in any manner without the express written permission of the publisher except for the use of brief quotations in a book review. Any person who does any unauthorised act in relation to this publication may be subject to criminal prosecution and civil claims for damages.

This is a work of fiction. Names, characters, places, and incidents either are the products of the author's imagination or are used fictitiously. Any resemblance to actual persons, living or dead, businesses, companies, events, or locales is entirely coincidental. Entirely. Except for those in the public eye who are referred to in a tongue in cheek way.

Cover design by Enni Tuomisalo of https://yummybookcovers.com[1]

Published by Pink Glitter Publishing. If you would like to receive (infrequent) email newsletters from the author, please email her at pinkglitterpubs@gmail.com. In return, she'll send you a free short story about the early days of Caroline and Ranald's relationship.

https://emmabaird.com[2]

---

1. https://yummybookcovers.com/
2. https://emmabaird.com/

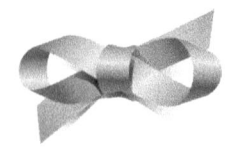

List of characters:

Gaby—a graphic designer of some talent and a woman who staked her future on moving to a small village in Scotland.

Jack—Gaby's boyfriend. Mean, moody, magnificent. Also bears a resemblance to Jamie Fraser/the actor Sam Heughan. His much better-looking younger brother, as Jack would tell you.

Mildred—their fabulous, and fabulously spoiled cat.

Katya—Gaby's best friend, a freelance writer, Pilates aficionado and talker of much sense.

Dexter—her boyfriend, an American too fond of hyperbole and long working hours.

Caitlin Cartier—a 'self-made' reality TV star billionaire at the age of 22, thanks to the beauty company she set up. Some of you might think she is based on a real-life person. The author refers you to the front of her book where she tells you everything in this book is fiction and any resemblance to real-life characters coincidental. Entirely.

Hyun-Ki—a hyper-talented South Korean graphic designer. Loves cats.

Mhari—a 'friend' of Gaby's and to date the nosiest woman in the world.

Lachlan Forrester—Mhari's on-off boyfriend. Upon reflection, he prefers the 'off' status.

Psychic Josie aka Dr McLatchie aka Caroline—Jack's mum, a GP who has embraced her side hustle as a psychic full time, the side hustle she freely admits is a complete fraud.

Jolene—a New Zealander expat and new mum with weird taste in boyfriends.

Stewart—boyfriend of the above. Worshipper of all things porridge and alcoholic.

Ashley—owner of the Lochside Welcome in Lochalshie, where you will find one of the world's most Instagrammable toilets, and a man desperate for business.

Nanna Cooper—Gaby's gran and the woman who could manage Brexit if only those daft politicians stood aside and let her.

Zac—posh, blond. Unspeakable.

CHAPTER 1

"Yes!" Jack punched the air, surprising the people around him who jumped back in alarm.

"Yes what?" I piped up. We'd found a spot in the field's edge which wasn't so crowded. This year's Lochalshie Highland Games had not drawn in as many people as last year's event, which had been graced by the presence of one of the biggest reality TV stars in the world, but it was still busy. Mother Nature had granted us a warm, sunny day too, rare in the north-west of Scotland.

From where we sat, I could see the tops of heads as dancers competed on the stage and the queue that snaked all the way around the park as people waited to see Psychic Josie, international medium consulted by all the stars. (As she herself put it.) From time to time, the bagpipes sounded. Earlier that day, the local pipe band dressed in regimental tartan marched down the High Street to start the games, and a few of them hung around piping tunes for the dancers and hammer throwers.

"The results are in!" Jack showed me his phone. As a long-time resident of Lochalshie, Jack held the record for best caber tosser in the area. And, as I often told him, the best-looking caber tosser. Shockingly judgemental of me to say so, but the competition wasn't high. Meeting any of the other contenders on a dark night guaranteed nightmares.

Jack's screen showed the Lochalshie WhatsApp group—the first and often the only source of up-to-date news for the area. Angus had sent out a rude message questioning the accuracy of the result but was one hundred percent certain the village's biggest tosser had won.

"I've regained my pride," Jack said. "First again."

Last year, he didn't win—distracted thanks to his pursuit of me. He was back in the game this year. The sun caught the red in his hair and made it gleam. I fell in love with Jamie Fraser's far more handsome and younger brother, and I still tingled when I looked at him. The Games competitors all looked the part—kilts, Timberland boots and tight T-shirts. Biased I know, but no-one wore a kilt better than Jack. He had the knees to carry it off. And the biceps to show off a skin-tight black T-shirt, and the calves that displayed socks to full adv—

"Gaby?"

I snapped to attention. Tempting as it was to sneak off home for a little tumble, we were committee members. Our job today was to help organise the Highland Games and ensure everything ran smoothly.

I ruffled his hair. "Good," I said. "I only date winners." Whispered, "Sleep with."

He laughed and leaned over to kiss me, a tiny peck on the lips that took me back to our first kiss on this same day one year ago. Once upon a time, I lived in Great Yarmouth with my boyfriend of ten years who was, not to put too fine a point on it, a douche bag. Chance took me here—the village in the middle of nowhere—when I signed up for cat-sitting services. As a fanatical Outlander fan, I'd been delighted to discover the village contained Jack, Jamie Fraser's (better-looking) double. We didn't hit it off at first, but the path of true love never does run smooth as the cliché goes. When we got together months later, it was all the sweeter for the wait.

And what a year it had been.

"What's the prize, oh champion tosser?" I asked Jack. "One thousand pounds?"

That was the cash prize last year. In my head, I'd spent the money already starting with a long weekend in a luxury hotel somewhere in the city where I rediscovered retail therapy and the two of us romped on a bed we didn't have to make afterwards.

"Ah… ten pounds and a wee dod o' shortbread."

Oh well. Last year's generous donation was a one-off. Though it seemed cheeky to force the winner to make his own prize. Yes, my boyfriend not only tossed cabers with aplomb, he was a dab hand in the kitchen. His shortbread had won the best bakery entry overall in the village's version of the Great British Bake Off, which had taken place earlier this afternoon.

"We'd better make our way over there," I said, "so you can have your picture taken receiving the prize for best caber toss." And then upload it onto the village website and Facebook page. If it's not on social media, it never happened right?

The Games were almost finished. The crowds had drifted away, and the stallholders were packing up. I'd seen plenty of people carrying bags brandishing the names of local companies—those selling soap, candles, hand-knitted jumpers, food and everything else artisan and craft-sy. Jack's stall advertising his authentic Outlander (ish) tours of the Highlands had taken sheet-loads of sign-ups to his mailing list, which promised a good start to next year's tourist season.

We picked our way over the field. Torrential rain the week before had turned it into a quagmire. The sun had come out today and the day before, making them the best ones of the summer so far. A miracle. The muddiness was due in part to building work going on nearby. The Highland Games took place in the large greenfield area next to the Royal George hotel. It had been bought last year by a company determined to expand. And the field was under threat. Next year, we'd need to find somewhere else to hold the games.

"Jack!" Angus waved us over. He sat at a table in front of the roped-off area for the actual games. Kids mucked about, trying to turn over the smallest of the tractor tyres. A few of them managed, which was more than could be said for me. I tried taking part in Highland Games activities once—the result a broken windscreen on an expensive car thanks to losing control of a too-heavy hammer.

"Fancy a go at the tug of war?" Angus said, standing up. I had to strain my neck to look up at him. He was also a rugby prop—a truly terrifying prospect to face. No wonder he doubled up as a bouncer at our local pub.

Jack squeezed my hand. "Nah. Gaby and I were going to head home and—"

Just what I'd been thinking too. But Angus butted in.

"New team put themselves forward. Calling themselves the Royal George champions."

Rivalry between the Lochside Welcome and the Royal George, the two pubs that bookended the village, had always been fierce. This year it was worse than ever. The expansion of the hotel threatened the Lochside Welcome—our favourite pub. The George never usually bothered with the tug of war. This year they must be trying to prove something. Honour was at stake.

Jack turned to me, eyes glinting. Often, I had to pinch myself. My mind would feverishly run through his many plus points. Red-head! With lovely knees! Jamie Fraser or rather Sam Heughan look-a-like but better... Then, I'd give my mind a ticking-off for being so shallow and make myself list the good points that didn't relate to his appearance. Kind! Maker of fantastic shortbread! Considerate! Fun to be with.

...a-may-zing between the sheets.

We'd seen little of each other during the past week. It being August, the tourist season was in full swing and Jack left most mornings at sparrow's fart, not returning until nine or ten o'clock at night. He was off tomorrow and we'd planned to sneak away from the games early and... catch up.

"You go," I said, prodding him forward. "And make me proud."

He and Angus exchanged eyebrow-raises—an 'as if!' thing I guessed. The Highland Games champion caber tosser and hammer thrower along with the other rugby boys, and Stewart who fuelled himself on industrial quantities of lager and porridge. What could the Royal George team throw at that?

Jolene wandered over to join me, baby clamped to her front. Macmillan Junior was a month old and—luckily for him—had inherited most of his mother's eight percent Maori genes. A tiny dark head nestled against Jolene's chest and snored gently. She'd put those baby headphones on him to protect against the bagpipes.

"How's Tamar?" I asked, resisting the impulse to stroke his little head. As a later in life cat lover, I wasn't sure what you did with babies but I assumed they didn't enjoy being stroked the way cats did.

"Fine," Jolene said, reaching her arms behind her so she could stretch out her back. "Though I wouldn't mind heaps more sleep at night, eh?"

Like many New Zealanders, most of what Jolene said sounded questioning.

"And is Stewart...?" Pulling his weight. A delicate question. Stewart's second home was the Lochside Welcome. I didn't know how much that had changed since the arrival of baba. Or if his attendance there had increased—a reluctant father too eager to leave the demands of parenthood to the woman.

She grinned—large straight white teeth gleaming, and the movement highlighting the dimples she had on each cheek. "Devoted. Tamar's his perfect audience. He doesn't mind listening to Stewart for hours at a time. Works a treat to get him off to sleep."

Oh to be a baby! If you nodded off when a person started banging on about the mysteries and marvels of coding as Stewart loved to do, no-one considered it impolite.

"Blast it!" Jolene's tone changed. Alarm. She pointed across the field.

I followed the direction of her fingers—the Royal George and a line of people who'd walked out of it. The tug of war wasn't always about bulk and size, but having heavyweights on your team was an advantage. Every man swaggering out of the hotel was three times the height and width of a normal person. Except for the end guy who looked familiar though I wasn't close enough to see.

"Right," Jolene said, unbuckling her baby harness. "He's been fed and changed, and he's fast asleep."

To my dismay, I realised she meant me for me to hold Tamar. Oh heck. Before I could mutter, "Gosh, are you sure?", she strapped the baby to me, dropped a kiss on his head and strolled over to the Lochside Welcome team.

That was the thing with Jolene. She was far fitter than your average person and stronger too. All the way through her pregnancy she jogged and weight-lifted—all the better to pop your baby out in under two hours, as her GP (and my almost mother-in-law Dr McLatchie) told me later.

The team members lined up, eight on each side, one behind the other and a thick strand of rope lying to the side of them. Word must have spread. Those crowds drifting off home drifted back inside the park gates. Whistles, cheers, boos and catcalls started up.

I booed myself when I worked out who the Royal George's end man was. Zac Cavanagh, one-time resident of Lochalshie, would-be boyfriend of my best friend and murderer. Come on, the Lochside Welcome team!

"The rotten, sodding cheats," Laney Haggerty hissed beside me. Owner of the local riding school and a cousin of Ashley, proprietor of the Lochside Welcome, she had skin in the game. "Channel 5 is filming the World's Strongest Man in Inverness. The Royal George has bussed them all in. I hope their steroid-filled biceps explode under the strain."

I could hardly bear to watch. These monsters dwarfed Jack, Angus and the others. The teams picked up the rope, the centre line above a marking on the ground. Jolene, face grimly determined, was third in line. Jack was behind her, his face equally so.

Big Donnie—and even he looked tiny next to the George's team—held a whistle and conferred with the teams' drivers. He positioned himself at the line marked on the ground, raised his arm in the air and dropped it, blowing the whistle at the same time.

The teams' drivers yelled instructions. "It's no' just about big bulging muscles," Laney said, eyeing the other team in their wife-beater vests with distaste. "A team needs rhythm too so they harmonise their traction power."

I nodded as if I understood what she meant, my eyes fixed on the middle of the rope as it moved one way then the other. The whistles, cat calls and jeers grew louder. Laney gripped my hand and Tamar stirred, his little mouth opening and shutting before he twisted his head the other way and returned to baby snores.

A faint cheer but a much louder boo sounded as the George's team yanked the Lochside Welcome's four metres over the centre line.

"Best of three!" someone yelled, and the teams nodded.

Second time round, the driver's pep talk must have worked. After what felt like the whole field willed on the Lochside Welcome team to "heave!", the George's overgrown athletes stumbled over the centre. Tamar's baby headphones did their job. The ear-shattering cheer that went up didn't disturb him.

So, one-all. Laney started muttering the Hail Mary under her breath.

Once more, the teams lined up, feet dug into the ground and scowls all round. Jack twisted his head and blew me a kiss. I blew him one back and concentrated on bargaining with everyone—God, the universe, Big Donnie even, any old Celtic god whose spirit still hung around.

Please. Let. Them. Win.

And if they did... An idea took root. What about if I...? Yes, yes, yes! The team's win would be a clear sign from the universe. Approval, even.

The George's too-big crew hauled the rope over to their side so easily, our team fell forward—the ground yanked out from underneath them. The boos rose once more. I cursed, upset because the universe had just signalled disapproval for my plan. The omens had seemed so promising too.

Laney shook her head. "No way," she said, ducking under the rope that fenced off the field. She marched over to Big Donnie. He blew his whistle once more and called both teams back.

"What did you say?" I asked when she returned. "Those rotten cheats cheated again," she said. "Did you notice the guy second at the back? He had the rope over his shoulder. Not allowed!"

Big Donnie conferred with the teams' drivers. Both sides gesticulated wildly, but another cheer went up when every team member returned to their positions. A replay then. Beside me, Laney muttered, "Hail Mary, full of grace, the Lord is with thee..."

The ground wouldn't help the Royal George. Those overgrown heavier than average bodies were ankle-deep in rain-sodden soft soil. The cry, "Heave!" started up once more, and both teams grasped the rope and pulled.

Laney bargained. She'd resume regular chapel attendance; even get up at 8am to attend mass every morning. "What are you going to do, Gaby?" she asked as we watched the rope nervously. "Give up pizza and chips for two months?"

"No! I'm going to do something much better."

"... blessed art thou amongst women, and blessed is the fruit of thy womb, Jesus... Oh aye? What are you going to do?"

I tapped my nose.

This time, the universe listened. Seconds later, the George's giants fell forward and everyone around us exploded—yelps, hoorays, claps and wolf whistles. Time to fulfil my part of the bargain.

I ran and then slowed, mindful Tamar might stir (he was still, miraculously, asleep) towards the victorious team. Jolene got to me first, her poor hands red raw and the palms bloody but the smile lighting up her face showing she felt no pain. I offloaded Tamar and Stewart joined us, monologuing about porridge and its amazing capabilities.

Everything flew over my head. There was only one person I had eyes and time for. And there he stood... again, the sun catching the glint of his hair, longer than usual but a perfect length to run your hands through. The sun that back lit him and set his profile in sharp relief. And those dark eyes when he turned towards me...

The perfect place to ask, right? The modern woman did not wait for a man to make his move. She jumped in and asked what she had been thinking about for... ooh, an age. Circumstances now presented me with the perfect moment. Universe approval, remember?

"Jack! Will you do me the great honour of becoming my wife—husband, husband, slip of the tongue!"

Jack's brow wrinkled. I watched two emotions chase their way across his face. Puzzlement and... oh, was that dismay?

"Did she just ask Jack tae marry her?"

Argh—yikes. The crowds had died away, so the small number of people around us had heard me loud and clear. An audience hadn't been part of my original plan for good reasons. My phone pinged. Easy to guess the cause—the Lochalshie WhatsApp group updating with the news. I couldn't see her, but the WhatsApp number one updater must be nearby.

In the background, a lone piper sounded, and traffic noise drifted over as cars made their way out of the village. All I heard was silence.

A man who didn't impulsively yell, "Yes, yes, a thousand times yes!" and punch the air.

Tamar chose that moment to wake up, loud cries that pierced the air.

You and me both, Tamar. I'd misread the situation completely. Was it possible to recover from such a public proposal when someone turned you down...?

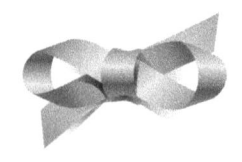

CHAPTER 2

My phone pinged once more. The wretched WhatsApp group. A speech bubble hanging on the screen: "He's no' said aye!" and "Why no'? She's a lovely lassie!" The thing where people pretend kind concern while at the same time revelling in your misfortune and embarrassment.

I cringed and considered my options. My best friend is a style-it-out expert. I channelled her. Nothing came through. Jack faced me, his expression back to a blank. It looked neither pleased or displeased. In the days before we were an item, I reckoned he would make an expert poker player.

He took my hand. "C'mon, Gaby. Let's go."

Let's go? LET'S GO?! Around us, people murmured, asking the same question I did, I guessed. Dude, you've no' answered the lassie's question. Are ye gonnae marry her or no'? Out of the corner of my eye, I spotted Zac—Lochalshie's one-time resident. He raised his hand to wave at me. I ignored it. I make a point of not acknowledging murderous scumbags.

Jack tipped his head to the side, gesturing towards our house a mere three minutes' walk away. I nodded gratefully. Perhaps he wanted me to do the proposal properly—get down on one knee and ask. At which point, he'd punch the air and say, "Yes, yes, a thousand times yes." Throw in, an "Are you sure, Gaby? I don't know if I'm good enough for you."

Stewart, who had yet to develop social awareness skills, jogged behind us followed by Scottie his West Highland white terrier. "Are youse off the pub?" he asked. "Jolene says Ah can have one pint if Ah promise to change wee Tamar's nappies for the next ten days."

"No!" I snapped. "We've got stuff to talk about."

When Jack smiled, fingers squeezing mine, relief washed over me. Thank goodness. Yes, he longed to settle down to a detailed discussion about wedding venues, menus, cakes and whether or not I opted for the full meringue dress-wise.

Someone called out Jack's name. Ashley. The Lochside Welcome had done a roaring trade so far today on half-price pizzas and cocktails invented especially for the games. He didn't need our custom. I pulled Jack's hand, still unnerved by the non-answer to my question.

"I'd better see what he wants," Jack said. "Sorry."

As we headed over, Mhari sidled up. The Lochalshie WhatsApp group updater extraordinaire. Mhari was one of the first people I met when I moved to Lochalshie. Her nosiness was legendary. There wasn't a single aspect of a person's life Mhari thought worth ignoring.

"What's happenin'? Are you getting married or no'?" she asked. her face arranged into what she thought invited a person to confide.

"None of your beeswax," I snapped back. Impulse took over. "We're off to the Lochside Welcome to celebrate."

Might be a celebration—might be a drink to drown my sorrows. Another hand squeeze.

"Bad news," Ashley said when we reached him. His normally friendly face looked strained and he shot killer looks in the direction of the Royal George. Extensive refurbishment of the hotel had been carried out at the beginning of the year, finishing only the day before. Once a shabby Edwardian place favoured by coach parties of touring OAPs making the most of their free bus pass, these days its car park was chokka most of the time.

"I'll tell you about it in the pub," he added, dropping his voice. "Free pizza and chocolate cake thrown in."

•• ✤ ••

TEN MINUTES LATER AND a large helping of Chocolate Decadence in front of me—created in honour of the reality TV star Caitlin Cartier and utterly delicious—Ashley told us what he knew.

'Us' being Jack, Stewart, Jolene and Tamar, Mhari and I. We'd taken up stools at the bar. Tourists and visitors occupied the tables at the back, Ashley's staff running back and forth delivering the wood-fired pizzas the Lochside Welcome specialised in. Mhari and Jolene had nabbed their own teaspoons and kept trying to swipe bits of my cake. What was it with women not ordering their own? I guarded it as well as I could.

"The appeal's been overturned," Ashley said as he poured Stewart a pint. "So those evil witches get their way."

Those 'evil witches' was how everyone referred to Lois Berringer and Angeline Manson, the millionaire property moguls behind Hammerstone Hotels and new owners of the Royal George. Last year, they'd come to the village and pretended their acquisition of the place would be a brilliant thing for everyone.

Spoiler—it wasn't. The only beneficiaries were Hammerstone Hotels who appeared to be on a mission to edge out all the local competition. Already, they'd pinched a lot of passing trade. Now, they'd be able to up the ante. Their first planning application had been to convert part of the field/playing park into a glamping site for stressed millennials and Gen Y-ers. After a lot of shrieking and shouting, we had persuaded our local councillors not to pass it. The application went to appeal.

Doom and gloom.

"I'll never drink there," Stewart declared supping his pint. Admittedly, Stewart spent more than your average punter but what difference would it make?

"And I'll make sure every coachload of tourists I pick up gets dropped off for lunch here," Jack threw in. He helped himself to a blob of fudge icing from my cake. At this rate, I'd be lucky to eat half of it. I dropped a bit and Scottie dived for it. Stewart whisked it away before he ate it seeing as dogs and chocolate did not go together. When he stuck what he had recovered from the floor in his mouth, only two people shook their head in disgust. We were used to him.

"They're planning this big launch," Ashley fumed. "So I've heard. Celebrities and everything. Those glamping tents are so warm you can even camp in winter!"

Gosh. So far, I'd experienced one Highland winter. Jack's heating bills shot through the roof. As a former soft southerner, I found the Arctic chill unbearable. And anyway, in the meantime, WHERE WAS THE ANSWER TO MY PROPOSAL? The phone in my pocket vibrated. A hundred or so people asking Mhari via the WhatsApp group, "Well? Has he said 'aye' yet?"

"Gaby," Ashley said, moving along so he stood opposite me. His eyes gleamed. "Would ye like another bit o' cake? Or what about some chips?"

Jack nudged me. Once upon a time, in our pre-dating days, we'd come to the Lochside Welcome for food, and ended up in a chip-off. It's like a boxing match only uglier. People pretend they are happy to share chips. When they are as good as Ashley's. this is never the case. I crammed ten of them all dipped into garlic mayo into my mouth at once to win the competition. Did Jack now remember this fondly? Or did he think to himself, "Hmm. Can I spend the rest of my life with a woman who will always nick my chips?"

"No thank you," I replied, passing the remains of the cake to Mhari.

"I've had this idea," Ashley added, "to bugger up their launch."

Jack turned his head my way. The paranoid bit of me—all of me at present given that he still hadn't answered my question—detected full-scale panic in his eyes. They'd widened, his eyebrows signalling a warning and his mouth stayed straight—no upturn of corners or the flash of teeth that showed when he was happy or pleased. He must have worked out what Ashley was about to ask, as had I...

"We've no' done weddings before," Ashley continued.

I blinked. Jack did too.

"Dunno why," Ashley pointed at the view in front of him. The Lochside Welcome's beer garden sat right on the edge of the loch, as you might expect from its title. On a nice day—though there weren't that many of them—wedding pictures would be superb.

"If you two got married here and invited the entire village, that would be a kick in the teeth for the George. And show off the Lochside Welcome as the best wedding venue in the area? I know you're supposed to get married in the lassie's home town, Gaby, but wouldn't you rather do it here than Great Yarmouth?"

Oh heavens... so now, not only did I have a boyfriend I'd proposed to and put under pressure by doing it publicly, we were duty-bound to marry to save the Lochside Welcome. Stewart, Jolene and Mhari loved the idea. They threw in their own suggestions. Lachlan Forrester could provide the wedding car. (Stolen, probably.) Mhari could do my hair. Ashley could create a wedding cake in my honour this time, instead of Caitlin Cartier, aforementioned reality TV star...

And still no answer from Jack. None of them seemed to have noticed that. No point in a wedding if only one person turns up, hmm?

Jack grabbed my hand. "C'mon," he whispered. "Let's talk."

We slid from our stools. Mhari moved too as if to follow us and I glared at her. Outside, the sun had sunk in the sky colouring it a lovely pinky-orange shade. We took the furthest away table. I felt four pairs of eyes on our backs—our friends, pushed up against the window and trying to listen in.

"Not the end to the day I'd planned," Jack said, and my heart sank.

"Listen, don't worry. I'm sorry it slipped out. Didn't mean for it to happen that way and it doesn't matter, and we can come up with another plan for Ashley. How about dirty tactics, I start spreading rumours that anyone who stays at the George gets food poisoning. I mean, Katya threw up after eating Zac's food, so that might wo—"

When I'm anxious, my mouth runs away with itself. The kiss silenced me, taking me back to our first time. Also beside the loch, also just after the Highland Games. Lips light at first and then demanding. My mouth parted underneath his and I surrendered to the here and now; jolts of electricity firing off in all directions—my throat, my chest, further down...

A kilt makes a man much more accessible. I was just about to reach under it when Jack broke apart, grin in place. "That's more like the end of the day I planned," he said. "Thought I'd get us warmed up."

STILL no answer. Even if the interlude had been extremely pleasant.

"But, but..." I hated how feeble I sounded.

"Oh? Don't actions speak louder than words then?" A sly wink and a grin. He'd been winding me up all along.

"You!" I said, planting one hand on his chest and shoving him away. "Are the biggest, rottenest bas—"

Another kiss, and this time his arms enfolded me, crushing me tightly to that T-shirt and kilt.

"Of course I'll marry you! You pipped me to the post. I had this plan where I asked you at the end of the tourist season. We went to a hotel, one of those ones with a big log fire, I got down on one knee all traditional like, and said, Gabrielle Amelia Richardson, will you—"

Relief can make you giddy. When he kissed me again, my head spun.

"Get a room!" someone called out. Jolene, I decided, and we didn't need to because all too soon we would head back to the house where marvellous, mind-blowing things would take place. After which, I *might* casually bring up the idea of a themed wedding. An Outlander one.

Ashley ran out bearing an ice bucket and a bottle of champagne. He stopped at the table next to us and wiped away a tear. The rest of our friends rushed outside to join us.

"So, so?"

"It's a 'yes' from the mean and moody one," I said, earning me a dig in the side.

"I'm so happy for youse both!" Ashley said, whipping off the foil top and wire cap. The bottle opened with a soft pop. Stewart downed what was left of his pint and held his glass out. Ashley ignored him and poured champagne for me and then Jack.

"Aye, so," he said, once I'd taken a fortifying gulp. My emotions had zig-zagged all over the place in the last couple of hours. "The Royal George's launch and your wedding?"

"Mmm?" I murmured, distracted. The groom-to-be had slung his arm over my shoulder. Out of sight of everyone else, his hand did discreetly clever things, fingers gently brushing against the super-sensitive bits of me.

"...so that gives you just over three months. Plenty o' time, aye?"

Jack and I snapped to smartly.

"What?"

"The launch of the Royal George," Ashley said. "It's December 21. When you get married here. I can't wait to create a pizza 'specially for it!"

CHAPTER 3

Despite our best intentions—and all that anticipatory action we'd built up earlier in the day—we didn't stumble out of the Lochside Welcome until well after ten o'clock.

When Ashley told us the date of the Royal George launch, Jack and I exchanged horrified grimaces. Engagements were all well and good but they were supposed to last ages. We'd hold a party for our friends, everyone would bring us a present (hopefully), we'd hashtag #engaged all over the place, plan our wedding in perfect detail three years ahead of the event and bang! We got married. Three-and-a-half months—or fifteen weeks—must miss out a lot of those key steps. Bad form, for example, to ask people to come to an engagement party (armed with pressie) and then demand their attendance at your wedding a few months later (again armed with pressie).

Greedy acquisition stuff aside, didn't wedding organisation take longer than twelve weeks? Like, a lot longer. Didn't photographers get booked up a year in advance? And weren't you supposed to take months searching for the perfect dress? My proposal had not even included a ring. Mhari had already noted the absence of anything on my left hand.

Jack tightened his hold on my hand. "Aye... okay, Ashley. The Lochside Welcome it is!"

A cheer sounded. Everyone had been listening in, and all those who'd been inside drifted out to join us. Cameras flashed left, right and centre, making me feel as if I was a celebrity. Every single app on my phone beeped—even the BBC weather one (felt like) as folks reacted to the news. Someone pointed out the length of time it had been since the last wedding—years, decades even. Funerals, on the other hand…

Ashley said the champagne was on the house—for me and Jack anyway. He whisked the bottle out of reach of Stewart, who only ever drank out of pint glasses no matter the drink. But everyone kept toasting us and it was only polite to raise our glasses when they did so. Jack's mother appeared too—once the village's GP and now in demand as self-proclaimed Psychic to the Stars, Caroline McLatchie.

"Jack! Gaby!" she exclaimed, throwing her hands in the air. "You've made me the happiest woman in the world!"

Fresh from her packed stall at the Highland Games, she still wore her psychic costume—long tasselled skirt, peasant-style smock top and her hair tucked under a turban. Caroline had kept her side line secret for years. But ever since Caitlin Cartier outed her as the source of amazingly accurate advice, she was proud to tell everyone about her lucrative sideline. I say 'amazingly accurate' because my (almost) mother-in-law once confessed to me she made it up as she went along. Modern life made it easy for the would-be fake psychic. All she needed to do was check out people on social media, read their body language and say she sensed pain and indecision. Worked ninety percent of the time.

"Didn't you see it in the stars then, Mum?" Jack asked. He took a dim view of his mother's activities and often had to rein her in. This year at the Highland Games, for instance, she wanted to charge people £50 for a ten-minute consultation in her tent. Psychic to the Stars prices and all that.

She flapped a heavily ringed hand. "I never use my powers to look at my own family members."

Convenient.

Ashley's promised pizza never materialised so by the time we left, my feet appeared to be working independently of my brain.

"I love you, you know," I said as we headed back to the house, darkness around us. "And I'm the luckiest woman alive!"

"I know. And watch your st—oh, too late."

Crap. Literally. I'd trodden in it—a heap of steaming dog poo outside Jamal's General Store. Despite his combing through his CCTV footage looking for the culprit who made a habit of this, the irresponsible dog owner had never been identified.

"How romantic!" I wailed, wiping my feet back and forth on the grass. "Just as I was declaring my love. And by the way, aren't you the luckiest man in the entire world?"

He winked and grabbed my hand. "C'mon. The luckiest man in the world wants to—"

My phone buzzed—a tinny ring sound I'd given my best friend so I could prioritise her calls and messages.

"WHAT THE..."

Choice expletives followed. Oh dear. Despite leaving Lochalshie months ago, Katya must still be a member of the Lochalshie WhatsApp group. Or our friends' social media posts hashtag GabyJackEngaged gave it away and all before I'd spoken to her. My phone showed eight missed calls.

By this point, we'd arrived back at the house.

"Katya," I mouthed to Jack as he opened the door and I pressed the call back button. Mildred, waiting behind the door, miaowed angrily, her fluffy ginger and white tail waving huffily in the air. Her name was nothing to do with me. We inherited her when her previous owner needed to go into an unenlightened nursing home that did not allow pets. She liked me. Jack she tolerated. Just. That was the deal with cats. If dogs think they are human, cats regard themselves as gods.

"Sorry-sorry-sorry-sorry times a million trillion billion," I said as soon as my oldest friend picked up. Jack rolled his eyes and retreated to the kitchen followed by the still-complaining Mildred, miffed because we were so late feeding her. "But aren't you pleased for me?"

"Marriage is a sorry institution that props up an outdated patriarchal system."

"Thanks, Katya."

"Kidding—well, half-kidding. I'm delighted for you. Have you set a date?"

"Ah, now there's a thing," I dropped onto the comfiest armchair in the room and tucked my legs under me. The phone call would take a while. Jack's expression had changed back to inscrutable, and I wished yet again that I'd done the proposal differently. In private. Nowhere near a landlord with a desperate plan. He pointed to the upstairs bedroom and left again.

There was another wish. In my proposal fantasy, I said the words, he punched the air with joy and we then spent the evening in bed doing filthy things. When I'd first met Jack, I entertained an intriguing fantasy where I imagined his body half-naked and wrapped in a pristine white towel. When I first got to see it, reality surpassed my expectations. Every time I saw him in the buff now, he still made me gasp.

"Twenty-first December," I told Katya.

"Good stuff," she said. "We can have your hen night in September, and you've got more than a year to do Pilates three times a week so your pelvic floor muscles are in excellent shape for a honeymoon that—"

"Katya. It's December this year."

The silence lasted far too long.

"OMG. Why? Are we living in 1922? Are you pregnant and you're marrying so your shame doesn't show too much as you walk up the aisle in a baggier than normal dress?"

"No!" I squawked. "I am *not* pregnant!"

Upstairs, a bang sounded. If bangs could sound part horrified part terrified part relieved that one did.

Mildred butted my hand with her head wafting stinky cat food breath my way. I adjusted position so she could sit on me.

"So why?"

I outlined Ashley's offer / emotional blackmail plea for us to marry in the Lochside Welcome to knock the shine off the Royal George's official launch. And mentioned that I'd seen Zac.

A hiss. "How is the lying git?"

"I didn't speak to him. I don't, as a rule, talk to murderers."

"But your wedding. It's so soon," she said. "I mean... well, I had something to tell you. Dead important in terms of career development."

"Aren't you already wildly successful?"

True. Katya had ghost-written Caitlin Cartier's autobiography stretching it out for 80,000 words despite Caitlin being a mere 22. She'd received a fat fee in advance. The book was due out anytime now, and Katya had negotiated royalties too. She was about to hit the stratosphere. Caitlin now considered Katya a bosom buddy, thanks to the autobiography. They exchanged DMs all over the place. I might have been jealous, had Katya not told me Caitlin considered 750 other people who also worked for her in some capacity as close mates.

"Not me. You."

"Me?"

She explained. I listened, excitement mounting. Gaby, the underpaid, underappreciated graphic designer finally getting the recognition (and money) she deserved. I ended the call.

"Gaby, please hurry up! I want to celebrate properly!"

I raced upstairs. An unbelievable opportunity... How it fitted with me walking up the aisle in three months' time was another matter.

"SO YOU'LL BE FINISHED at seven, right?"

"Yup. They're spending the day on Skye and then we'll be back on the mainland for six o'clock. I'll drop them at their hotel and I'll meet you at the Plockton Inn at seven."

Mildred sat on my small suitcase and eyed me balefully. She knew an owner who was about to disappear for two days when she spotted one. But our two nights away now were a necessity. Two weeks after I'd proposed, and Jack and I had spent ten hours together if I didn't count sleeping—him zonking out as soon as he got in at night.

To be fair, Jack had warned me from the beginning the tourism season was bonkers. And this year, he'd been busier than ever. So busy, I'd yet to tell him what Katya had said to me on the night of the proposal. When we finally ended up in bed that night, amazing things happened just as I hoped. Breaking the mood would be such a waste.

"Tonight's the night, Mildred," I said. "And, um, can you shift off my case so I can put my super-sexy underwear in it?"

Ever tried reasoning with cats? It rarely works. I picked her up for a consoling cuddle and she scratched me in return. Mildred hated being left on her own. I'd arranged for Mhari to look after her, even if I risked having her poke her way around the house looking for anything secretive. I'd hidden as many incriminating items as I could. She wasn't able to stay tonight but she could do tomorrow. Mildred must have realised a night alone was on the cards.

When Jack had said last week he'd be away yet again at the weekend, I stamped my foot. A day later, he sent me a message with a link to the Plockton Inn. "Fancy a night here, gorgeous?"

Too right. Set in a sheltered bay overlooking Loch Carron, Plockton outdid even Lochalshie with its village charms. I'd plugged the location into my phone and Google maps was about to take me there now. I had previous for taking too long to get anywhere in Scotland—the views distracted me—so I set off in plenty of time.

Just as well. Eilean Donan Castle demanded I stop the car, get out and visit it. Then, a group of Americans caught my attention chattering excitedly about Outlander and if the castle had been used during filming.

I bustled up, keen to show off. "No," I said, "but it was in Highlander—the film with the sexy Frenchman and that woman Beatie thingie who has never been in anything since!"

And then didn't it only turn out 'that woman' was leading the tour, the imaginatively named Scottish Film Locations. "Five seasons of Poldark!" one of her party snapped at me. I spent the rest of my visit to the castle ducking out of sight every time she and her group appeared.

Still, the road to Plockton was enchanting weaving its twisty way through tiny hamlets and farmland. Highland cows, their horns scarily long and pointed, sat on the road and didn't seem inclined to move. I peeped the horn and waited. And waited. By the time I got to Plockton it was five past seven. The inn was the first hotel as you drove in. Jack's minibus was nowhere to be seen.

I checked in and headed up the stairs. The room looked onto the high street, beyond which you could see the loch. Signs at a jetty for a seal tour promised your money back if said seals didn't appear. I dumped my suitcase on the bed. "Perhaps," I told my reflection, "I should ask Highland Tours for my money back for the non-appearance this summer of my boyfriend!"

Last year, the tourist season was tailing off when Jack realised I was the woman of his dreams. (He'd been slow on the uptake.) As soon as October kicked in six weeks later, he was all mine for months. Goodness it had been fun. In theory I was working, having negotiated a remote working deal with my boss at Bespoke Design. When your boyfriend dangles keys in front of you and says, "Hey, shall we drive out to Oban and get some fish and chips?" who says no?

Or even better, he dispenses with the keys and dangles himself. "Gaby, I'm bored... shall we go to bed for a while?"

This year, the summer season began gently, but then the bookings stacked up. Throughout May, June, July and August we'd spent so little time together, Mildred sometimes hissed at him when he came in, arching her back, her fur all puffed out. Who was this stranger? Don't get me wrong. Those end of the week get-togethers were exciting. But for the past two weeks we hadn't talked about the wedding once. Or Katya's revelation. And yesterday I'd only gone and said 'yes' to it...

"Think of the money," Katya said when I umm-ed and ah-ed again. "And how brilliant the job will look on your CV."

"Room service!"

I'd recognise that deep, gruff Scottish voice anywhere. I ripped off all my clothes. This must be one of those role-playing scenarios. Plockton was about to reignite our relationship in a wonderful way. I pulled the bobble off my ponytail and shook my hair out. No time to apply make-up but at least I'd shaved everything in readiness.

"Come in!" I thrust out my arms. "Ta da!"

"Your boyfriend sen—"

Difficult to know who was the more horrified—me or the teenage boy holding an ice bucket and champagne. He flushed the exact colour of his scarlet waistcoat, and I discovered that yes when you blush, it can go head to toe. I crossed both hands over my chest, realising too late that left everything else on show.

"Ahem."

Jack materialised behind the teenage waiter who appeared to have frozen to the spot. If he'd been half a minute quicker, this would never have happened. I fled to the en suite and bolted the door. My heart hammed in my chest as I prayed that the lad got temporary but total amnesia covering the last five minutes of his life. Or he was struck dumb and illiterate from this moment forth, unable ever to describe what he'd seen.

I heard Jack and the traumatised teen exchange murmured words, and the bedroom door closed as someone hurriedly made their way downstairs.

A knock sounded on the door. "You can come out now."

I sat on the bath, its porcelain doing a grand job of cooling down my still burning hot in embarrassment skin. Yes, bottoms felt shame too. "I think I'll just stay here."

His voice dropped to a whisper. "You can't. I've just seen the best view in Plockton. If you don't open the door right now, I'll have to batter it down."

An offer I couldn't refuse. Still, Jack might have put more effort into stopping the upward tilt to his mouth. He kept straightening his lips, but the corners moved upwards of their own accord as he watched me edge out, worried Teenage Room Service boy might have hidden himself under the bed.

Jack pulled the naked me into a bear hug and laughed like a loon for far too long.

"Gaby, the look on your face. That poor fella's shell-shocked."

"Shell shock!" I squawked, my face pushed into his shoulder. As I began to recover from the indignity, it struck me there were advantages to this being naked already lark. Hands, for example, could make the most of it, moving up and down leisurely and slowly, making the tiny hairs on my skin stand on end.

"Aye, the family that run this place are God-fearin' souls. You might be the first in the flesh naked woman he's ever seen. You've done the lad a huge favour," Jack said. His voice changed, the words becoming laboured. "And now, seeing as you are…"

Later, we sat up in bed sipping the champagne. "Do you want to order room service?" Jack asked, turning on the TV. "I dunno if I can be bothered moving. Though if we do, both of us will be fully dressed when the food arrives."

At that, he gave me one of those sideways glances. I knew the story would be dredged up for the rest of my life. The time Gaby mistook an 18-year-old waiter for her boyfriend and swung open the door buck naked. Heck, he'd probably even tell it—

"You're *not* to mention this at your stag night," I said. "Or, absolutely not three hundred times no, at the speech you make at our wedding."

He turned onto his side and propped his head on his hand. "Not fair! It's the best story ever."

I thumped him, then ran my finger down his nose, moving gently over the slight bump where he'd broken it at the Highland Games a few years ago.

"Is this all moving too quickly? We, um, don't have to get married. Well, I'd like to eventually but we can wait."

Time to check in with my intended. Why had neither of us mentioned the 'w' word since my proposal? Part of my reasoning behind the 'spur-of-the-moment' ask at this year's Highland Games had been something that happened the week before. Jack had come in after work and caught me watching a repeat of *Don't Tell The Bride*, the programme where the groom-to-be has to organise the entire wedding including choosing the dress. (Always the most contentious bit.) I'd whipped the remote control from underneath me and offered to change channels, but he waved the offer aside and sat down.

"Nah, I quite like this programme. Just out of interest, what kind of dress would you want? And what's your favourite cake?"

I took that as my green light. He likes *Don't Tell The Bride!* He's asking me marriage-related questions! Ergo—he can't wait for me to walk down the aisle towards him. I should ask him soon.

And then he threw me by winding me up after the all-too public proposal. Imagine the cruelty of making a girl wait so long for her answer!

"I want to get married too Gaby. I just... now it's a bit like a runaway train. Every time I go into Jamal's shop, someone tells me they're fair looking forward to our wedding, and do we have a wedding list yet so they can buy us something before all the cheaper presents get snapped up and they're left with the thousand pound telly or something."

"We wouldn't do a wedding list." That seemed the easiest thing to say. 'Runaway train' alarmed me.

Suddenly he was on top of me once more, his body heavy, familiar and comforting. I stared up into those brown eyes I loved and watched a lock of auburn hair fall forward onto his forehead.

"And we do need to help Ashley make the Lochside Welcome the venue of choice for all brides to be."

He kissed me. "Though I doubt any of them will be as daft—I mean, delightful as you."

More kisses, in part to stifle my protests at that character assessment. M'lud, I'm as sensible as the next woman. My best friend testifies to that. When she isn't telling me I'm bonkers.

As he seemed to be in an agreeable mood, I cleared my throat.

"So, I have this thing to tell you." Spit this out as quickly as possible, Gaby, I told myself.

"Dexter has offered me a job with Blissful Beauty in London. Big promotion, tonnes of money for things like weddings. Isn't that amazing?! But he really needed an answer. Like, yesterday and I said yes."

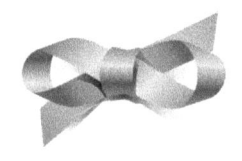

CHAPTER 4

"You said yes? To a job in London? Without discussing it with me first?"

I worked for a graphic design agency. Two years ago, the agency landed the contract of its dreams. Blissful Beauty, reality TV star Caitlin Cartier's skincare and make-up company, hired us. The company wanted to launch in the UK. They needed a local design agency to create their UK-specific site—the agency I worked for. Dexter was their marketing manager and now the boyfriend of my best friend. After a lot of to-ing and fro-ing, they'd lived in Lochalshie for five months before the company recalled him to London.

Those five months had been fun. We teamed up all the time. Dexter was the opposite of Jack—enthusiasm on legs and keen on talking. And my best friend and I loved living close to each other, which we'd done for most of our lives until I moved to Lochalshie. When she said they were moving back to the capital, I cried for days.

Now, an opportunity had arisen. Blissful Beauty dominated the make-up market. They needed more in-house designers. Dexter had worked with me. He wanted to put my name forward for second-in-charge design person. (He didn't call it that—the job had a much fancier title using words I had to look up afterwards.)

But. The killer thing. Blissful Beauty encouraged remote and flexible working, as Dexter had proved with his stint living in Lochalshie. Just not when an employee started. So, I would need to work in their UK HQ for at least six months—in London.

"Gaby, this is an awesome opportunity!" Dexter said when he Skyped me to talk about it. "Like, any graphic designer would kill for this. It would be beyond brilliant if you joined our team."

Dexter loved hyperbole.

Katya wandered into the room behind him and waved at me. "Beyond brilliant," she echoed. The opposite of Dexter, Katya never used such words lightly.

"After you've worked with us, you can take your pick of any graphic design job in the world! And did I mention the salary?"

He did then. My jaw dropped. It was four times what I currently made. I wasn't ambitious but it would be stupid to turn down the job.

I repeated everything Dexter had said, emphasising the 'only six months in London' bit and how much the salary increase would help pay for a wedding. Expensive things, weddings, weren't they?

"You still should have talked about it with me before saying yes," Jack said, getting out of bed and pulling his jeans on. The earlier, lovely mood had disappeared.

"I wasn't one hundred percent sure I would take it until yesterday."

Not one hundred percent, but probably 97.5.

He grunted something in reply and rubbed his stomach. Jack with food in him was far more agreeable. I crossed my fingers that the inn lived up to its TripAdvisor reputation.

"With any luck, that poor guy's not working this evening," I said as we made our way to the hotel's bar lounge for dinner. Sadly for me he was. He froze when he saw us come downstairs, eyes running up and down my body. Checking I was fully dressed, I supposed. At least he didn't seem to have told anyone. The bartender took our drink order with a straight face.

Jack chose the table closest to the window where we looked out at the loch. The sun was setting, and it silhouetted the palm trees. Yes, palm trees in Scotland. I know.

He fiddled with his knife and fork. "We won't see each other."

"We don't now."

"Aye, but the season is almost finished. And I'm thinking of taking someone on for next year so I'm not away as much. And what about the wedding? How will we be able to plan and make arrangements when one of us is miles away?"

"Easy! I'll get onto it next week. Do as much as I can."

Was that possible? Could you book everything you needed in seven days and then do nothing until a week before the big day itself?

A waiter approached our table, asking if we were ready to order. "What are the specials?" Jack asked, glancing at the board on the wall too far away for us to read.

The waiter cleared his throat and looked at me. "Dressed crab. Done to a Jamie Oliver recipe—you know that guy who used to call himself the Naked Chef?"

I shot the traumatised teen a furious look. When he started to laugh joined by the waiter and the bartender, Jack—the traitorous wretch!—guffawed with the three of them.

CHAPTER 5

Psychic Josie, also known as Dr McLatchie, insisted on taking us out for a meal to celebrate our upcoming nuptials, as she called them.

"No need, Caroline!" I said when she mentioned it. "We've got a lot on."

True. After everyone had laughed far too long and hard at me in the Plockton Inn, Jack cheered up and admitted the extra money would come in handy. I was off to London with his blessing. But I only had a week to pack my stuff, sort out what wedding arrangements I could and move to London.

Caroline waved away all my objections, so the week before I was due to fly to London we ended up in the Lochside Welcome once more. As the night coincided with the pub quiz due to start an hour later, the hotel was jam-packed.

As Jack and I made our way through the tables, everyone congratulated us and said how much they were looking forward to the wedding. Which would have been okay if I'd known them well. A good few of them I didn't recognise.

By the time we got to our table, Jack's smile was a faded remain—a ghost-like flicker that was more like a grimace. Mine was fixed in place too.

"Sit doon, sit doon!" Caroline leapt up when she saw us. Ranald, her husband and Jack's stepfather, sat beside her sipping from what looked like his third pint. He found crowds and people trying and coped by drinking copiously and hiding in corridors or the toilets.

He muttered, "Congratulations," and asked if we wanted anything to drink, heaving himself up to make his way to the bar.

"Jack, son," he said as he handed over a beer and a diet coke. Something must have struck him while he'd waited for those drinks and he looked horrified. "I dinnae have to make a speech, do I?"

"No, no!" Caroline waved a hand. "It's usually the father o' the bride that does that. Will your dad be happy to speak about you, Gaby?"

Ah. No, given that I did not plan to invite him. He and my mother split up years ago. He was an okay part-time father but I did not fancy the stress of having him and my mother in the same room.

"I don't know if we'll bother with speeches, will we, Jack?"

"No," Jack shook his head. "Let's not."

"Oh no, no," Caroline said. "Folks expect a wee word or two. They'll be awfy disappointed if they dinnae get to listen to any silly stories. Who's gonnae be your best man, Jack?"

"Er."

A shout came from the bar. "I'll dae it, Jack!"

Stewart.

"Ma Jolene can help wi' the speech."

Oh dear lord, no. We couldn't expose our guests, a captive audience, to Stewart who'd talk about anything and everything in detail and for hours. Porridge, coding and the ever-increasing number of midges in Scotland would all feature. Plus, he'd drink the bar dry beforehand in preparation.

"Lachlan," Ranald said. As he was someone of so few words, the determination in that one startled us. Lachlan Forrester, Mhari's on-off boyfriend, was Ranald's nephew, and he was fond of him. Still, again Jack and I hadn't imagined an old school wedding. I didn't even have an engagement ring yet. We'd thought our big day would be about the two of us—no fuss, no extras and a few friends. And in my ideal scenario, all of us would be dressed up to resemble

Outlander characters, a priest nearby to verify our hand-fasting ceremony.

The ideal scenario I was yet to share with Jack.

"Um," Jack gulped his beer. Whoever he chose, it would offend the other. And we hadn't even started on bridesmaids yet. Again, I thought 'bridesmaid' would be singular and Katya. Going by the general expectation, perhaps not. Were Jolene and Mhari flicking their way through magazines and choosing dresses as we spoke? Or would little nieces and cousins appear left, right and centre demanding to be flower girls?

Speak of the devil, the nosey one herself pushed through the crowds.

"Hiya—I dinnae like to to intrude."

Huh. A lie of a sentence. Mhari liked nothing better than poking her nose in where it wasn't wanted. She didn't wait for a reply and pulled up a seat opposite me. Lachlan hovered behind her. Fingers crossed, he'd heard none of the best man conversation. That decision would require high-level diplomacy on Jack's part.

"Aye, so the wedding," Mhari said, her right hand twirling strands of thick auburn hair round and round. "Who's organising your hen party, Gaby? I fancy a wee jaunt to Ibiza. It's a lot cheaper in October."

My mouth opened and shut far more times than was elegant.

"Hen p-p-party?" Visions of it swam in front of me. Dear lord. Mhari would make me wear L-plates and have us all drinking Prosecco on the flight and annoying every other passenger. The vision intensified to the point where the plane made an emergency landing in Marseilles and grim-faced policemen escorted us off the plane straight into a French jail, complete with damp walls, bars on the window and rats in the cells.

"Ibiza," Caroline joined in. "Aye, that's the ticket. I've always wanted tae go to that Pacha place. Plus, there are loads of celebrities in Ibiza—all of them in need of sane and sensible advice from a renowned psychic."

Great. She planned to use my hen party to hustle for business. Time to nip this in the bud.

"I won't have time to go to Ibiza," I said. Jack gripped my hand under the table and squeezed hard. "I'm off to London in a week's time, remember? So I can't take much time off. A hen party isn't doable."

Mhari tutted, and the doctor shook her head. Protests started but Jack shot the two of them such a fierce look they shut up. I knew this wasn't the end of it, but at least for now we wouldn't get any more outrageous and expensive hen party suggestions.

Ashley drifted over, his Lochside Welcome apron dusted with flour straining over a substantial girth. "I've created a wedding pizza," he said, clapping his hands to get everyone's attention. "In your honour."

"What's on it?" Jack asked. My fiancé was a pizza traditionalist. Four cheese and/or ham at a push.

"It's a sourdough base I make three days beforehand," Ashley said, "and then I top it with home-made tomato sauce, mozzarella stamped out with a heart cutter and I cut Parma ham into strips and make them into G and J initials. Fantastic, eh?"

As everyone else seemed to think it sounded out of this world, I joined in with the cries of 'Brilliant' and 'Can't wait to try it'. The Gaby Jack wedding pizza would be more expensive than the usual ones, Ashley added. Ham-shaped initials, it seemed, were costly things. And he had no plans to offer us this pizza created in our honour for free this evening so we could taste test it.

Normal pizzas ordered, he left us to it. As Mhari and Caroline put their heads together to discuss their ideas for our wedding and Ranald sipped his beer and zoned out, Jack turned to me. "The runaway train, hmm?"

That phrase again, loaded with meaning and none of it good. "I just wanted..."

"I know." Then he startled me, slinging an arm around my shoulder and leaning in close enough to whisper in my ear. "You, me, a few people—preferably no-one else. Plenty of time for parties afterwards, seeing as I plan to live a long, happy life, all the better with you by my side."

Jack didn't much go for 'I love you' and the soppy stuff. He was Scottish, for heaven's sakes. The best most Scotsmen could manage as far as I knew was drunkenly telling their mates they loved them or weeping copiously when their football team lost.

But sometimes, sometimes he came out with words that took my breath away. And stopped every doubt in its tracks. That dark red hair and those brown-y-black eyes I'd noticed from the start. The arm that hung on the upper part of my arm made the tiny hairs there stand on end. Ach, the sooner those pizzas arrived, the better. I had no intention of staying here any longer than necessary.

Jack shared my mood, wolfing down his pizza in record-quick time and earning a cautionary warning from his mother about what happened to people who ate too quickly. The former GP specialised in dire medical warnings. We scrambled to our feet, knocking back the offer of dessert and thanked Caroline and Ranald for the meal. At the bar, Big Donnie took the microphone from Ashley. The pub quiz was about to begin—the perfect time to make our escape.

"Race you home?" Jack asked, cocking an eyebrow at me as soon as we got outside. "Winner gets..." He lowered his voice to describe the rest.

Blimey. Now there was a gold-plated incentive. We flew off, me with the advantage seeing as I'd eaten less pizza than him and I wasn't weighed down by two pints of lager. But Jack was a foot taller and had longer legs—a definite advantage.

It was a close call, but I put my hand on the front door first when we arrived minutes later, laughing and panting hard.

"Ha!" I crowed, "so I'm going indoors where I'll take off—"

My phone rang, its beep loud and insistent. Jack shook his head and mouthed 'leave it,' which was tempting as he was about to fulfil the far-too enticing offer he'd made already. But it might be serious. My mum, say, calling about my nanna who was recovering from pneumonia.

Dexter. Serious too.

I held up a finger. "One minute."

Jack pulled up his T-shirt to flash me a tantalising glimpse of rock hard abs. He unlocked the door and called out a greeting to Mildred, who yowled in response, an indignant cry for food.

"Gaby, hey! How's my super favourite designer?"

"Um, okay?" I shut the door behind me, lingering in the hallway and wondering where this was leading.

"Thing is... we kinda need you to start soon as."

'Soon as' turned out to be Monday. As in three days' time. I'd already handed in my notice. Melissa, my boss, didn't sound that sorry to see me go. Her aunt's best friend's sister had a fresh-from-college son who could take my place (and be paid peanuts). She owed me eight days' holiday too, so I'd be able to bring forward my Blissful Beauty start date.

"I can rearrange my flight," I said, "But I'll need to run it past Jack."

I came off the phone to deathly silence.

"Um, Dexter needs—"

"Don't bother, Gaby. I heard it all."

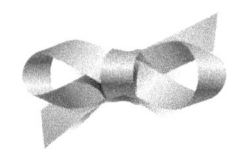

CHAPTER 6

"This is the last call for Passenger Gabrielle Richardson travelling on Flight EZY206 Glasgow to London Stansted. I repeat, this is the last call for..."

Blast it. I hugged my rucksack tightly to me and bolted to the gate. Yet again the Gabrielle Amelia Richardson penchant for (un)punctuality had struck. I'd planned to be at the airport two hours before the flight—Jack driving me to Glasgow where we would do the whole romantic thing. He snogged me, hugged me and wiped away a (manly) tear.

Instead, because I was now flying to London a week earlier than planned, I'd had to make my own arrangements to get to the airport. Jack had a one-day Outlander tour booking the next day. He couldn't possibly cancel it to take little ol' me to the departure gate for our teary farewell.

Post the Dexter phone call the night before, he'd stamped out of the living room whistling on Mildred. (He'd taught her to come to him when he whistled Flower of Scotland—mainly because he always fed her if he did.) She swished out of the room after him into the kitchen. Cupboard doors opened and banged shut.

"Again," he said when he came back, stony-faced. "Please can we discuss things before you decide anything?"

"It's an emergency," I said. "Blissful Beauty's brought forward the launch of a new skincare range and they need the graphic design to support it. What else could I do?"

Then I wittered on about how often we would see each other. I'd fly up to Glasgow every second weekend. He could pop down to London. If you thought about it, the situation would be an improvement on the current one.

"And Skype!" I said. "We'll do that every night. Goodness, we can even do sexy Skype chats where I'm naked and you're naked, and we tell each other—"

Mildred chose that moment to throw up her too-hastily scoffed cat food. A comment on how vomit-making she thought those Skype chats sounded. Or perhaps a reminder that as our fur baby she was too delicate for the details.

Puke cleaned—post the usual argument about whose turn it was—I channelled my inner persuasion powers. We would be fine. The location was temporary. I'd make wedding arrangements from afar. Jack could help too, seeing as we were a modern couple where all the stuff wasn't just left to the bride-to-be, and in three months' time, we'd be on our way to wedded bliss.

"Less than," Jack said. But he'd pulled me to him on the couch. "It's only eleven weeks away now."

"Right! Before I go tomorrow, I'll make a list of everything we need to do."

I meant to start that list too, make it extra pretty by designing it in Adobe Illustrator and adding cutesy pics of Jack and I. But the London job took over. Two minutes after he hung up, Dexter decided I'd already started. He sent me a tonne of emails outlining what I would be doing, stuff about the ethos of the company and how they worked. I read through that email with dread mounting.

How they worked? Hard. Bespoke Design, the agency I'd just resigned from, was strictly nine to five. The first line on the 'work for us' bit of their website said, "Nine to fivers? You're not for us. But while we expect our employees to work hard, we want them to play hard too..." Plus, they liked their designers to be 'on call'.

I thought of my new salary. All the better to buy the wedding dress of my dreams. And splash out on a honeymoon in a destination that took eight hours to fly to, right?

The wedding to-do list never materialised, but at least I'd been able to leave Jack a long list of instructions relating to Mildred's care. He pretended he tolerated her, but I'd caught him kissing her on the odd occasion when he thought I wasn't looking.

Without Jack to take me to the airport, I ended up getting the bus to Glasgow forgetting how long it took. When it ended up on a 25-mile diversion because of a landslide on the A82, another half hour added itself to the journey. By the time I got to Glasgow airport, I was hot, stressed and weepy. "Why, why, why did you say yes to this job," I muttered to myself as I bolted across the concourse, heading for the gate. "You silly moo."

The plane was full. The passengers near me me included 1) a super unhappy baby, 2) a man who'd never heard of antiperspirant, and 3) a woman who kept clutching my hand and telling me flight horror stories where planes plunged to the bottom of the sea. By the time I got to London, I was a quivering wreck.

"Gaby!" Katya met me at the airport and flung her arms around me. We hadn't seen each other in months. As always, she looked amazing. My best friend could walk through bargain basement Primark, pick out five items and put them together in a way that made them look designer. Me? I'd look as if I'd spent weeks living rough.

We had arranged for me to live with Katya and Dexter in the Blissful Beauty flat, located in its HQ. Unlike every other Londoner, my commute would take... ooh, three minutes.

"How are the wedding plans going?" Katya asked as we boarded the Stansted Express.

"Okay. The venue's booked."

"And your dress? The photographer? Flowers? Cake?"

"Not yet, but I can arrange it from here, can't I?"

Katya's brow wrinkled. The train was jam-packed. As I stared around me, I tried to remember when I'd last seen so many people in such a compact space. Lochalshie had less than a thousand inhabitants. The twice daily bus that trundled through it never had more than five people on board.

"I s'pose. Though aren't photographers booked up months in advance? Anyway, I've come up with some ideas for your hen night. I'll email them to you."

Argh. The hen party that refused to die.

"If I must have one, no cocktail master classes," I said. "Or, and you must swear on Dexter's life you won't do this, an army assault course where we have to crawl through mud while a power-crazed Sergeant Major yells at us."

Katya was into fitness. An army assault course would be her idea of fantastic fun. I caught a tiny flicker of disappointment in her eyes. Hmm. The army assault course *had* been an option.

Forty-five minutes later, and we were in the centre of London. Again, the crowds startled me. Everyone, but everyone rushed and pushed past me. I pictured Lochalshie High Street and me sauntering down it—the loch view to the right, the pastel-painted little houses to the left. I shook my head. Tears threatened.

"Isn't it fabulous to be back in civilisation?" Katya asked, pointing at the surrounding crowds. "I enjoyed living in Lochalshie, but when Dexter and I came back here, I realised I'm a city girl at heart."

"Coffees," I said, determined to make the most of my new city status. "So many of them. Everywhere. And very good."

"Clothes shops. Everywhere. And most of them not selling tweed or woolly jumpers."

"Weather," I continued. "Warm and dry six days out of seven."

The escalators took us down into the depths of London and the Piccadilly and Bakerloo line. It was a Saturday. I tried to imagine what the city was like during rush hour and failed. Even at three o'clock every single carriage was rammed full of people.

Located just off Regent Street, the Blissful Beauty flat was on the top floor of an Edwardian-style town house, the HQ took up the entire two floors underneath and the shop was on the ground floor. Katya let us in, telling me it might take a few days to adjust to the noise. Despite triple-glazed windows, London traffic sounded throughout. I'd spent more than a year living in a silent night village. This would take some getting used to.

My bedroom was the smaller one at the back. Whoever had organised the flat's décor and furniture had gone for pared back minimalism—creams, whites and blacks, the pictures on the walls perfect examples of corporate art chosen to blend in rather than grab a viewer's attention. I unpacked my rucksack and thought of Jack, Mildred and our messy home with its blue-y green walls and the oil landscapes he painted in his free time. Tears threatened again.

The front door opened, and a voice called, "Katya? Gaby?"

Ah. Dexter. He must have been doing overtime in the office below the flat. When I met him, he was an eighty hours a week man. Last year, a stress-related illness forced him to cut back on work, but Katya told me he'd started working full time again. Dexter's idea of full-time work didn't match most people's.

"I've got someone I'd like you to meet?"

Someone from Blissful Beauty then. A glance at the mirror in the en suite bathroom told me I wasn't fit for human presentation. I pulled a brush through my hair and hastily applied make-up—the Blissful Beauty bronzer and lip plumper, products sent by angels to help women like me fool people into thinking they've just had ten hours' sleep and eat a wholesome, fresh diet at all times.

From the living room I heard chat—three people joking together. Whoever this person was they had a sense of humour. People who laughed a lot made the working environment much nicer. I let myself into the room and Dexter, a man who favoured old-fashioned courtesy, leapt to his feet.

"Gaby! Awesome to see you! I'd like you to meet your new boss."

He gestured to the man beside him who'd also stood up.

"This is Hyun-Ki Choi. Hyun-Ki, meet Gaby Richardson."

A firm hand gripped mine, the eyes merry and... flirty?!

CHAPTER 7

Hyun-Ki Choi—or 'Hunky' as I christened him in my head—was already the lead designer in a multinational company. I stared at him far too long, astonished someone so young could be in such a high-up position.

"Pleased to smee-meet, meet! you," I said, returning the handshake. Nerves always made me sound half-witted. Katya snorted behind me. Here was the thing. I adored Jack and thought him the best-looking man in Scotland if not the UK, but window shopping did not count, right? And Hunky—I mean Hyun-Ki—was easy on the eye. I put him at just over six foot. Dark brown, almost black hair framed an oval-shaped face, clear skin and perfect cheekbones.

"Pleased to smeet you too," he said back, winking at me and biting his bottom lip. He spoke English with only a faint trace of an accent. Just as well. I was nowhere near fluent in Korean. Katya often joked she wasn't sure English was my first language either when she read the emails or messages I sent her.

"How old are you?" I burst out. "Sorry! Shouldn't ask things like that."

He grinned once more. Koreans must favour the same approach to dentistry Americans did. He had the same white, dazzle in the dark teeth Dexter sported.

"I'm used to it. Twenty-two."

Oh well. Five years younger than me and older than I'd guessed but still ever so young. He must be a design genius. And I'd be working alongside him. Despite Dexter's enthusiasm, I knew Hyun-Ki's skills would far outstrip mine.

"We wanted someone who knows the South Korean market inside out," Dexter said, sitting down again. Everyone else did the same. "And Hyun-Ki specialises in hyper brand-focused design."

I nodded thoughtfully, pretending I knew what he meant. At Bespoke Design, we used to specialise in websites for farmers. I always added a bit of straw or a pitchfork to the pages. Did that count as hyper-brand focused design?

"And the South Korean skincare market is huge—worth $13billion a year."

Next to him, Katya rolled her eyes. She was too familiar with Dexter's reverence for the South Korean market.

"... so we needed an expert on the ground, and you two will be working closely together to ensure Blissful Beauty can maximise its presence and visibility in..."

I zoned out. To be fair to me, my alarm had gone off at five that morning and the journey had been exhausting even if all I'd done was sit around all day.

"We can talk about it on Monday," Hyun-Ki piped up. "When Gaby starts work. I can't wait to work with you."

He smiled at me, and I returned it gratefully.

"Me too, Hunky—no, Hyun-Ki. Hyun, *Hyun*. Oh, silly slip of the tongue there. Goodness me, I must be much more tired than I realised, but working with you, Hunky, Hyun-Ki, *Hyun-Ki!* will be amaze-balls, incredible, totally brilliant..."

As often happened during the (many) embarrassing moments of my life, beside me Katya shook her head in sorrow and sent out telepathic messages. *Richardson, Richardson! Shut up.* Luckily, she decided to step in before Hyun-Ki fled from the flat screaming and Dexter changed his mind about hiring me.

"Do you want to join us this evening?" Katya asked. "We are going to take Gaby out and reintroduce her to the joys of city life via the London Eye and dinner in a hipster restaurant."

He shook his head regretfully. "Can't. I'm sorry. I've got my English grammar night class this evening."

"But your English is amazing!" I said. It was, the words spoken carefully and the accent adding a lilt to the consonants.

"Thanks, but I'm still struggling with past perfect continuous tense. That, and the use of the past participle."

Katya and I waggled eyebrows at each other. As I was the designer, I had an excuse for not knowing what he was talking about. What was Katya's? Last month, I'd read an article online about South Korean teenagers and their school days. The day began at 8am, finished at 4pm and after that most students took a break for dinner before heading out for lessons in private crammers. No wonder they had such high pass rates in exams.

I forced myself into new girl keenness. "What time do you want me to start on Monday?"

At that, he looked apologetic. "I start at seven am? But you don't need to. Would eight o'clock suit?"

Good grief. Most mornings at seven o'clock I was either a) fast asleep with Mildred parked on my chest, or b) having adult time with my significant other. I didn't know what the world looked like at seven am. The only consolation was that I wouldn't need to factor in two hours of travel—your average Londoner's commute to work.

"Splendid!" I said. Another nerves/excitement effect, making me spout stupid words. Next I'd be saying 'Jolly Good' and 'spiffing'.

"I'll see you on Monday."

And with that, he was off. My weekend plans took on a different hue. I'd need to Google 'hyper-brand focused design' for a start so I didn't look a complete idiot come my first day at work. And I ought to find out about past participles. Just in case my boss wanted to ask about them.

Katya stood up. "Do you want to get changed, Gaby? Before we go out? And what about some make-up too? I've got all the latest Blissful Beauty stuff if you want to borrow it?"

. . ⚜ . .

"COOL, CALM, FOCUSED—HYPER-brand focused, in fact."

As I brushed my hair, I repeated the words several times. If I said it often enough, wouldn't they be true? The nerves had set in for sure. On Saturday, Katya and I spent too much money paying for a go on the London Eye and then at the hipster restaurant which served up vegan food they charged steak and lobster prices for.

On Sunday, I flicked my way through various website articles about modern design trends and the latest software. It triggered a meltdown.

"I can't do this!" I wailed to Katya as we sat in the living room. The traffic noise had kept me awake most of the previous night. Would Bespoke Design take me back if I begged, and could I flee back to Lochalshie with my tail between my legs? Katya murmured soothing noises and made me look at some of the websites I'd designed over the years.

"That one!" she said, pointing at the screen. "Absolutely brilliant. You'll be fine."

"What about offices? I've been working from home for more than a year now. You know, in pyjamas most of the time. Sometimes, I don't even get out of bed."

Katya inspected my new pyjamas. Tartan ones to remind me of Lochalshie. "You're a designer. No-one will care if you turn up tomorrow in your PJs."

Maybe not. But bunking off to go and eat fish and chips or, even better, running upstairs chased by your boyfriend when he had wicked intentions on his mind, was definitely out the window.

Jack phoned. "You made it then. How is the big smoke?"

"Smelly, evil and overrun with people."

"Fair enough. Mildred says 'hi' by the way. She's on an enforced diet and looks a lot better already."

I made him show me her and she miaowed piteously at the screen. "Darling! I can't help you. Jack, please, please can you buy her one of those feeders that dispenses biscuits every hour? She'll starve to death if I'm not there."

Unlikely. The last time I'd taken her to the vet, she'd treated me to a long lecture about obesity in pets and its dangers. But poor little Mildred, forced to go from treats six times a day to breakfast, dinner and a long interval between.

Sunday night ended up no more restful than Saturday. Added to the constant traffic noise and people too keen on leaning on their horns, I had those anxiety-racked dreams. In one of them, I forgot everything I knew about design. In another, I tried to get to work and kept taking the wrong turn in corridors that led nowhere. Even Jack's Monday morning message—'Go get 'em, Tiger!', accompanied by a picture of him and Mildred—failed to cheer me up.

The Blissful Beauty building didn't have stairs—only a fire escape on the outside, so my commute took all of thirty seconds in the super-smart lift. The mirrors reflected a white-faced woman with a messy ponytail. When the lift came to a stop, I jumped, nerves jangling. And even though my journey to work was so short, I hadn't made Hyun-Ki's seven am start. It was closer to eight o'clock.

The HQ office held no surprises. Open plan, iMacs left, right and centre and break-away rooms with table tennis and orange space hoppers where overworked executives bounced off their stress.

Everyone else was already in place. I cursed and vowed to set three alarms tomorrow morning so I made the seven o'clock start.

"Gaby! Over here!"

Hyun-Ki didn't seem bothered by my lateness. He beckoned me to where he was standing, pointing at the iMac next to his. Goodness, we were close together. His iMac was set on a standing desk as was mine. Oh heck. I knew sitting all day wasn't good for you, but I was used to it.

Hyun-Ki bounced on his toes, the enthusiasm of a man who's already had his first two espressos of the day. He handed me a coffee. "Black, no milk, no sugar. That's how you like it, right?"

"Thank you!" Someone had done their homework.

"Look!" he said, pointing at his screen. Expecting an amazing page template for the latest Blissful Beauty campaign, he was on YouTube instead. And one of my favourite channels—Cat Man Chris.

"I saved it for you!"

We watched reverentially as Chris (a man who ought to be knighted) single-handedly rescued thirty-five kitties from a hoarding situation and transported them to the vet. By the end of the film, he'd found forever homes for all of them. Chris pleaded with viewers to adopt not shop, and I blinked. Tears on my first day of work—terrific professionalism.

"Guys!" Dexter's voice sang out. Another one far too cheery for first thing on a Monday morning. I whipped round and tried to block his view of the screen.

"Oh! Cat Man Chris," he said. "I've seen that one a few times. That tortoise-shell tabby is so cute, right?"

"Yeah," another voice popped up—a woman my age I guessed who sat at the far side of the room. Three other people stood up and came to join us. I appeared to have found my people. The first five minutes were taken up by a long discussion of the best cat films on YouTube, recommendations for which channels you should subscribe to, and an exchange of pictures of our pets.

"Everyone, this is Gaby!" Dexter said eventually. "She's come to join our team and help make Blissful Beauty the best skincare and make-up company in the world."

He threw his arms out as he said it, almost knocking over the wax life-size model of Caitlin, blowing her audience a kiss through filler-enhanced lips.

"Make-up and skincare so good..."

A pause.

"You don't need to cover up!" the team chorused, me joining in as soon as I realised I was supposed to. Words said, they whooped and high-fived each other.

"Go get 'em team!"

Then, I had to stand next to life-sized (tiny) Caitlin and throw my arm around her for a photo for Blissful Beauty's Instagram account. I'd met her last year and she ably demonstrated the rule celebrities are always much shorter and thinner in real life. Dexter uploaded it: New #designer Gaby joins our team #makeupmarvels! Smiling face with heart eyes emoji.

Blissful Beauty was an American company. They believed in all this motivational shizz. Did every morning start this way, where we stood up and chorused the mission statement before settling down to our ten-hour day broken up only by the odd five minutes bouncing on a space hopper while we threw around ideas?

Dexter burst out laughing, Hyun-Ki and the others tittered too.

"Gaby, your face!" He clapped me on the back. "It's okay. We've all worked in the UK for a while, and we know you guys hate that stuff. Hyun-Ki's idea of a joke to make you feel welcome."

Phew. The guilty party smiled at me, raising his coffee cup in a mock salute. Cats AND practical jokes. This would be okay.

Ten exhausting hours later and I revised my initial assessment. Hyun-Ki might love cats, gently teasing a person and smell delightful (our desks were close together; difficult not to notice) but our similarity ended there.

"I've set up some practice pages for the skin-brightening serum launch, Gaby," he said once I'd finished my first coffee and took my place at my new desk. "Can you see what you can do with them?"

The version of Adobe Design Blissful Beauty used was a beta one, so advanced it wasn't yet on general release. I struggled my way through it, too terrified to ask Hyun-Ki how to do this, that and the other. When I finally completed the first one in what felt like hours later, I turned my screen to face my citrus and wood-smoke fragranced boss.

He nodded. "Not bad for a first attempt."

My heart sank. Damned by faint praise.

"Now, if you just want to…"

There followed a long list of instructions, confirming my earlier suspicions about what it would be like to work for Blissful Beauty. Back-breaking. Exacting. And it was already six o'clock. No-one had left the office.

As I struggled my way through page one version ten, Dexter wandered over.

"Hey that pic of you I put out earlier—the one of you with Caitlin? It's got more than two million likes. Awesome work, Gaby. And everyone's asking when the new bronzer comes out."

Gosh. Fame at last, eh? The power of celebrity even a wax model of one. Apparently, Madame Tussauds had made the one in the office but Caitlin had rejected it as too "unrepresentative" (read: unflattering), which was why we had it.

"Do you wanna see?"

I took Dexter's phone.

OH FLIPPIN' HECK.

I hadn't put on enough make-up—prompting comments about the new bronzer and how much it brightened up skin as Caitlin's wax face clearly showed. However, that was minor compared to the worst of it.

Gabrielle Amelia Richardson, the voice started up in my head, you've BALLOONED. At this rate, I would be waddling up the aisle in three months' time.

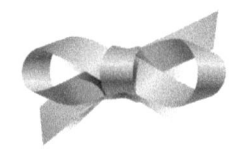

CHAPTER 8

"How was your first day at work," Jack asked when I finally got hold of him on Skype at nine thirty that evening from the living room in the flat.

"Hideously hard," I said. "They work like slaves. I'd forgotten how horrible it is to work in offices. And my day was made much worse by that photo. Did you see it?"

Jack shook his head, pulling up the Blissful Beauty Instagram account on his phone so he could look at it. The blasted thing had burned itself onto my retinas. Twice the size of Caitlin, grey-skinned, far from gorgeous and the whole world appeared to have seen it. A day is nothing in social media time. Since Dexter had shown me the picture, likes had leapt a further half a million.

"It's just a bad photo," he said. In the background, Katya nodded agreement. We were too used, she said, to taking at least thirty photos of ourselves before we ever put anything online these days. And then feeding them through software that evened out skin, whitened eyes and teeth and slimmed you down if necessary.

"Gaby," Jack said, shaking his head in disbelief as I continued to moan. "You're fine. I think you're gorgeous. Don't you remember the hotel a few weeks ago…"

He broke off, seeing as Katya was still in the room. She took the hint, backing out of the room.

Alone, Jack looked tired. He'd had a long day too. The Glencoe trip started at five in the morning for him. And now he had Ms Whiny to deal with, though come to think of it the blame for my ballooning lay partly at his door. I'd gone up a couple of dress sizes since hooking up with Jack. He cooked brilliantly. And we spent a lot of time in the Lochside Welcome eating Ashley's amazing pizzas and his triple-cooked chips. Jack almost always gave in when I finished mine and started on his.

Men ought to come with a health warning: expect a good stone or two to add itself to your waist. Which was fine. Just a bit dismaying when you pictured wedding photos due to happen in ten weeks.

"I just want to look... brilliant for you."

He shook his head. "Gaby, I can't cope if you turn into a Bridezilla."

His tone was sharp and I bit back an impatient reply of my own. So much for our romantic (dirty) Skype chats.

"You don't need to do anything. Promise," Jack added, the words softer this time and sweet. I blew him a kiss, wished him good night, added that in an ideal world I'd teleport myself up there every morning, and hung up.

My fingers hovered above the keyboard. Time for a little Google research. Plan decided, I went to find Katya who was making a stir-fry in the kitchen.

"Can you help me with a wedding weight loss plan, Katya? That photo makes me feel sick."

She paused, wooden spoon aloft. "Fine. I'll take you to Pilates tomorrow. And make you a few vegan dishes if that makes you feel better. But, and I'll say this only once: There. Is. No. Need."

• • ❦ • •

"RIGHT. YOU WANTED EXERCISE. I'll give you exercise."

Katya met me from work at seven thirty (seven thirty!) two days later and said I could tag along with her to an advanced Pilates class. My mind registered alarm. Advanced? Way back when we lived together in Lochalshie, Katya set up classes in the village hall. She'd focussed far too much on abs stuff, but otherwise they'd been fun. As Mhari, Jolene and even Stewart were regular attendees, laughter featured a lot. According to Katya, laughing during Pilates made it harder on the stomach muscles so she encouraged the hilarity.

"Where is it?" I asked, as we headed left toward Conduit Street, people still leaving work and thronging the pavements.

"Not far. Are you okay about getting married, by the way? You didn't sound happy the other night."

The woeful fat picture meltdown. "Fine!" I said. "Timing's a bit tricky, that's all."

What else had I managed to arrange, she asked, rolling her eyes when I told her. Precisely nothing.

Queen of the to-do list, Katya started ticking off things on her fingers, stopping when she saw my expression.

"Okay. At the weekend, we'll sort stuff out. I know! What about wedding dresses? We could mooch round some of the fancy shops to get some ideas."

That sounded doable. "No meringues," I muttered and Katya gave me one of her best "as if" eyebrow raises. She might regard marriage as an outmoded patriarchal institution (partly) but I knew my best friend would lead me by the hand to an outstanding dress.

She stopped in front of a glass-fronted building a few doors down from Sotheby's. "Here we are." On the first floor, treadmills looked out onto the street. Grim-faced Londoners pounded them while on the floor above, people pummelled punchbags.

"Don't be alarmed by the seriousness," she said. "The Pilates class is at the back, and the woman who does it is lovely."

Inside, the changing room on the ground floor hummed with hair driers and showers going full pelt. And... oh no, plenty of women happy to wander around naked, many of them displaying extreme lady bush gardening. I concentrated on keeping my gaze as high as possible.

"Katya, I..."

"Through here," she said, ever the professional and gaze not sinking below shoulder level. She put a finger to her lips, and pushed open a door at the back of the changing room, hidden from sight by a row of lockers.

"London's best-kept secret."

It opened up into a small studio with barres, mirrored walls and men and women sitting on the floor chatting to each other. They looked reassuringly normal, one or two of them calling out "Hi's" to Katya. Another room opened up beyond the studio, which had—glory be—cubicles where you could change.

I came out of my cubicle at the same time as Katya. As usual, she looked a million times better than I did. I knew she didn't buy designer exercise gear, but whatever she wore looked the part. My natty Asda leggings and an old T-shirt of Jack's weren't going to cut it in the style stakes.

"Tomorrow," she said, looking me up and down, "we'll go shopping after work and buy some half-decent workout clothes."

"Fine!" I muttered.

The studio had filled up, every inch of space occupied by a mat while a grey-haired woman with the most extraordinary flat stomach and Michele Obama arms made her way round the participants asking after their health.

Katya introduced her to me.

"Madge, Gaby. Gaby, Madge."

Madge gripped my hands and told me it was an honour to welcome me to her Pilates class. Did I have any injuries, illnesses or life stress situations that might affect my mobility or peace of mind...? 'Life stress' hung there for a couple of seconds.

"I suppose so," I said. "I've started a new job working for a guy much, much younger than me who's a complete perfectionist and so demanding it's—"

Next to me, Katya coughed. "Behind you!"

I turned my head. Yes, there at the back and sending an apologetic look in my direction was my super-young, super-demanding boss. Immaculate too, head to toe in sleek-fitting workout gear, down to those weird toe socks that take hours to put on.

"Hyun-Ki," I croaked. "How... fantastic to see you!" I pulled at the front of my old Highland Tours T-shirt. It did nothing for my chest or stomach.

Madge, her welcome to the class chat complete, told us to stand at the foot of our mats and take deep breaths. In one two three, out one two three, as she wandered around, prodding people's shoulders and telling them to stop hunching themselves up. Not so advanced after all. Still, I made an effort to suck in my stomach, too aware of Hyun-Ki behind me. When Madge ordered us to do the downward facing dog, I sent silent prayers to heaven—please let my knicker line not be visible, and also my bottom not to look too lardy from this angle. As it might be, according to the evidence on Instagram.

Ten minutes later, I told Madge how much I hated her in my head. Gentle, my foot. She said 'darling' and 'I wonder if you might try it this way' a lot to disguise the steel core of her. She wandered/wondered in my direction far too often, tweaking every position I held and making it three hundred times more tricky. Every muscle screamed at me. If this was what it took to get wedding-ready in ten weeks, I faced two and a half months of hell. When she finally said Namaste (the international word for "and this is the end of the yoga/Pilates class") I just about kissed her.

Lord only knew how I was going to get up off the floor. My legs had disconnected themselves from my torso, currently lead-filled as the light in the room shimmered above my head.

"Wasn't that awesome?" Hyun-Ki stood above me, bright, white toothed smile so dazzling I had to put my hand up to protect my eyes.

"It's so hard to find a Pilates teacher in London who understands core strength so thoroughly."

He held out a hand to help haul me to my feet, as Katya had gone to talk to Madge about doing Pilates teacher training. I doubted Hyun-Ki would be able to pull me up and for a second, an image fluttered to mind—where he tumbled on top of me instead. I blushed. Disconcerting, but that image appealed far more than it should to an about-to-be married woman.

I got up slowly, one leg buckling as I did so.

Katya and Madge wandered over to join us.

"Gaby, hi!" Madge said, putting her hands on either side of my shoulders. Little did she realise she was propping me up. "How did you find the class? I hope it de-stressed you. People quit their jobs, you know, when they come to my Pilates classes. It gives them the inner strength they need to realise it's not worth working their socks off for power-crazed tyrants."

I jumped in. "Ah, it's not so bad really! Hyun-Ki is such an understanding guy. He knows he'll need to take his time with me before I can..."

What? Flounder around digging an even deeper hole for myself?

"Oh?" Madge folded her arms. "You two work together. Well, Hyun-Ki be nice to her. She's got other stresses too. Katya tells me you're getting married in a few months' time?"

I sensed, rather than saw disappointment from Hyun-Ki, so I guessed myself forgiven for the too demanding boss comments. He shuffled next to me, eyes automatically darting to my engagement ringless left hand. (To do, list, Gaby. Add engagement ring.) Dexter's sum-up of me obviously had not included the personal stuff. As it shouldn't in a workplace.

"Yes... um, I wonder if..."

"Pilates is a blessing for the bride-to-be!" Madge said, tipping her head to the side to appraise me. Did a before and after picture run through her mind—one she could put on her website afterwards as a testimonial to the powers of core training? "I'm sure Katya has told you the benefits of pelvic muscle strength when it—"

"Brilliant, yes, brilliant!" I said. Did these people have no shame? Happy to discuss my body bits and their squeezing power in front of my boss?

"Many people focus purely on Pilates' aesthetic effects. The Pippa Middleton effect, unfortunately," she waved a hand in dismissal. All very well, I thought, for the woman with the world's flattest stomach and Michele Obama arms to say.

"I'll see you Friday, then?"

Two days away. If I still lived.

I nodded feebly and we headed out, Katya and Hyun-Ki swapping notes on their favourite exercises. All of them by the sounds of it. Outside the gym, the air hit me and my legs wobbled once more. My last meal had been years ago and my stomach moaned in protest. I held my hands out. They shook too, and the thought of the walk back to the Blissful Beauty, short-ish as it was, made me want to cry. Could an Uber come and pick us up or would Katya insist on walking, persuading me this was all part of the big Gaby Improvement Plan?

Hyun-Ki slung his backpack over both shoulders. "I'm off to an advanced programming class. See you tomorrow, Gaby!"

"Bye!" But the effort of raising my hand to wave goodbye proved too much. Dizziness overcame me and I dropped to the ground.

I came to minutes later. At least that's what I assumed. Katya and Hyun-Ki's faces hovered above me, their conversation disjointed and disconnected.

"... working hard..."

"...low blood pressure..."

"... said she wasn't but pregnant?"

That one I did understand. "I'm not pregnant!"

Hyun-Ki held my head in his hands, long fingers cool and soothing. "Is it a delayed reaction to the past few days? Starting your new job and working too hard?" he asked, dark brown eyes watching me carefully.

"No." I knew what had caused it. Admitting it would make me look stupid. And Katya would shout at me. She folded her arms anyway and regarded me balefully.

"Gaby. What have you had to eat today?"

Foiled. I did my best to look truthful. "Tonnes!"

After that hideous picture appeared in on Instagram, I typed 'Crash Diets that are Dead Easy But Super Effective' into Google on the basis that Google will find you anything you want. And it did. Sixteen Eight, otherwise known at Intermittent Fasting. You skipped breakfast, thus cutting down your 'window' of eating to a mere eight hours and the weight magically fell off you.

So the article claimed. The trouble was for the past two days, the relentless Blissful Beauty working regime hadn't left much time for lunch, so I'd figured I might as well do Twenty-two Two or whatever. One super empty stomach was the result.

Katya raised a perfectly groomed eyebrow. "Okay. Not much."

She bullied the truth out of me. And told me I was stupid. At least she didn't shout.

"I know this great Korean place nearby," Hyun-Ki said. "Lots of rice, fish and veggies. Healthy and low fat. Shall we go there?"

Me fainting had made him miss his advanced programming class. I apologised but he shrugged, saying he didn't rate the teacher anyway and was thinking of quitting the class in favour of the super-advanced one. Katya checked the time on her FitBit.

"You go," she said. "I should get back. Check Dexter is okay."

And the rest... without gooseberry me in the flat, she and Dexter could do all sorts of things. In my head, I promised her I'd stay out for at least two hours.

Hyun-Ki threaded his arm through mine. "Think you can manage to get there without fainting again?"

"I'll be fine."

It struck me that we must look like a couple. Did going out for dinner with him on my own sort of count as a date? *No, Gabrielle Amelia Richardson,* I told myself firmly. It doesn't. You are off to have some food with your boss / rescuer. Nothing intimate at all.

Pity too much of me seemed to like the idea.

·· ⚜ ··

AS PROMISED, HYUN-KI'S favourite Korean restaurant was close by—a bustling place where people perched on stools next to the window or sat at long, narrow communal tables. K-pop boomed out, a song that had hit number one last year. The venue wasn't date-like in the slightest.

We sat down. "Can you order for me?" I didn't know Korean cuisine so decided to leave it to the expert.

"Bibimbap! Our most famous dish. Rice, vegetables, meat, sauce and a fried egg. The version they do is the best outside Seoul."

"Sounds lovely." Looked fantastic too. Around me, waiters carried huge steaming granite bowls of the stuff. If a girl needed to break her twenty-two hour fast with something, that meal ought to be a big one. And it wouldn't matter because I'd done the fast bit. None of the articles I'd read online said anything about the food or the amount you ate in your eight (two) hour window.

Dishes ordered, along with green teas, Hyun-Ki relaxed against his chair. "Hey, I'm sorry if I've made you do too much. I know I work too hard and I kinda expect others to do the same."

"Oh no, no, no! It's fine." Only a tiny lie. In the past few days, I'd worked harder than I'd ever done. Tricky too, adjusting to office life once more. And the breakneck pace didn't look like letting up any time soon. Nothing wedding-related had been done either. Every time I reminded myself of that, my mind fizzed in panic. I dealt with it by humming 'la, la, go away'. An excellent strategy. Not.

"How long have you been at Blissful Beauty?" I asked Hyun-Ki, wondering if he had been earmarked by some talent scout while still at school and then fast-tracked into the management programme.

"Four months. They took me on as a junior designer and I worked my way up."

He laughed at my expression—aghast. How, how, how could you work your way up in four measly months? Hyun-Ki must be exceptionally talented.

"But I've only been in London for a month."

He'd come over, he explained, from the US. As a seventeen-year-old, he'd moved to the States to go to university—one of the Ivy League ones too. His degree was in law, and he'd done design on the side as he loved the arty, creative bit of it whereas his parents felt artsy stuff wasn't intellectual or well paid enough.

"Your food!" A waiter put two bowls down, adding a side dish of cucumber and a plate of fried chicken. Warm clouds of spicy-smelling, gingery steam rose from them, and I inhaled greedily. Was it impolite in South Korea to dive into a bowl of food and shovel it in? I was about to find out when Hyun-Ki picked up his phone, the latest and priciest Samsung Galaxy model.

"We should get pictures for Instagram! Everyone loves the food pics on the 'gram."

My stomach rumbled in protest.

"Lean across!"

He held the camera across so the two of us could grin up at it above our bowls of food.

"Um, will the pics look okay?" I muttered and he promised he was a whizz with filters and photo-editing tools. Ten photos doctored, fired off, labelled and hash-tagged, he picked up his spoon, stirred the sauce into his bowl and took a big mouthful. I breathed a sigh of relief. Spoons facilitated greed much more easily than chopsticks.

"You proved them wrong, your parents," I said once I'd finished my third mouthful. Goodness, it was delicious. Crispy rice on the bottom, ginger and pickled cucumber adding sharpness and strips of steak for taste.

He sat back. "Nope. I'm only the head designer for the South Korean side of the business. If I was top man in the LA HQ, they'd be impressed."

Blimey. South Korean parents sounded impossible to please. When I'd told my mum I was moving to London because I'd got a new job and how much I'd be getting paid, she screamed and said she had no idea where I got my talents from. And then asked how I was going to manage planning a wedding from a distance.

"Eat the cucumber," he said, pointing a chopstick at the dish. "It's fermented so super-healthy."

I picked up a piece of fried chicken instead.

"So, getting married huh?"

Ooh. I hadn't been expecting the question and tried to answer before I'd finished swallowing the chicken. Hyun-Ki leapt up when I coughed, my face turning scarlet. He moved to my side of the table and wrapped his arms around me.

"Are you okay? I'm a trained first aider! I know how to do the Heimlich manoeuvre."

So did I. It wasn't a gentle move, risking cracked ribs or even broken ones. Hyun-Ki's arms felt too safe and cosy, and oh so tempting for a girl who might want to lean her head back and enjoy it.

"No need." The chicken dislodged itself and Hyun-Ki dropped his arms quickly. He hurried back to his own side of the table. We both pretended nothing had happened.

"Yes. In December."

"Aren't you too young?" he asked, an echo of the question I'd asked him when we first met.

"I'm twenty seven," I said. "Five years older than you."

What did his eyes say to me—'so what?' Doesn't mean anything, my inner voice said. Vanity tells you the 'so what' is because he's indicating the age gap would not make a difference. If we were to go out, say. Jack's face hovered above me, dark eyes flinty and his mouth in a hard line. This would not do.

"Have you got a girlfriend? Someone back in South Korea or the US?"

A big sigh. He ran his hand through his hair. "Nope. I haven't had time for many relationships."

No wonder. Too busy studying and trying to conquer the design world.

"And I can't work women out. What do they want, Gaby?"

"But you're so gorgeous!" I burst out, my mouth and brain working out of sync. His eyes flashed surprise and something else, and I flushed scarlet. What a thing to say to your boss. Now he was going to think I spent my time drooling over him.

"Um, well... I can't speak for all straight women, but we, er do like guys who are kind. And um, principled. Interested too. Katya says you can tell a nice guy straight away if he asks you lots of questions."

Hyun-Ki nodded, his expression relaxed once more. "There's this dating guru who's offering—"

My phone vibrated and I pulled it out. The notifications showed that my Instagram account had gone mad, and the Lochalshie WhatsApp group had twenty or so new messages.

Hyun-Ki's too-flattering photo of us, grins in place and heads touching and my name tagged in. Mhari, Jolene, Stewart and ten others all wanting to know who I was with, and was Jack happy about it?

The man himself? No message, no missed call, no voicemail.

CHAPTER 9

A non-guilty girlfriend phones her boyfriend and doesn't mention what appears to be an incriminating photograph. Because she has no need to. As far as she is concerned, the picture isn't evidence of anything at all.

Our food paid for—Hyun-Ki insisted, saying he never got a chance to spend everything he earned—we said an awkward goodbye outside the restaurant. His eyes flickered away from mine a few times. Dear oh dear. He probably thought I had a big crush on him and was wondering how he was going to deal with it as my boss. As well as knowing I thought him a tyrant.

Katya called out a cheery 'hello!' when I got back to the flat, but didn't come out of her bedroom. At least I'd kept my promise and stayed away for a few hours. I flopped onto the bed in my room and phoned Jack.

He took an age to pick up and my heart thudded in response. Oh heck, had he seen that pic and was he…

"Gaby."

"Jack! Babes, so amazing to talk to you!"

Babes?! Urgh.

"How has your day been?"

"Long. I was up at four thirty this morning to pick up the latest group. When we went to Doune Castle, all of them wanted selfies with me. My jaw aches from smiling so much."

Doune Castle was one of the venues on Jack's Outlander-themed tour. Such requests were not unusual. Tourists often asked him to stand on the castle ramparts and stare into the distance.

"I'd just fallen asleep."

I checked the time. Yikes, it was eleven thirty already. The Pilates class and the meal out had taken much longer than I'd realised. No wonder my boyfriend sounded so grumpy.

"Sorry, sorry! Just wanted to talk to you because I miss you so much."

He yawned down the phone. "Yeah. Me too."

Better. No mention of pictures of heads too close together or questions about the exact nature of my relationship with my new boss. A non-guilty girlfriend says nothing. Because there is no need.

By the time I put the phone down, the low-level anxiety had disappeared. Almost. Promised, yet again, that this weekend was the one I'd sort out wedding arrangements, hinting that Jack might like to do some of the work. He knew the kind of cake I liked, for example, thanks to that conversation we'd had when he came home to find me watching *Don't Tell the Bride*. He sighed and muttered about his one weekend goal to spend the bulk of it in bed, a dream come true bar one essential element.

Me.

· · ✿ · ·

DESPITE PROMISING MYSELF I would get up early, I slept till noon on Saturday. Five long days, two Pilates classes and the lack of sleep earlier in the week kicked in and knocked me out. At least London's constant night-time noise no longer bothered me.

"Afternoon sleepy-head!" Katya announced when I made my way into the kitchen and stumbled my way toward the kettle. "I've made you a healthy brunch. And I've put together a list of wedding dress shops we can visit. Also, there's a wedding fair in one of the posh hotels near here. We could drop by to get some ideas."

"Mmm-hmm." I eyed my brunch warily. As a most of the time vegan, Katya wasn't likely to have made me a bacon sandwich. "What is that?"

"A green rainbow smoothie bowl. Spinach, avocado, almond milk, apple, mango and berries."

Urgh. I managed half of it before giving up; Spinach and avocado first thing too much of a tough call.

Unsatisfactory brunch completed, we headed out jumping on the Tube so we could get to the hotel first. The Crowley Townhouse was in Knightsbridge, its door manned by two members of staff dressed in purple and gold livery. They tipped their hats at us as we entered and said the wedding fair was in the main function room down the corridor.

My experience of hotels was cosy, family run places. Nothing cosy or family-run about the Crowley Townhouse, its ceilings high, panelled wood walls so polished you could just about use them to check your make-up, and carpets your feet sank into. The function room featured sparkling chandeliers, towering marble columns and floor-to-ceiling windows which looked out over a garden. In the corner, a string quartet played something soft and classical.

A woman at the door handed us a leaflet—The Crowley Townhouse Wedding Package. Katya skim-read it and ripped it up. "How many people do they think will book this ridiculously overpriced venue? I didn't think there were that many Russian billionaires in London."

"How much was it?" I asked. She shook her head, pointless for me to know. It would only make me panic all the more. Not sure if that was meant to reassure me or not.

"Who shall we talk to first?" Katya said. At the front, a poster on a board listed the stalls. Florists, bakers, photographers, beauticians, hen party organisers, bands, videographers, dress-makers, milliners, wedding favours and plenty of things essential for the modern wedding. We were surrounded by couples—had Jack been available, I doubted he'd have come with me to this—and well-spoken women with loud voices saying 'Darling!' a lot.

"Cakes," I said. With any luck, they'd be offering samples. Something that might take away the lingering taste of that smoothie. Katya pointed at a stall at the far end that was less busy than the others and we drifted over.

"Hello!" The guy in charge of Jake's Cakes, pounced on us, manic grin in place. "Who's the lucky lady then?" he said, staring at Katya. He collected himself. "Or perhaps you're both the lucky ladies, hmm?"

"God, no," Katya said, rolling her eyes. "If I was gay, I'd have chosen someone far better."

I protested. Plenty of lesbians out there thought me a terrific catch, weeping, in fact, at the waste to womankind me marrying Jack was. Two women walking past caught Katya's eye and winked at her. "Too right, love."

And I'd always believed the lesbian community to be super supportive.

Jake's Cakes owner picked up a plate loaded with samples. The day looked up. Normally food samples are teeny-tiny but he'd put actual slices on his plate. I helped myself to one of them and took a big bite.

It took far too long to swallow, the texture rubbery and the flavour like a health bar that has sat in the cupboard for years. Jake—I presume it was he—watched me anxiously. My expression, unfortunately, must have given away everything I thought.

"What's in that?! It's disgusting!"

Oh dear. The ingredients included truth serum.

Jake looked as if he might cry. I apologised profusely. The cake had taken me by surprise, I said. That was all. I'm sure it was very delicious. (Just that I wasn't going to risk trying it again.)

"It's an allergy cake," he said. "It's sugar-free, gluten-free, egg-free and vegan. The plant-based food industry has exploded. I thought going into the vegan wedding cake business would be a sure-fire way to hit the big time. Maybe I need to work on the recipe a bit more."

Was it possible to make a cake taste nice if you didn't put eggs, sugar and flour in it? To make up for the faux pas, I wittered on about how plenty of people would love his cake. Then, as I still felt guilty, I made him wrap up a slice of the chocolate version in a paper napkin to take with me as proof. Katya took a slice herself and told him it was the best vegan cake she had ever tried. We moved off.

"Was it?" I asked and she shook her head. "No, it was disgusting but I had to make up for you telling the truth, didn't I?"

The next stop at the opposite end of the room was a florist, her table covered in elaborate table decorations in pinks, purples and whites. Her leaflet also contained a price list, once more way out of my league.

"When are you getting married?"

"December 21."

"Gosh. That's a bit tight—only fifteen months to get everything booked."

When I corrected her, she stared at me aghast. "What have you managed to organise?" she asked. When I admitted only the venue, she put her hand in front of her mouth. "Dear oh dear oh dear..."

"Can we go?" I asked Katya as we wandered off. "This is hideous and everything is so expensive. Let's visit the dress shops instead."

Katya nodded, and said she'd found two shops close by. A great plan, but it turned out shop number one was appointments only and particularly on a Saturday afternoon. Shop number two's assistant welcomed us with open arms and told us to call her Alice, once more assuming Katya was the bride to be rather than me. Corrected, she asked when the wedding was. This time, I let her assume I meant

December next year. She ticked me off anyway for not starting my search before now, and led us through to the back room.

There, a small changing cubicle was at the back, two full-length mirrors stood in the middle and the wall-to-wall rails were hung with huge white dresses in plastic covers. I'd specified no meringues. These looked far too voluminous.

"Now, do you want to slip your clothes off in the changing room and we can try some dresses on?" Alice said.

I hadn't remembered that bit about shopping—always wear your best underwear. The mismatched bra and pants drew gasps from Alice before she remembered I was her only customer on what should have been a busy Saturday afternoon and she waved her hands. "I love that you young people are so relaxed about the details!"

Katya flicked her way through the dresses on the rail. She and Alice conferred, disagreed and examined four or five of the dresses again.

"This one!" Katya said, "No," Alice shook her head and yanked forward something hanging further down the rail. "This is the one!"

A million years later (felt like), the two of them edged towards me, each holding one dress.

"Underwear off!" Alice yelled, pushing a pair of paper underpants at me. My bra and pants would ruin the line, apparently, and spoil my view of the dress. It took me an age to change, the petticoats, mid-arm sleeves and tight fit making it a struggle to get on. Changing room mirrors always made you look hideous. An overstuffed sausage stared back at me.

When I came out, Alice and Katya exchanged looks.

"No," Katya said.

Alice, I could tell, wanted to protest. The dress had been her choice. She walked around me a few times, tilting her specs back and forth.

"Try the other one on."

Katya's dress. And a lot easier to pull on than the last one had been. A long v-neck off-white chiffon dress with silver braid under the boobs and around the waist, the material gathered in folds around my hips, giving me the perfect hour-glass figure. Alice had lent me a pair of silver sandals and a tiny white clutch bag to complete the look.

This time, the mirror was far kinder. My grin touched both ears. I twirled around a few times, delighted with the vision in front of me.

When I pushed aside the cubicle curtain, Alice and Katya gasped.

"Only trouble is I'll freeze to death," I said. "December wedding, remember? In a part of the world that gets very cold in the winter."

"Too bad," Katya snapped, Alice nodding along. She turned back to the rails, pulled out a silver floor-length fur coat she assured me was fake and draped it over my shoulders.

"This!"

"So, how much is the dress and coat?" I asked.

"Very reasonable!" Alice said. "You'll see the price label when you take it off. Once you come out, we'll book you in for a proper fitting and we can talk about the deposit and payment."

Katya took photos, promising to send them to me and my mum.

Bracing myself to tell Alice when I planned to get married, I went back inside the cubicle and took the dress off, picking up my T-shirt and hoodie.

The label of the dress was tucked away on the petticoat down the bottom. I crouched to read it, eyes widening. Three thousand pounds! Oh dear. I had crossed my fingers it might be closer to just over four figures. The coat was the same again. I took my phone out of the front pocket in my hoodie and fired off a quick message to Jack. How much money did he think it was reasonable to spend on the dress?

Something spilled from my pocket, its contents tumbling out onto the dress train. I bent to pick it up and stepped on it instead. That blasted piece of vegan chocolate cake. Squashed flat onto the dress, it proved impossible to remove marking the off-white material with a nasty brown stain that looked remarkably like...

That scene in the film *Bridesmaids*. Remember?

Panic set in. I twitched the curtain open a fraction and caught Katya's eye, pointing to the front of the shop and mouthing that we needed to get out of here asap.

"Do you have a card I can take?" she said, turning to Alice. "I have another friend getting married and I know she'd look amazing in that first dress Gaby tried on."

The woman nodded, saying she would pick one up from the back of the shop. She disappeared and I thanked the stars for a quick-thinking best friend. I pulled back the changing room curtain. Katya and I bolted out of the shop running down the street as fast as we could and stopping only when we were too far for her to chase after us.

I put my hands on my thighs, breath coming in gasps. "I-dropped-chocolate-cake-on-the-dress," I said, words coming out in pants. "And it left this ruddy great mark on the train. I thought it best to clear out."

"Only you, Gaby."

Predictably, Katya found it hilarious. I checked my phone. As it happened, Jack's idea of a reasonable amount of money to spend on a dress came nowhere near the price of the v-neck chiffon example. Just as well now that I'd burned my bridges with the shop, but the dress would have made me the belle of the ball. Which was what you were supposed to be on your wedding day.

"Do you want to go anywhere else?" Katya asked, but the thought of more overpriced stuff, people rolling their eyes when I told them when I was getting married and bumping elbows with

Saturday afternoon shoppers filled me with dread. When I said 'no', Katya didn't push me. Turned out she wasn't finding it enjoyable either.

Back at the flat, I Skyped Jack and told him the dress story hoping it might make him laugh. All he managed was a small smile, his early rise once again making him crabby.

"Talking of overpriced dresses," he said, "what is the budget for this wedding?"

I stared at him on-screen, his eyes hooded and his face stubbly. Even though Jack was a red-head when his beard came through, the hair there was dark brown. I longed to touch him. Mildred strolled across the screen, her furry body blocking the view though not quite as thoroughly as she usually did. I hoped she'd adjusted to less than frequent feeding.

"I jotted some figures down," Jack said. As someone who managed his own business, he knew much more about budgeting than me. "Based on rough estimates for the basics and no fancy extras. You don't want to ask your mum for a contribution, do you?"

"Nope," I shook my head. When Katya sent her the pic of my (not now) wedding dress, she'd asked if she could pay for it. Bless her, but my mum was on her own and she worked as a receptionist at the local GP surgery. My older brother Dylan decided long ago independence was overrated. Why bother with your own flat when you could mooch at your mother's, rent-free, meals and laundry supplied? I couldn't ask her to pay for anything. She'd need to splash out on a mother-of-the-bride dress and plane tickets for her and my nanna as it was.

"And I can't ask my mum and Ranald. They gave me tonnes of money when I first set up Highland Tours years ago."

Ah. I'd been banking on help from Caroline and Ranald. His farm business and her psychic sideline were lucrative. They could a) afford it and b) would love to help. Blast Jack's worthy principles.

"Still, we can use our savings can't we?" I said. True. When I'd first moved to Lochalshie, I spent hardly anything thanks to the lack of shops and a dire social life. When I got together with Jack, I continued the savings habit.

"Wouldn't it be better to spend your savings on a holiday somewhere exotic?" Jack asked, a man who looked as if he badly needed one. "In a really hot, sunny country?"

He shivered. I peered closely at the screen.

"Jack—what's going on?"

"Nothing!"

"Why have you got so many clothes on?"

He wore a fleece over the top of a polo neck, and a thick scarf around his neck.

It came out in a rush. The boiler had packed in just as a rogue cold snap hit the Highlands. As a result, Jack had no heating and no hot water. No wonder Mildred kept wandering across the screen. She was doing her best to soak up heat from the laptop. Jack was trying to tough it out, reluctant to buy a new boiler when we had a wedding to pay for. Anyway, he said, weren't cold showers meant to build your character?

"No, no, a thousand times no," I replied. "My savings. How much does a new boiler cost?"

Fifty quid? A hundred?

"Depends. Lachlan offered me one for £600."

Ouch. That would be for the dodgy, off-the-back-of-a-truck version too.

"And a proper one?" I said, bracing myself.

"Just over two grand."

A figure that would wipe out two thirds of my savings, more money than I'd ever had in my entire life. But I planned to return to Lochalshie in the near future and cold showers featured nowhere in those weekends. I offered to pay for all of it. He beat me down to half the sum. We argued some more, me pointing out that no heating in a home counted as neglect of our cat, and he eventually gave in.

Jack smiled, the brightness of it breaking through pallor. The smile gave him a dimple on his left cheek. Oh to kiss it!

"Thank you. The wedding budget then. I've got £3,000 in my business account, minus half the boiler costs. Want to see how much I reckon a bare minimum wedding will cost?"

"Yes."

He held up a piece of paper to the screen. On it a list of items, an estimated cost and a figure at the bottom circled in red.

My calculations had been way off the mark. How on earth were we going to afford this?

CHAPTER 10

"Are you sure?" I asked, unwilling to believe a 'bargain basement' wedding would cost even that much. Boy, the industry must be full of rip-off merchants.

Jack nodded. "'Fraid so, Gaby."

"The venue is free."

He'd taken that into account, he told me.

"Well, we've only got the food to pay for, right?"

"Ashley's had leaflets made up advertising his wedding packages," Jack said, holding up the proposed leaflet. The design professional in me tutted. And I would *not* have used that font in a million years. Comic sans—honestly.

Jack opened the leaflet and I read the prices, alarm mounting. Even if we subtracted the costs of the venue, the package detailed a dizzying number of other things. Wine per guest, champagne to toast the bride and groom, table for the cake, red carpet as you walked in, wedding breakfast, evening buffet, covers for chairs. Chair covers?! Good grief.

"Er... if we go for the cheapest food package that works out as £30 per guest, so doable? And we can do without lots of things—cars, photographers etcetera. Katya says you can get a wedding dress for less than £500 on vintage auction sites."

From the sharp intake of breath, I gathered Jack hadn't realised that counted as 'cheap' in wedding dress world.

"Have you written out your guest list yet?" he asked. "Every time I bump into someone, they seem to think they're coming. In my head, I invited Mum, Ranald, Jolene, Stewart and Tamar, Mhari and

Lachlan, and Jamal and Enisa. Then a few from your side and that was it. By the time we add up all the people who think they are coming, the numbers will be closer to one hundred and fifty."

Double it. According to my mum, everyone in my home town of Great Yarmouth thought they were coming too—all very excited at the thought of a winter wedding in Scotland.

"Sod them," I said. "I'm only going to invite a few people from Great Yarmouth and you can..."

Jack's eyebrows did that little upwards downwards dance—the 'Gaby has just said something silly' one he'd perfected over the last year. Fair enough. Did I want to try living in a village where the people you didn't invite to your wedding took against you? We would never be able to leave the house again.

"But there's my new salary too. Four times what I was earning before. I could spend the next three months living on beans on toast, which might help the wedding diet too, though my office colleagues might grow to hate me."

Another sigh. And not even a smirk at the baked beans joke. "Again, I think you'd be better spending it on a holiday. Or property." He rubbed his eyes.

"Jack—do you want to marry me?" I couldn't help myself. The words burst out. Everything he'd said so far had made him sound like a man trying to wriggle out of something.

A pause.

"Yes. I just didn't imagine it would get so complicated."

Me either. A fabulous dress, an engagement ring that made everyone gasp in admiration and close family and friends. But then much as I wondered and tut-tutted at the expense, another part of me longed for it all. Wouldn't it be amazing to have an unlimited budget and be able to do the whole wedding shebang? From the dress, to beautiful flowers, thoughtful favours you gave away to guests and yes, even blasted chair covers.

Anyway, I wouldn't discuss any more wedding stuff now. It was time to discuss more immediate matters, such as when me and my groom-to-be next met up. We'd been apart for more than a week—longer than we'd ever been since first getting together.

"Next weekend then?" I said. "I can't wait for you to come to and we can paint the town red."

Or pink-ish. Seeing as we had a bargain basement wedding to save up for and wouldn't be able to throw away money on frivolities such as meals out, a boat tour on the Thames or any of the other lovely things I'd imagined us doing..

"Ah... I was going to get to that."

My heart sank. I knew what was coming.

"A last-minute booking came in, and I can't afford to knock it back. Especially now that we've got the boiler to pay for and the wedding is going to be so much bigger than planned. Sorry, Gaby."

I stifled back a wail. "How about if I come to you?"

No point, Jack said. He'd be away from 6am until 9pm Saturday and Sunday. We would see precisely nine hours of each other—seven or eight of which would be in bed where sadly little action would take place thanks to the two of us being flat-out exhausted—before I needed to return to London.

"The following one then?" I said, and he nodded fervently.

"Promise." We reached out hands to touch the screen. I blew him kisses and cheered when he pretended to catch one.

"Good night, Jack."

· · ✿ · ·

THE WEEK FLEW PAST in a blur. Hyun-Ki wanted me to create animations and posts for all Blissful Beauty's social media feeds. As well as working on the thousands of pages that made up that website. I'd managed to drag myself into the office at seven am every morning—and I still never made it there before him—where he'd be waiting with a coffee and a killer smile.

"I call him the Delicious Dictator in my head," I told Katya. "Always so nice and charming. And then he presents me with this mile-long list of things to do."

At least I was spending hardly any money. Or seeing much of London, apart from the few streets Katya and I walked three times a week to get to the Pilates class. And the city's constant traffic noise no longer bothered me. When I collapsed into bed every evening, I fell asleep the minute my head hit the pillow.

Ashley phoned me on Friday afternoon.

"Gaby, how're? How're?" His voice boomed out and I shot Hyun-Ki an apologetic look. He waved a hand in dismissal so it looked as if I was allowed to take a personal call.

"I've been working on the canapés," Ashley announced. "The ones you can offer your guests when they come in?"

Er, what? Safe to bet canapés was yet another 'extra' and not included in the overall catering costs.

"I've done one in your honour and one in Jack's. Want me to send you pics? They'll go really well with the champagne. Have you worked out how much of that you want—half a bottle per guest? More?"

I muttered I needed to discuss it with Jack. With our budget, we would need to skip the champagne and offer the guests tap water instead.

"Another thing! I wanted to talk to you about my niece, Lara? Did ye know she's a photographer—awfy good at weddings. Have you got a pen handy and then you can jot down her number?"

I obeyed, heart sinking all the more.

"Mind you phone her this afternoon. She's very in demand. Gets booked up awfy fast."

I came off the phone and turned to Hyun-Ki.

"Er... do you mind if I phone this photographer. She's—"
"Awfy in demand."

I laughed. He'd impersonated Ashley brilliantly.

Lara answered her phone immediately. Almost as if she'd been waiting for the call. The background noise sounded suspiciously similar to what had been going on behind Ashley a few minutes ago.

"Gaby, hi!"

She followed up a too bright and breezy greeting with all the out of this world things she could do for me photographically. Engagement shots—had we thought of those? I visualised one of those too big framed pictures of couples some people displayed in their living rooms. My fingers always itched to take out a black pen and deface them.

"Ah, no thanks."

Never mind then, what about a half-day or full day for the wedding? She could start with the preparations—me, my mum, matron of honour and bridesmaids (who were all these people?) putting on our make-up.

"The key, Gaby," she explained, "is that I'm a journalist, not a director. I move around the room unobtrusively taking pictures. You don't notice I'm there and that means great, natural-looking pics."

As an expert in photo editing, she added, all final pictures would be flawless. I'd look so amazing I wouldn't recognise myself.

Hyun-Ki screwed up his face and I stifled giggles. We were graphic designers; both of us experts in Photo-Shop. I was perfectly capable of touching up my own photos thank you very much.

I steeled myself to ask how much these excellent services cost. Just as well—otherwise I might have fallen off my seat. Lara kept talking, too aware of the number one golden rule for sales. The longer you can keep someone's attention, the likelier you are to sell.

Hyun-Ki took the phone out of my hand. "I'm sorry," he said. "But I'm Gaby's boss and she is not allowed to spend so much time on personal calls. She will be in touch."

He gave me the phone back. "Was that okay?"

"Thank you," I said, the relief overwhelming.

"And you won't need to use Photo-Shop," he added, fixing his eyes on mine and then looking away.

Ooh.

"You should phone some other photographers. Find someone who's a bit cheaper."

Personal calls weren't a no-no after all then, or maybe Hyun-Ki found it diverting. Thought to himself, "Gosh. British people. *So disorganised and inefficient.*"

I searched for photographers in the Lochalshie area and found two nearby. Both of them quoted prices well below Lara's rates, but when I mentioned the date, one of them burst out laughing and the other whistled.

No way, Jose. They were booked up eighteen months in advance. I phoned two others who weren't nearby. They added travel expenses to their fees before telling me December 21 was a no-go.

When Hyun-Ki wandered off to chat to Dexter, I phoned Lara back and booked the bare minimum. Half-day only, no hard copies, no wedding album presentation box and she could leave off the photo editing as I'd do that myself. She agreed, sniffing hard as she did so, and made me promise to put down half the deposit the next working day.

I opened the email Jack had sent me the other day, the one where he'd attached the budget estimate. Lara's fees ate up a fair chunk of it. I would wait until we were face to face before I broke the news.

Hyun-Ki had returned to his desk. He spun around in his chair to face me, wafting over pine-scented wood smoke and coffee. As it was half-past five, he must have given himself permission to finish for the weekend. What was on his agenda? Another advanced Pilates class or a programming course? What about his English lessons? While he jam-packed his time with self-improvement, the single women (or men, who knew?) missed out on a seriously beautiful guy who happened to be nice too. When he wasn't cracking the whip at work.

I took in his outfit. He'd changed clothes—from the typical jeans and slogan T-shirt designer combo to a bold, striped shirt and Vans skater trousers matched with hi-trainers. I'd always had a soft spot for hair that flopped forward as his did now. A girl who a) wasn't engaged to be married or b) in front of her boss might lean forward and push it out of his eyes.

"What are weddings like in South Korea?" I asked. "Are they this stressful?"

"No idea," slim shoulders lifted elegantly to his ears. "I've never organised one. Gaby..."

The words came out in a rush. Hyun-Ki had booked a place on (yet another) self-improvement course taking place at the nearby Staffordshire Hotel. Thing was... would I come with him, please, please, pretty-please.

"What's the course?"

He swallowed hard, the movement making his Adam's apple bob up and down.

"A dating boot-camp. Run by an amazing woman who has all these videos on YouTube."

"Who?" I croaked.

"Christina the Dating Guru."

Christina also known as Kirsty. The previous owner of my first cat, the beloved Mena, and also of Jack.

Oh dear.

CHAPTER 11

"I'm engaged to be married—I'm not the target audience for a dating boot camp, surely?" And especially not one run by Kirsty.

Last time I'd seen her was the day Jack and I got together, following some choice words Jack made to her when he'd discovered her plan. She'd been 'writing' a self-help book at the time Called *How to Hook a Commitment-Phobe in Ten Easy Steps*. Jack was the supposed commitment-phobe. Not so. It was more a case of not being able to stand the woman in question. Kirsty's plan was for her to reunite with Jack and therefore provide the final chapter where she proved her stupid methods worked.

If Hyun-Ki wanted relationship advice from anyone, Kirsty was the last person he should ask. I found it hard to believe women did not drop at his feet, but this was the guy who spent all his spare time self-improving. Inexplicably, Kirsty's dating guru website and YouTube channel remained popular—the videos she uploaded stacking up likes and shares in their hundreds of thousands.

"No," I said, "Kirsty's Jack's ex. I met her through a cat-sitting website when I looked after her cat for her. Jack was the love of her life."

He hadn't been. She'd only liked him because he was so easy on the eye and every time she put up a loved-up shot of them on Instagram, it attracted massive likes. Still, 'the love of my life' was something Kirsty liked to say a lot. I left out the Kirsty book detail. Hyun-Ki did not need to know the course he had spent so much money on was run by a woman whose love life was an abject failure.

"Please, Gaby," he said, that blasted lock of hair falling further forward and covering his right eye. He glanced up under his eyelashes. A killer move.

"I'm... nervous. I'd like someone there with me."

"I'm not booked on." If the course was anything like as popular as her website, it would have filled up months in advance.

"I phoned earlier," he said, "and someone dropped out at the last minute. I'll pay for you."

I snorted. As if I was going to come along AND pay for advice I didn't want or need.

"When Kirsty sees me, she'll probably throw me out."

"It'll be busy," Hyun-Ki said. "We'll sit at the back and you can put your hood up... and I'll buy you dinner beforehand."

Ah. The beans on toast wedding economy diet was no fun. And I've been ruled by my stomach for a long time.

"Not McDonald's," I said. "Or Nando's."

"Neither," he promised, his face lighting up. "Another Korean place. Better than the other one."

· · ❦ · ·

THIS TIME, THE RESTAURANT was off Leicester Square and busy, given it was a Friday evening. As we weaved in and out of people on the streets, a longing for the quiet of Lochalshie punched me in the guts. I'd done two weeks in London—only another twenty four or so to go until I could escape back there.

Hyun-Ki pushed the restaurant's door open and found us a table at the back. Flagstone floors, and the brick and wooden beams made it hip—just not very cosy. Jack, I guessed, would be in the Lochside Welcome weeping into a pint because he missed me so much. Hopefully. If I closed my eyes, I could imagine the roaring fire, the bar in the centre where you could always find Stewart and Scottie, and the ever-present smell of pizza.

"What made you sign up for a dating boot camp?" I asked Hyun-Ki as we sat down.

He fiddled with his napkin. "The testimonials are brilliant."

Hmm. And made up too, probably. Katya told me there was a thriving industry out there that specialised in fake reviews—from books, to restaurants, hotels and diet programmes. When Kirsty had tried to run her ten steps to hook a commitment-phobe by me, I couldn't believe anyone would fall for them.

A waiter appeared, keypad in hand. "Two bowls of galbitang," Hyun-Ki said, "and two shots of Soju."

Galbitang, he explained once the waiter had left, was beef short ribs soup, and Soju the country's national drink.

Shots? Dear oh dear. The last time I'd tackled spirits had been an ill-advised experiment at Stewart's instigation. He wanted to prove that a big bowl of porridge lined the stomach so well, gin didn't even touch the sides.

Oh, it did. And did so again when it came back up an hour and a half later.

Food presented and another thirty or so pictures for Instagram fired off until Hyun-Ki got the one he liked, we knocked back the first Soju shot. It didn't taste of much but it didn't burn either.

"To you!" I said, toasting him with shot glass number two. "The best designer in the whole world!"

"To you!" he nodded gravely, "the two hundred and second-best designer in the whole world."

I kicked him under the table.

By the time we left the restaurant, the shots had persuaded me a dating boot camp was just the thing for Hyun-Ki. He might even find a suitable date that very night. If so, I would need to vet her. I appointed myself Hyun-Ki's bodyguard—ready to fight off all predatory women who might like his high-earning potential too much.

"Bodyguard?" Hyun-Ki said, opening the door and then standing back to let me out first. "You can guard my body any time!"

Outside, he clapped a hand over his mouth. "Sorry!"

"That's okay," I said, threading my arm through his. There was a lot to be said for a little light flirting. "Anyway, this course might be good for me too. I might pick up some tips and Jack will love me even more!"

"Doesn't he love you loads already?" Hyun-Ki stumbled over the words. He must be as tipsy as I was.

"Totes loads!" I said, apologising profusely to a woman I'd just bumped into. She glared, which only made us howl with laughter. On the way to the hotel, we had to stop three hundred times (felt like) to take photos of anything Hyun-Ki thought was a London landmark. A lot of things counted. A phone box, a street sign, the skyline, Liberty's, the Apple store (of course) and the Oxford Circus Tube sign.

The Staffordshire was a boutique hotel not far from the Blissful Beauty store. A doorman in purple and gold livery guarded the door and eyed our outfits disdainfully. Hyun-Ki poked his tongue out at him once we were safely in the revolving door, which made him look about twelve years old—definitely not a guy in charge of a multimillion dollar design budget.

In the lobby, a woman with a clipboard and earpiece checked her list. "You're late. Names?"

She pointed at the stairs and told us to take the first room at the top on the right. I put up my hoodie and pulled the strings around my face tight, tucking my hair out of sight. "Have you got sunglasses?" I whispered as we climbed the stairs. Yes, people who wore sunglasses indoors deserved to be lined up against a wall and shot, but if Kirsty recognised me, she'd throw me out the window. Five floors up.

Hyun-Ki handed over a pair of oversized designer Oakley glasses. I plonked them on. They took up half my face. The lighting in the hotel, already dim, darkened further. I stuck my hand out, trying to find the stair rail. It landed instead on Hyun-Ki's... argh! I'd just groped my boss.

"So sorry, sorry, sorry, sorry. Can't see!"

I saw a flash of teeth—a smile rather than a growl. Not offended then.

Christina Collett's Dating Boot Camp, the sign outside the door announced. Pity I hadn't nabbed one of the office's red pens then I could have scribbled her real name on it. Kirsty Begbie. Not half as glamorous, eh? Her face beamed a megawatt smile; next to it a list of the promises she made for those attending.

We slid in as quietly as possible, edging our way along the back wall. Rows of chairs, almost all of them filled, faced a small stage where Kirsty stood. I swallowed back jealousy. "A person's appearance," as my Nanna Cooper liked to say, "is the least interesting thing about them." And I agreed with her but heck, Kirsty dazzled. Her hair was pinned up, tendrils curling around a swan-like neck. The scarlet body-con dress matched her colouring and her skin glowed.

She caught sight of us. "Hi there! Thanks for joining us. I've only just started. There are two spare seats at the front."

Shoot. I jammed the glasses more firmly in place and we took our places. The woman next to Hyun-Ki handed us a clipboard for us to tick off our names and fill in one line about what we wanted to achieve.

I took the board and pen, the flaw in Hyun-Ki's otherwise foolproof plan immediately obvious. My name there in black and white. Kirsty wouldn't be involved in the admin of her dating boot camps, so she probably hadn't seen the list. But if she was going to read out the reasons people gave for attending, exposure threatened.

"Love, I just want genuine love and someone who wants the real me, who is prepared to fight for me," I made sure the 'Love' bit covered my surname and handed it back.

"... so we're going to focus on getting healthy and dating healthy!"

I zoned back in on what Kirsty was saying. She kept looking at me and smiling. Had the disguise not worked? And why did she seem so pleased to see me? I shuffled on my seat and crossed my fingers the smile was just to make newcomers feel welcome.

"... and we're going to improve your boundaries, communication, connection and intimacy through interactive games and drills so you learn how to be the best gift possible!"

She took the clipboard and read out some of the reasons people gave for coming along.

"I can't get past the three-month mark."

"Guys always go off with my friends."

"I always choose douche-bags."

"Women only seem interested in my body."

Hyun-Ki's? I dug my elbow into his side and whispered, "Big-head." "Not me!" he muttered back.

"Love, I just want genuine love and someone who wants the real me. Who is prepared to fight for me."

Crap. My made-up statement. Kristy/Christina settled her gaze on me, smiling from ear to ear. I dropped my eyes to the ground. Dear oh dear oh dear.

"Genuine love? Isn't that beautiful, everyone? A person who wants someone to see and love their real self! Thank you so much for sharing. Whoever you are."

As she looked at me directly, she knew fine who'd written that reason. It dawned on me why she was so pleased to see me. She thought Jack and I were no longer together. Huh.

"Now. Let's split into groups of two and role play."

The screen behind her changed to a new slide setting out the roles we were meant to play. Hyun-Ki angled his chair towards me and we faced each other. He glanced at the screen, where it said, "Person A. You've just met a guy/gal you find attractive. Act out what you say and do and then swap. Person B. Do you find the words and actions persuasive?"

"I would never have agreed to this if I'd known role play was involved," I hissed. "You owe me big time."

Hyun-Ki held up his hands. "I know, I know. Sorry. Shall I do person A first?

"Hi." He flashed me that killer look again where his hair flopped forward and he looked at me under his eyelashes. "I'm so pleased to meet you."

Over-acting, I decided, was the only way to get through this.

"Me too!" I put my hands on his knees. "You're so gorgeous, but I'm only interested in real people, y'know? Someone who gets me heart and soul, pet!" Always adopt a bad Geordie accent to add to the fun.

Hyun-Ki grinned. "That's all I want too!"

"But how can we find it? Genuine love, whey aye? How do we know when it reaches out and bites us on the bottom?"

Hyun-Ki snorted. "What if the bite is from a snake—poisonous and not proper love?"

Ha! He was going to play along too. The evening improved 100 percent.

Walking around the groups, Kirsty stopped at us. "This is so beautiful," she said, clutching a hand to her chest. "So moving. Keep going."

Five minutes later, having declared ourselves irrevocably glued together by the strong venom of love, Kirsty clapped her hands.

"Great work, everyone! But two people really nailed it." She picked up her clipboard. "Hyun-Ki Choi and... Gaby someone?" Her nose wrinkled and she paused. Maybe she didn't know who I was after all.

"Please would you mind coming up here and sharing your role play so we can all learn?"

I shook my head furiously, but Kirsty ignored me walking to our seats and taking us both by the hand. "Come on. We're with friends. And everything that happens at the dating boot camp stays at the dating boot camp."

The only way to get through it was to ham it up even more. I threw myself into the part, throwing in as many 'pets' and 'whey ayes' as possible and grabbing Hyun-Ki's hands in mine to finish as I asked (begged) him to marry me, love's venom so irresistible.

Applause rang out. I bowed.

The evening continued along the same lines—three more role-playing exercises interspersed with useless tips and finished with a plug by Kirsty for her new app, *Love Loser to Winner*, free or £5.99 for the version without ads.

Because Hyun-Ki insisted on gathering up every single leaflet and tip sheet which he said would help improve his English if nothing else, we were among the last to leave.

"Hey!" Kirsty called over just as we got to the door. I stiffened. "You do all the talking," I muttered as she sauntered over.

"So glad you felt you could come along!" She thrust her hand out to shake mine. I'd been rumbled after all. Still, I hadn't expected her to be nice to me, given the Mena/Jack situation.

"I don't suppose you'd write me a review? A testimonial would mean so much to me."

Why would my opinion count for so much?

"Imagine," she said, giggling. Mhari once said Kirsty spent all her time online telling women to be 'all tinkly-laughy'. True. "If you found your third husband thanks to me!"

Eh?

"Because you're quite right. You have to fight, fight, fight for your love."

What?

Hyun-Ki started to whistle—a pop tune it took me a while to recognise. Then it hit me. Oh dear heavens. Kirsty thought I was Cheryl Tweedy in disguise, famous as much for her high-profile break-ups as her pop and TV presenting career. No wonder Kirsty had been so delighted to see me. Boasting the High Princess of Pop rated your love advice was bound to bring more people to those boot camps.

I nodded, said thank you as quietly as I could and turned to leave. And banged into the door, closer to me than I realised thanks to my still darkened vision. An ominous crack sounded—argh, I'd broken Hyun-Ki's expensive Oakley glasses. I pulled them off to inspect the damage and wondered how much of the wedding budget could justifiably be spent on a new pair.

"Gaby!"

The tinkly-laughy voice banished, Kirsty's sunny smile turned to a malevolent stare as she recognised me. "You killed my beautiful little Mena!"

Hyun-Ki stepped back, his face horrified. "What?"

"My cat!" Kirsty wailed. "Gaby was looking after her for me when she died. I hold her solely responsible!"

CHAPTER 12

I thrust my hood down. "I did not kill Mena! Hyun-Ki, you know how much I love cats!"

True. By now Hyun-Ki and I had our morning ritual, where we prepared ourselves for the day ahead ooh-ing and ah-ing over the latest uploads by Cat Man Chris, Kitten Lady or the Cat Man of Aleppo. And I shared every photo of Mildred that Jack sent me, asking my boss if he thought the poor wee thing was too hungry. Hyun-Ki described Mildred as big-boned rather than obese as that insensitive vet had said.

"Besides," I added, "Zac killed Mena, remember? When he was staying in your house? Knocked her down when driving too fast down the high street in his fancy-pants flashy sports car. And didn't bother to tell anyone. We only found out when Jamal saw it on his CCTV."

Zac, one-time resident of Lochalshie and back there now for the launch of the Royal George. Despite being hated by everyone in the village.

"She was in your care at the time!"

'In my care at the time' rankled. Kirsty, once she'd given up on Jack, upped sticks and left. Never said anything to me about taking on little Mena full-time. By that point I didn't mind as I adored her, but Kirsty complaining after the fact was seriously cheeky.

Hyun-Ki butted in. "Gaby's right. C'mon, let's go." He took hold of my arm and made to steer me away before I said something much worse to the tinkly-laughy one. Tempting indeed. We stomped out, managing to hold back the laughter until we were out of the room.

"Honestly," I said as we stood in lift, "did you get anything out of that boot camp?" I could see his face in the mirrored glass, dark eyes glinting and mouth straightening and turning up.

"And I'm sorry about the specs." I held them out. The jolt had broken one of the lenses and cracked the bridge.

He shrugged and took them off me. "No worries. They're knock-offs. Maybe I should take myself—or life—less seriously? I'm going to use that snake line for sure, though. I'll put it on my Tinder bio."

"Definitely," I said. "The women will fling themselves at you. Desperate to find out if the snake is as ginormous as they think it might be!"

As soon as the words were out of my mouth, I wanted to claw them back. His mouth dropped open and shut once again. The two of us matched each other for redness.

"Snake venom, snake venom! If the poisonous bite is as big as..."

Spade, hole, earth—keep digging, Gaby.

Hyun-Ki's eyes met mine in the lift. He nodded. "Yes, of course. I knew that's what you meant."

When we reached the ground floor and the lift door opened, Kirsty was waiting for us. She must have flown down the stairs.

"Gaby!" Back to tinkly laughy again. "I know little Mena's demise was not your fault. I'd always kept her inside so the poor thing wasn't street-savvy. Still, you weren't to know"

Then, she eyed me in a way that made me very nervous. "So are you and Jack still together? You don't need dating advice, do you?!"

More tinkly-laughy stuff.

"No," Hyun-Ki answered. "She came along because I begged her. Gaby and Jack are totes loved up. They're engaged to be married."

Kirsty's wide-open smile faltered for a few seconds and then lit up once more.

"Brilliant! What wonderful news. Have you picked your dress?"

A quick glance at my left hand. "And where's your engagement ring?"

"I've not got around to ring shopping yet," I announced grandly. Dress shopping, flowers, cakes, invite list compiling... I shook my head to dislodge the panic that started up. "But maybe—"

Kirsty stopped still. "Weddings—super expensive, huh?"

Not 'alf. I thought of Jack's budget and how much of it I'd already spent without us having agreed the guest list. So far, it looked as if we could afford ten people to be there by the time everything else had been paid for. What did unpopularity look like? Me, walking down the high street in Lochalshie as people lined the street either side, boo-ing and hissing because we couldn't afford to invite them to our wedding.

"Um, yes?"

Kirsty clapped her hands, the movement making her pinned-up hair wobble. "I have this super-amazing, super-awesome suggestion! Shall we go order a wheatgrass shot?"

· · ⚜ · ·

YES, KIRSTY'S IDEA of celebration was a tiny glass of a thick bright-green liquid that tasted like the gloop Nanna Cooper drained off the tins of marrow fat peas she ate to "keep her regular".

We perched on stools at the bar and Kirsty outlined her idea.

"I want to set myself up as a virtual wedding planner and I need a case study."

Virtual? Didn't a wedding planner need to be onsite to deal with hotels and florists etc.? Kirsty waved it away. Her business grouped weddings together so everyone could share their experiences and chat to each other.

Maximise her income, more like. If ten people signed up for her services at a time, she'd make ten times the money.

"I have all these contacts—people who will provide everything for free so they can showcase what they have to offer. Flowers, cakes, hairdressing, make-up, cars, harpist, DJ, toastmaster, stationery, accessories, rose petals to scatter on the bed..."

Sat across from me, I suspected Hyun-Ki's expression reflected mine—jaw dropped open in disbelief. Harpists? Accessories? A toast master? Jack's budget hadn't included any of those. We were clueless.

"But I'm not sure we want—"

Another hand wave. "Everyone says that at the start and then they realise a wedding only happens once." Tinkly-laugh. "Or so it should! And why not make it as special as you can? You're so lucky, Gaby. Marrying Jack. When I first met him, I used to imagine our wedding day all the time and how fantastic it would be."

Oof. Guilt trip there for me. When I first met Kirsty, she did her best to persuade me to help her get Jack back and I ended up with him instead. My life changed completely—from moving to Lochalshie in the first place, to staying there permanently, becoming obsessed with cats and meeting my one true love.

"All the expense and hassle spared, Gaby!" Kirsty added, eyelashes fluttering between me and Hyun-Ki.

I pictured Jack's face when I told him Kirsty wanted to be our wedding planner... Thunderstruck?

But all that free stuff. A solution to our popularity problem as we would be able to invite everyone who expected to attend... And, the vanity thing, a designer dress even better than the one I was forced to abandon in that shop after my unfortunate accident...

We could bin the measly budget estimate Jack had drawn up. *"Wouldn't it be better to spend your savings on a holiday somewhere exotic?"* A Caribbean island six months from now when I'd completed the Blissful Beauty probationary period, Jack and I swinging in hammocks while aqua blue sea lapped white sands. I could taste the sweet and coconut-y cocktails already.

"What would I need to do?"

Kirsty downed her second wheatgrass shot. "Nothing much, Gaby hon! We'll document your wedding journey online. The odd video for YouTube. We could do one where we practise your make-up for the big day.

"And we'll need a whole section about the wedding diet. I have nutrition training and I can advise on what to eat so you look amazing in your dress and your skin glows."

She squinted at me. "The before and afters will look so different."

Hyun-Ki coughed. "Gaby's perfect as she is. *You* thought she was Cheryl Tweedy."

Kirsty widened her eyes. "Of course. You're so beautiful. I'll only be polishing up perfection." Said with all the sincerity of one who knows who the best-looking woman in the room is. "And everyone always wants to know what diet a woman follows before she gets married."

Mine? Dead easy. Beans on toast. With butter when I was being extravagant.

"I know!" Kirsty said, glancing about her. "Why don't we do an initial video here? We could sit at one of those booths and discuss what you want from your wedding and I'll advise. My iPhone is brilliant for videos."

She tapped it on the bar. Sure enough, Kirsty had the latest and most expensive iPhone.

Hyun-Ki coughed again. "I've got the newest Samsung Galaxy model. It's far superior. And the editing software is brilliant too. I could shoot the film."

National pride was at stake. Samsung phones came from South Korea.

"I don't think…"

"It's just to practise!" Kirsty said. I'd forgotten how... forceful she could be. Before I knew it, she'd bundled me over to a booth in the far corner, Hyun-Ki following behind us phone in hand.

"I'm here with Gaby," Kirsty announced, smiling directly at Hyun-Ki's phone, "who is getting married in December."

"Show everyone your engagement ring, Gaby!"

"Er..."

She grabbed my hand. "No ring! Goodness me, you urgently need the services of a wedding planner, don't you? Imagine everything else you haven't thought about!"

An hour later and it was done. I'd thought the first take fine, but Kirsty insisted on re-shooting five times to ensure the video "truly represented" (read: flattered) her. I mumbled replies to her questions and tried not to resemble a rabbit caught in the headlights. At least I finished with a plug for Jack's Highland Tours telling everyone if you wanted the authentic Outlander tour of Scotland, book my about-to-be husband.

"So, why no ring?" Kirsty asked again. Fake astonishment battled glee.

It was a good question. Where was my engagement ring? I didn't remember a discussion taking place but if it had, was the ring was of those things Jack and I thought unnecessary for modern dudes such as ourselves? But now she'd plonked the thought in my head, I really, really wanted a ring.

"No time," I muttered. Also code for "far too bleedin' expensive".

"I have a silversmith friend who's just started an online jewellery business. I can get you a free ring too...?"

So long as I put a pic on Instagram #gabyengaged! Along with the website address. Welcome to the modern influencer wedding.

Hyun-Ki and I left, Kirsty promising she would be in touch once she'd spoken to her website manager, the YouTube uploader and her silversmith friend the following week.

"This is going to be such fun, Gaby!"

Hyun-Ki beamed too. "Samsung is running a new course on film editing starting next week. I can sign up for that to make your films super-professional. Brilliant!"

And I got a free-ish wedding. Win-win?

• • ⚜ • •

MY PHONE RANG AT SEVEN o'clock the following morning, dragging me out of yet another anxiety dream where I walked up the aisle, naked, everyone laughing at me. I stretched out a hand to pat for my phone on the bedside table and hoped the noise had not disturbed Dexter and Katya. None of us got up early on a Saturday—our work schedules through the week were too hectic.

"Gaby. Something's happened and I need to—"

Cancellation of the last-minute booking? Happy days!

"Jack! Fab! What time does your train come in and I can meet you?"

He paused. "No, sorry. I've still got that booking. It's just..."

An all-too familiar beep sounded. The Lochalshie WhatsApp group his end. I always switched off the notifications at night. Mhari updated it so often three am pings as another message came in were standard.

The silence went on too long.

"Jack?"

"What are you doing with my ex-girlfriend? And why does she think she's planning our wedding?"

I sat bolt upright, startled out of sleep too quickly. A conversation I had planned for when we were face to face, not over the phone. A quick scroll through the WhatsApp messages showed a link to YouTube and a video where Kirsty told the world Christina the Dating Guru now offered wedding planning for her devoted followers.

"She promised me that video was a practise one! But it's actually a fantastic idea, Jack."

Ominous silence.

"Our budget covers practically nothing. She can get all this free stuff and in record-quick time—a harpist, favours, petals on the bed and even an engagement ring, Jack!"

"I can buy my own fiancée an engagement ring, thank you very much."

"Of course, of course but the point is if Kirsty gets us all this stuff, we can spend our savings on the sensible stuff. Like the boiler or another Highland Tours van. And what about a holiday on a nice Caribbean island, you, me, blue skies, not a care in the world?"

Mildred miaowed loudly in the background.

"See? Mildred loves the idea!"

"Kirsty's devious, Gaby. You know that."

"So am I," I said. "Deviously trying to arrange the world's cheapest wedding."

"You are the least devious person in the world."

I took heart. And decided it was time to change the subject to far less controversial subjects, such as the following weekend.

"Hyun-Ki says I can take a half-day next Friday so I'll be able to fly to Glasgow that afternoon. If you can pick me up at the airport, I'll be in Lochalshie for six o'clock and we can have a whole three nights together!"

There were super-early flights from Glasgow to London on Monday mornings. If I got one, I could make the office for nine o'clock, and work through till nine pm.

Another silence.

"I meant to tell you before but I can't pick you up on Friday—sorry. I'm taking a group to Clava Cairns; that spot where Claire travelled back in time to the 1700s in the Outlander book, and I won't be back in Lochalshie until seven o'clock."

"Jack!"

Oh, this was too bad. He'd cancelled me this weekend and now the extended weekend I'd planned wouldn't be that long after all. I itched to see Mildred too. Cat videos on YouTube were all very well, but nothing topped cuddling your own kitty.

"We knew this would happen when you took the job, Gaby."

Emphasis on the 'you'.

"You work all the hours God sends too," I snapped. "And.. and... ar-aren't you desperate to see me?"

"You know I do, Gaby-sketch."

Jack's silly nickname for me prompted tears. I missed him and Lochalshie, its tiny streets, lack of people and the loch with the gentle lapping waves. A vision of the village swam before me—Stewart and Scottie by the loch shores, the dog doing his mad barking at the ducks thing. Mhari coming out of the pharmacist's and making a beeline for me ready to ask 101 nosey questions. Jack driving through the village in his van, U-turning in the High Street, opening the doors and me flying into his arms...

"I'll make it up to you—honestly, all day Saturday and Sunday," he said, far too far away for a cuddle. "We can spend the entire weekend in bed if you want, only getting out of it to order takeaway pizzas from the pub."

"No good for my wedding diet," I sniffled, and he sighed. "You don't need to diet, Gaby! And do *not* let Kirsty tell you any differently. She's obsessed with her appearance."

Ah. Tacit approval for Kirsty and her money-solving solution for the wedding?

"Anyway, I've got to go," he added. "Tourists to pick up, places to go. Gaby..."

Oh-oh. More than anything else he'd said so far about what I now referred to in my head as our 'wretched' wedding, that one word frightened me. It sounded too... loaded. A guy bracing himself to say something he knew was hurtful.

"Yes?" I squeaked, wishing I was with him. Phone calls were all very well but nothing beat looking in someone's eyes. And wasn't I much more persuasive when I was in front of him?

"Nothing. It doesn't matter." Big sigh. "We'll talk properly when you're in Lochalshie next week. Enjoy your weekend."

Guaranteed not to now, hmm? Or the following week as I obsessed about what a "proper" talk was, and worried that it involved the killer sentence, "I've changed my mind."

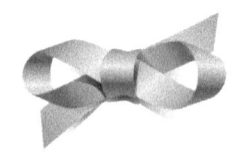

CHAPTER 13

"Hiya, Gaby! Ah seen you on YouTube wi' Kirsty. You looked a hundred times better once she'd finished wi' you."

Stewart, and as luck would have it, the first person I bumped into when I got off the bus on Friday evening. When Katya had lived in Lochalshie, she used to get the bus to Glasgow frequently and always described the journey as "bone-rattling". Every vertebrae in my back felt as if someone had danced there. Wearing stiletto heels. The last thing I wanted was a reminder of that blasted YouTube video.

Kirsty called me on Monday night, ecstatic because the video of us discussing my wedding had already got her tonnes of enquiries. Mad eejits all wanting her sage advice. "We must take advantage of the momentum," she declared, "and get another up soon as! What about a make-up one?"

As my London social life consisted of Pilates classes and nothing else—the capital is a ruinously expensive place to live—I said 'yes'. She met me in a salon in Knightsbridge and Hyun-Ki filmed her making me over. He seemed to have decided no-one else could be trusted to do it. And the Samsung Galaxy's superiority to the iPhone was a point of national and professional pride.

The makeover took forty-five sodding minutes. I couldn't believe anyone would keep watching it beyond the quarter-way mark when Kirsty said yet again that wedding make-up shouldn't be heavy or over the top. Applying 'light' make-up took forever and involved hundreds of products—serums, primers, concealers, highlighters, bronzers, eyebrow gels, pencils, blusher, mascara, lipstick and more.

A tiny bit of everything and a lot of blending. By the end of it my face tingled, unused to the application of so much gunk.

Still, when she uploaded the film the next day it got even more likes than the first one. "Amazing transformation", the most frequent comment. Then someone found that wretched video of me Mhari had filmed not long after I'd first moved to Lochalshie and I rescued Stewart's dog when he got into difficulties in the loch.

Thanks to the cold, when I came out of the loch carrying the dog I suffered an unfortunate wardrobe malfunction. My nipples were clearly visible. Most of the comments under that were LOLs, and *"Here she comes... the magnificent Nora Nipples!"*. "I coined that nickname," Jack once said, adding the clip was by far and away the best thing on YouTube.

He was joking about the nickname. I think.

"Jack's no' back yet," Stewart said, joining me as I walked towards our house via the lochside, Scottie trotting alongside us. Three weeks of London air had coated my nasal passages in grime—an urban myth that is true. You blow your nose after a few days in London and discover your snot is black. I gulped in mouthfuls of pure, fresh air. The sun was setting too, pinky-orange light touching the tops of Maggie Broon's Boobs, the locals' affectionate nickname for the hills at the other side of the loch.

"Oh. How disappointing."

"But he's got the heating fixed. Proper boiler too, no' one of Lachlan's stolen yins."

Glory be.

"D'ye ken if he's made up his mind about his best man yet?"

Argh—Stewart was angling for a decision. The real reason he had pounced on me. Jack and Stewart had known each other for years and Stewart would think that gave him first claim to best man status.

"Um... I'm not sure if—"

"Ah've researched speeches and Ah've got loads of great stories to tell."

None of them anything other than dead boring.

We'd arrived outside my front door, and the sight of it made my spirits rise. Mildred sat in the window glaring at Scottie. He whimpered and hid behind Stewart's legs.

"Brilliant to see you, Stewart!" I got my keys out and found my best 'goodbye now!' face.

"Aye, well. Ah'll be in the Lochside Welcome tomorrow night if Jack wants to talk to me about his stag night. Ah've got loads of ideas for that too. *Much* better than anything Lachlan can come up wi'."

I murmured something non-committal. Jack had promised we wouldn't leave the house.

Inside, the house warm and welcoming thank goodness, Mildred trotted towards me tail in the air.

"Little Scrumptious! Have you missed me?"

She miaowed loudly. Some people might interpret that as a 'yes'; others as a demand for food. I headed for the kitchen, noting how much tidier the whole house was without me there. The cat food cupboard contained biscuits—a new brand that billed itself perfect for overweight cats. I put a handful down for her and she shot me a disdainful look.

"Oh dear, Mildred. Shall we see if there's anything nice in the fridge?"

Answer—no. Two bottles of beer, half a carton of milk and the mouldy remains of a pizza. Mildred wasn't the only hungry one. I headed out for Jamal's store, promising Mildred I wouldn't be long.

"When's your hen night?"

Far too optimistic to think I could escape a visit to the store without bumping into someone else I knew. And it had to be Mhari, thumbs already flying over her phone screen. She sidled up to me.

"Better hurry up wi' the dates for that. If we go to Ibiza, you'll need at least a fortnight to recover."

"We're *not* going to Ibiza," I snapped, pulling open the fridge door and picking up a packet of ham for Mildred who went wild for the stuff. "No hen night, remember? Because I'm super busy in London."

"You have to have a hen night!" Jamal called out. "Are you only buying ham for the cat, Gaby? And you home after having left her for weeks and weeks. I've got a special offer on the venison. Ham's awfy salty. Bad for your wee cat's kidneys."

I rolled my eyes and agreed, putting back the Weight Watchers ready meal I'd chosen for myself and picking up a tin of beans and a loaf of bread instead.

"You cannae not have a hen night," Jamal continued, bagging my stuff up. "Jack's having a stag do. We're all off to Blackpool for the weekend. Stewart's got the T-shirts made up an' all."

Did Jack know any of this? Especially the bit where he agreed to appoint Stewart as his best man?

"December the first then," I said before Mhari decided to book Ibiza herself. "An evening thing. In London."

That ought to put her off.

"Brilliant. I'll organise a bus. Will you be paying for it?"

"No!"

"Oh well. Never mind. We'll borrow Jack's minibus as he won't be using it at that time of year, will he?" She turned to Jamal. "Tell Enisa to save the date."

I paid for my shopping and fled, ignoring Ashley who stood outside the Lochside Welcome and shouted something inaudible at me.

Back in the house, the organic venison convinced Mildred I was her best friend again. "We won't tell Jack, will we, Mildred?" I asked. "Seeing as he thinks you need to diet."

Seven o'clock and still no sign of the man himself. I was far too hungry to wait any longer for dinner. Beans on toast variety twenty one—pan bread, toasted, lightly buttered, a thin application of Marmite and beans on top. The gourmet version.

Meal polished off in record time, my phone vibrated. "Sorry. Crash on the A82 and traffic backed up for miles."

Oh honestly! Why couldn't people drive more carefully and avoid finding themselves in accidents thereby delaying the return of my beloved? Then, I ticked myself off. I'd morphed into a cold, callous city person already. Not in the least bit concerned about the poor person who'd crashed and if they were badly injured or even—gulp—alive.

Still, when Jack hadn't returned by ten-thirty I was back to selfish cursing of careless motorists and yawning my head off. Where was my joyous reunion? When I imagined it last week, it started with Jack at the airport, flinging open his arms as I emerged from the arrivals gate. Then, it downsized to Lochalshie High Street, me getting off the bus, Jack flinging his arms open. Finally, it was going to be me throwing open the front door, Jack grabbing me and the two of us snogging for so long I got stubble rash.

Scenarios one, two and three gone. "C'mon, Mildred!" I said, trudging up the stairs. "Let's go to bed."

I wasn't aware of Jack coming in, but at some point during the night I woke up to find him curled around me and fast asleep. The darkness made it impossible to see him, but his breath tickled the back of my neck and his arm curled over my chest. Mildred had tucked herself in beside me too, the two of them pinning me in place. I'd fallen asleep fretting about various things—unasked for hen and stag parties, the strain of living in London, whatever Jack planned to say to me this weekend—and now none of it mattered. I drifted back to sleep, a smile on my face.

. . ⚘ . .

"ASHLEY WANTS TO MEET us to discuss canapés and numbers."

Jack groaned. As promised, we'd spent most of Saturday in bed. And very enjoyable it had been too. We'd both slept till nine and then... well, poor Mildred didn't get her breakfast venison until eleven o'clock despite piteous cries at repeated intervals. My chin, neck and chest were covered in an angry red rash I didn't mind in the slightest.

Jack rolled onto his side, propping his head on his hand. "Bit of toast and pate and mushroom vol au vents for the vegetarians and vegans. Guest numbers still to be decided. Nothing more to be said."

"Much as I'd love to spend the rest of today in bed with you," I moved my hand further down to emphasise the point. Jack's pupils dilated further, his nipples stiffening in response. "Perhaps we ought to meet him. And stop Mhari and Stewart getting any silly ideas about imaginary hen and stag parties."

I filled Jack in about Stewart's plan for Blackpool and the T-shirts.

He screwed his face up. "What? I haven't spoken to Stewart in ages. And I'm not going to Blackpool."

"And I'm not wasting any of the wedding budget on Ibiza," I said rolling out of bed. Jack tried to grab me, but I wriggled out of his way.

"One hour in the Lochside Welcome tops. Then we come home and..." I mimed something so explicit, he lay on his back and muttered about cruel, torturous girlfriends denying their fiancés basic human rights by making them wait.

Moans over, he threw off the duvet and got up. I'd forgotten how Jack dominated a room. Partly it was his size, the tallness and breadth of him and his hair colour—that gorgeous red-auburn that managed to catch the light so it gleamed. The air around him always seemed to shimmer, and watching him pull clothes on was almost as enticing as watching him strip them off.

Showered, dressed and Mildred fussed over, we left the house. Jack's phone buzzed and his face darkened as he glanced at the screen.

"Anything wrong?" I asked, and he shook his head.

"Tell you later."

That reminded me. He'd said he wanted to talk to me about something the next time we were together. And it worried me. But now… surely the past few hours showed I had nothing to fear? If I left it well alone maybe it would disappear.

We walked past the Royal George, which looked even fancier than the last time I'd seen it. The hotel was an old Edwardian stately home that had been turned into a hotel in the 1920s. As it was expensive and old-fashioned, the hotel had never threatened the Lochside Welcome's status. But Hammerstone Hotels had ploughed money into the place. The stonework gleamed, the windows had been replaced and the grounds tidied up. Now the hotel looked exclusive and upmarket. And the car park was full. Jack shot the place a daggers look.

Everyone in the Lochside Welcome gathered around us when we came in. It being a Saturday night and only just October so still theoretically the tourist season, the pub was busy. Had the Royal George stolen many potential customers?

"Jack! D'ye want tae see the T-shirts I've had made up for Blackpool?"

"Ibiza, Gaby. I found this dead cheap deal—flights only and we stay in an Airbnb, just three nights so no' that much time off your work."

"Ah, Gaby, Jack. I'll need to know the numbers very soon." Ashley, always a large man, had thinned down considerably since the last time I'd seen him. Worry about the threat to his livelihood, I guessed.

Jack closed his eyes. "Let's leave. Now."

"One hour," I said squeezing Jack's hand, "one pizza. On me."

"I'll get our drinks," he said, heading for the bar. His phone beeped and that look I'd seen earlier passed across his face once more. Best I solve that little mystery as soon as possible.

Stewart and Mhari joined me as soon as I sat down at one of the tables near the bar. Without waiting for an invite. Ashley took a seat too, sighing as if the world sat on his shoulders. As he made his way back from the bar, Jack spotted them, screwed his face up and about-turned. I smiled when he did it again, face resigned as he headed over.

"They've got all these celebrities coming to their launch," Ashley said as Jack slid in beside me and put his phone on the table. No need to ask who 'they' was. "Promises to be the biggest event in the Highlands this Christmas."

"Naw, naw," Stewart said, picking up his pint. "That'll be Jack and Gaby's wedding. Ah was thinking. D'ye reckon Hello! magazine will want tae cover it?"

"Aye," Mhari said. "You could pretend Jack really *is* Jamie Fraser or that guy who plays him on the telly. Tell them it'll be packed wi' famous folks."

Jack kicked me under the table. How were we going to stop this getting out of hand? Mhari turned her phone to face me. "See," she said as I squinted at the screen. "The magazine's got this hotline you can call if you're famous and you want them to come to your wedding. Or what about Lara?" She addressed Ashley. "Your niece could gie them the exclusive pics, eh?"

Ashley nodded. "Yes, and take lots of the venue looking beautiful!"

"So yer best man, Jack, ah've rehearsed my sp—"

"If anyone says anything more about weddings," Jack snapped. "Gaby and I will elope to Gretna Green by ourselves, pick two random strangers off the street to be our witnesses and get married there."

Firmness and a show of authority always made me tingle. Even if a teeny-tiny part of me thought, "That sounds terribly dull..."

"No need to be so bad-tempered about it," Mhari said, getting to her feet. "And can we borrow your minibus on December 1 and take it to London?"

Ah. Another thing I forgot to mention to Jack. The alternative hen party I thought guaranteed to put Mhari off. She'd once asked Katya if London was bigger than Glasgow, and if so, she never wanted to go there.

"Not unless you contribute to my third party insurance," Jack threw in, as Mhari flounced off followed by Stewart, who promised he'd drop the T-shirts round tomorrow morning. Note to self: we would not answer the door.

Alone, I leaned back against the padded headboard in the booth. Ashley stood up. "Four cheese pizza was it?" he moved off, hint also taken about wedding discussions. Around us, several people told us how excited they were about the wedding. Jack's stony face stopped them saying too much more.

We ate the pizza in record time and fled to avoid any more wedding discussion.

"Are you okay?" I asked as we headed home, the wind picking up and making me shiver. "And sure about all this? Getting married and everything? I know Kirsty is a nightmare, but the money we save will make it all worthwhile, right? You said you wanted to talk?"

I steeled myself. My mum says you shouldn't ask questions if you are not prepared for an answer you don't want.

Jack bent his head. He matched Ashley for the weight of the world on his shoulders look, and I wondered what on earth was to come... My heart fluttered hard against my rib cage and my stomach churned.

Prepare for an answer you don't want.

Dark eyes met mine as he turned his head. I stopped, waiting for words that might destroy me.

"There is something I need to…"

Not ready, not ready…

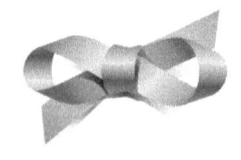

CHAPTER 14

The loud ring made us jump. I caught a glimpse of the screen as Jack took his phone out of his jacket pocket—Lachlan, the might be/might not be best man. "Sorry," Jack said, picking it up. "I need to check this."

I watched his expression change. He wasn't the easiest man to read but the furrow between his brow softened and I heard a gentle sigh—like someone breathing out after holding it in for a long time. When he twisted in his seat to face me, I sensed lightness and relief.

"What did Lachlan want?"

He shook his head. "Nothing important."

Obviously it was. "You're not involved in any of his mad schemes, are you?" On the surface, Lachlan charmed everyone but this was the guy specialised in licence plate changing and vehicle theft. Had he persuaded my beloved that if the two of them held up a bank he could pay for the wedding?

Jack squeezed my hand. "No. I'm not involved in any of Lachlan's schemes. I didn't even take that cheap boiler he offered me. Something from the other week. All sorted now."

He turned my hand over, studying it. "You said something the other day about engagement rings. I need to buy you one. Can't believe it's taken me this long to get round to it. Sorry."

Fabulous. I wanted to cheer from the rooftop. My boyfriend had nothing horrible to say after all *and* he wanted to buy me a ring, which we would not spend silly money on, oh no we would not. Tricky not to, though. After Kirsty's prompt, I Googled rings. Blimey, those things didn't come cheap. I hated myself for doing so, but I also Googled Kirsty's silversmith friend. Her rings dazzled; the prices eye-watering. We could have had one of those for free.

Big Donnie, a Lochside Welcome regular and on his way there by the looks of things, held a hand up in greeting.

"Jack! Great timing. I wanted to talk to you about your wedding to the lovely Gaby here."

Good grief. Did he want to apply for the as yet unfilled position as Jack's best man too?

"Couldnae help overhearing the stuff about your engagement ring," he said, smiling at us both. "My shop's open tomorrow. You can have your pick of rings if you gie me that picture of Kirsty, Jack?"

Ooh. Talk about killing two birds with one stone. *"Now Jack,"* I willed him silently, *"do the sensible thing and say yes."*

Jack looked from him to me, raising an eyebrow and giving me a small smile. If he wasn't easy to read, I was an open book. The answer to Donnie's question loud and clear on my face.

He shifted from side to side prolonging the suspense, that small smile there the whole time.

"Okay then, Donnie. The picture's all yours."

· · ✥ · ·

BIG DONNIE'S SHOP WAS in Oban, a town that got far more visitors in the summer than Lochalshie thanks to its bigger size. The shop was on the main street, two doors down from the restaurant we'd visited there last year when checking the town out for the night.

As it was the beginning of October, the weather had turned chilly. Rain-free but dark grey skies and a cold wind coming off the sea. It sent those on the streets eking out the last of the tourist season scurrying into the shops and restaurants.

"Fancy some fish and chips after we've got your ring?" Jack asked, tipping his head towards the restaurant as we passed it. Monaghan's had won Scotland's fish and chip shop of the year several times in a row and the smell of batter, chips and malt vinegar formed a cloud that scented the air all around it. My stomach rumbled.

"No. Wedding diet," I said and he shook his head, tutting. "Maybe they can rustle you up a salad or something."

Food denial aside I felt better than I had in weeks. The sudden proposal and the accelerated wedding plans, my doubts, the stress of working in London and being apart from Jack. All had taken their toll. Today, though, was much better. Everything was in line for our December wedding and the old happily ever after.

Jack held the picture of Kirsty covered in brown paper and a bin bag to protect it from the elements. My fiancé painted in the winters when he had no tourists to take around Scotland. He was, as the locals said, "awfy good" at it. Mostly, he stuck with landscapes but he'd painted Kirsty during their brief time together. The painting was out of this world—her skin shimmered and her hair sparkled, the light dancing on her head and shoulders.

Naturally, I hated it. In respect to me, Jack shifted the painting to the attic when I moved in with him. But he'd held onto it. And a long time ago Big Donnie, whose Oban shop specialised in antiques and fine art, had offered him £5,000 for it. Jack turned him down.

Now at last I could wave it a (not) fond farewell. Terrible pity if it got accidentally ruined in the shop. Say, someone spilled bleach on it or dropped it on a sharp spike, slashing Kirsty's face in half.

Past and Present Antiques' door chimed as we walked in. The window display appeared to be the only smart part of the shop. Inside, dusty chairs, tables with curvy legs and shelves stacked with blue and white crockery dominated all available space. What little sunlight streamed in picked up dust motes dancing in the air. I sucked in my stomach, too terrified to move. What if I knocked something over—one of those hideous pink and gold vases bound to date back to the Ming Dynasty and be worth thousands of pounds? Bye-bye any remaining wedding budget.

"Hello! You must be Jack and Gaby? Am I right?"

A thin old man thrust his arms out. Experience must have made it instinctive—one hand fitted through a tiny gap to the left, the other found the miniscule space on the right so he didn't disturb anything. He looked antique himself, the skin on his face and neck leathery and wrinkled, spare locks of white hair barely covering a pinky scalp.

"Yes," Jack nodded, the painting still clutched to his chest. There was nowhere to put it down.

"I'm Bert. Manager of this fine establishment. And I am to find you an engagement ring. Am I right?"

"You are," I said, realising belatedly the 'am I rights' were meant hypothetically.

"Show me the picture," Bert said, "and then I'll find you a ring that matches its value."

It struck me that he could produce any old Christmas cracker ring and tell us it was worth the same amount as Jack's painting. Pity I hadn't paid more attention to all those old heist movies my ex Ryan liked to watch. Didn't people do things in them such as biting diamonds or using them to scratch glass to work out if they were the real deal?

Jack turned the picture around and Bert edged forward through the desks and chairs, bending over so he could peer at it closely.

He stayed there for a long time. Jack and I exchanged worried glances over the top of his head. Christmas cracker ring here we came...

Bones creaking, Bert straightened up. "Beautiful, truly beautiful. As you can see, we stock some of Scotland's best fine art in this shop." He gestured behind him where paintings covered the wall space. Most of them featured hill and loch views, the odd stag here and there. Not my cup of tea, but who was I to argue with that assessment of the Kirsty pic and what it might net us, ring-wise?

Jack handed it over. "Aye, great. So the ring...?"

Bert vanished into a back store, returning with a velvet tray of antique rings. He lowered the tray onto the counter, beckoning Jack and I forward. I reassessed my opinion of Kirsty's silverware friend. These ones made hers look cheap and tacky. Hard to tell which one I loved the most.

"Wonderful," Donnie's shopkeeper breathed reverentially. "Am I right?"

"Well, Gaby-sketch," Jack said. "Which one do you like best?"

"That one," I said, having umm-ed and ah-ed over it and the ring alongside. The jewel in the middle glowed bright cobalt blue, surrounded by two rows of other tiny sparkling stones. Worried that ladies in the olden days had slimmer fingers, I picked it up and tried it on. Glory be. A perfect fit.

"Excellent choice," Bert said, nodding his head. "Sapphires are my favourite stone. And pear cut diamonds burst with internal fire, do they not? But you have chosen our most valuable ring, dear lady, and I'm not sure..." he let the rest of the sentence trail off. Obviously, the painting of Kirsty he'd drooled over wasn't that valuable.

"Never mind," I said, "No need to be greedy. What about that one?" I picked up number two choice, holding it to the light—the more conventional single diamond on a white gold band.

"Ah, what taste you have! Again, I'm not sure..."

"Another painting," Jack interrupted. "I've got one of the views of Oban harbour as the sun sets."

He whipped out his phone and showed Bert the picture.

The man eyed him beadily. "What about pets?"

On cue, a dog nosed its way through from the back room. An ancient greyhound by the looks of him. He sat by his owner and panted at us.

"This," Bert swept his hand down, fingers brushing the dog's head, "is Alfie. Could you immortalise him in oils? I've got plenty of photos of him."

"In return for the sapphire engagement ring?"

"And the Oban sunset picture."

"Done."

Ring encased in a tiny jewel box and envelope of Alfie pictures handed over, we made our escape before the clouds of dust in the place choked us..

"Thank you, thank you, thank you!" I said, "I'm sorry you've now got to paint a picture of a dog."

Jack drew out some of the pictures and grimaced. Most of them looked blurred. "I guess it could be a sideline for the winter months. Plenty of people out there who are as cat daft as you and willing to pay stupid prices for a painting of their pet."

I chose to ignore the lumping together of me, daft and stupid in the same sentence.

"Want me to put the ring on?"

"Yes please! Do you go down on one knee to do it?"

He gave me a sideways roll of the eye and dropped to the ground, flinging his arms out.

"Gaby, Gaby, light of my life! Love of my heart. Will you marry me? Say yes or I'll die of sorrow!"

What few people there were out and about on a blustery October day stopped and stared. One or two cameras came out.

"Yes, yes, a thousand times yes!"

Had we been in the US, spontaneous cheers would have broken out. Or someone might at least have clapped. As this was Scotland, our audience nodded among themselves and moved on. Jack put the ring on, easing it gently over my knuckle. I held my hand out to admire it. The sapphire ring knocked the first engagement ring I'd had into a cocked hat. Ryan had picked it without bothering to consult me. If he had, I'd have declared it disgusting. Another note to self—do not allow your nail varnish to get so chipped from now on.

Jack stood up and leant in to kiss me. "Please can I get fish and chips now?"

"Why not? I'll have steamed fish and no chips."

Pushing open the door, Jack turned to me, expression fierce. "You are *not* to nick any of my chips."

Gosh—the unjustifiable, suspicious nature of him.

The waitress who greeted us remembered us from last time almost a year ago. She took our coats and directed us to one of the tables in front of the big window that looked out onto the main street and the harbour beyond. The food was on Monaghan's, she said, as Jack's Highland Tour parties had all visited the restaurant in the past six months, keeping the place busy.

Orders placed, I stretched my hand out to admire my ring once more.

"I'll have to send a picture of this to Katya," I said, "and my mum. And my nanna. And Mhari I suppose, or she'll feel left out, and Jolene will want to see it, maybe even Melissa my old boss at Bespoke Design. Or I could just put it on Instagram, though that is the height of naffn—"

"Jack?"

We both looked up. The man who hovered next to our table looked oddly familiar. In his seventies I guessed, the wrinkled face at odds with his shock of white hair though the restaurant lighting bounced off it in places, changing its colour to red. He wore a tweed suit, the material faded in places and he wrung his hands together repeatedly.

I switched my gaze to Jack. A negative force field radiated off him, so powerful I leant back in my seat. Whoever this man was, he...

Duh, Gaby. Oddly familiar? Face shape and build almost an exact match? Once upon a time red hair?

Meet Jack McAllan Senior. Former husband of Dr McLatchie and father of my beloved, known forever as the man who used to beat her up until she took her young son and up and left him, met and married Ranald McLatchie and lived happily ever after.

"Can I sit down?"

His request coincided with the arrival of our food—a ginormous heap of chips topped with two fillets of battered fish, mushy peas and tartare sauce for Jack and my sad plate of steamed fish sitting on stir-fried veggies.

"Naw," Jack tilted his chin as soon as the waitress left, the move hard and challenging. "Ignore him, Gaby."

His accent always got stronger when he was angry. He swivelled to face the man.

"Leave us alone. Piss off back under the rock ye crawled out fae under."

I watched his eyes, his mouth and his jaw—the first two rigid, the latter a tiny pulse throbbing. The Brit in me cringed. Confrontation made me want to hide under a blanket, crawling out only when it was all over. I pulled my steamed fish plate toward me and tried to look neutral. La, la, la let's crush a few salt flakes on top of my fish and—

"I dinnae drink any more, Jack."

Jack grabbed the salt flake ramekin and crushed a few salt flakes of his own on top of his chips.

"That so?"

Uninvited, Jack Senior pulled up a seat and sat down. "Aye. I'm on the twelve-step programme and at the bit where I go back to the people I let down and say how awfy sorry I am."

Jack stabbed his fish, spearing a big bit of it with his fork and sticking it in his mouth. I stifled ignoble thoughts. If everyone's attention was elsewhere, could I pilfer a few chips? These were golden-brown, thick cut, drenched in vinegar and dusted with—

"I mean it! Leave me and Gaby alone!"

Oops, my chip musings meant I'd missed a crucial exchange. Jack gripped his knife and fork either side of his plate. I feared for McAllan Senior. Another wrong word and he risked a fork in the eye.

The waitress who'd greeted us so warmly made her way over. "Is everything all right, folks?"

Jack's 'no' came out at the same time as my 'yes'.

Lisa wrinkled her brow. "Can I get you extra tartare sauce?"

"Yes!" I said, my steamed fish badly in need of fat calories. And taste for that matter. Wonderful restaurant but they should stick to fish and chips if they wanted to build their reputation.

"Son," McAllan Senior bowed his head. "I've made an awfy lot of mistakes."

Jack continued to cram chips in to his gob, gaze rigidly fastened in front of him.

"I know the last time we saw each other wasnae good, and I deserved what happened. But I wish I could change the past."

Didn't we all? I'd have skipped spending all those years in Norfolk for a start. And ten years with a man I didn't love.

Something must have shown on my face, as McAllan Senior twisted in his seat to face me. "So you're Gaby, aye?" Quick glance at my left hand. "And you and Jack are getting married?"

I nodded. "Yes. In the Lochside Welcome."

Jack glared at me. What was I supposed to say?

"Bonny place to get married, Lochalshie." He scraped back his chair and stood up. "Well, I should leave you. It's nice to see you again, Jack, and you doing so well for yourself. And I'm sorry for everything."

He took out a card and laid it on the table. "That's ma phone number if you ever want tae get in touch. Even just to shout at me."

He clapped Jack's shoulder, my boyfriend doing nothing to disguise the flinch, and moved off, the door ringing behind him. The card sat on the table between us, both of us eyeing it.

"Goodness," I said. "Are you going to tell your mum?"

Jack ploughed his way through a large mouthful of fish and chips. "Nope. And neither are you. He can shove his twelve steps where the sun don't shine. Don't bother lifting that card when we leave either."

"Jack…" I said. "Um, should we talk about your dad?"

Curiosity killed the cat, or the nosey girlfriend in this case. But I burned with questions. The sum of information I knew about Jack's father was Caroline walked out on him when Jack was a young boy and moved miles away. He made a brief reappearance years later (not a happy reunion) and nothing since.

"No. Want to talk about yours?"

Quid pro quo. Neither of us could claim fond memories on the father front, though mine was merely neglectful rather than a wife beater.

"But… he says he's changed. What about second chances?"

The tic on Jack's jaw started up again, syncing with the tick-tock of the clock on the wall. Talk about a mood plunge. Total contrast to half an hour ago when we'd stood outside entertaining strangers with a hammy proposal.

"Please can we not talk about the waste of space that calls himself my father?"

Heartfelt. I nodded. Then eyed his plate. "Are you going to eat all those chips?"

"Gaby!" But the protest lacked bite, and I took it as a 'yes, you can stretch a sneaky hand across the table and help yourself to plenty of 'em'.

"Shall we make up our own wedding vows?"

Oh! Back to wedding talk and how fabulous. Originally crafted declarations where Jack told the world I was the best, most beautiful, kindest, sexiest light of his life and love of his world. I dipped his chips in tartare sauce, my eyes welling up at the thought of it.

"Yours will be, 'I, Gabrielle Amelia Richardson, take thee Jack McAllan, to be my lawfully wedded husband and before these witnesses I vow never, ever to steal chips from your plate again.'"

Huh.

But I pocketed the card when we did leave. Jack might regret leaving it in the cold light of day. McAllan Senior's plea seemed sincere to me, and I knew about the twelve-step programme through one of my mum's friends who'd done it a few years ago. She said the asking forgiveness bit was the trickiest part.

Back at the house, Jack poured me a G&T, the gin from a local distillery that harvested it own botanics and run by an old school friend of his. They might, he mused, provide a few bottles for the wedding so long as we took lots of pics, posted them on Instagram and hash-tagged #CraigellochGin left, right and centre.

"You don't mind if I clean the tour bus quickly?" Jack asked, waggling a bucket and sponge at me. Mildred miaowed at the two of us, a reminder that there was still organic venison to be eaten. I pointed gently at the fridge. Jack rolled his eyes but took the packet from her fridge and tipped its contents into her bowl.

Lovely stuff, gin. When you mix it with posh tonic water, a slice of cucumber and plenty of ice you float above yourself, hands gently propelling the cloud you lie on forwards. Everything becomes possible.

- No budget for anything but the most basic of weddings? We've got a social media influencer who is also a YouTube star about to make it A-MAY-ZING.
- The Stewart/Lachlan best man dilemma? We tell them to

fight it out among themselves and then declare the winner.
- Blackpool? Not happening.
- Ibiza? Ditto.
- Unwanted relatives suddenly turning up and promising reconciliation paired with happy endings...?

My family members were going to far outnumber Jack's at the wedding. My mum, my nanna, my brother and two of my nicer cousins. Whereas Jack would have Dr McLatchie and Ranald, and Lachlan and Lachlan's sister who weren't blood relatives.

I reached for my phone. "Hey, Mr McAllan! Thanks for talking to us today. Would you like to come to the wedding? Everyone deserves a second chance, right?"

There! Gaby Richardson, peacemaker extraordinaire. I took another mouthful of gin. Time enough to work on Jack and promise him our love transcended all the ills of the past, and that forgiveness was a mighty thing...

The front door opened and Jack stormed into the living room, his face fizzing. Mildred, sleeping on my lap, took one look at him and leapt to the floor, scuttling into the kitchen. The cat flap on the back door pinged open and shut.

"Gaby! What the—"

Turned out I'd sent it to the wrong Jack.

Whoops.

CHAPTER 15

Some choice words followed. I'll say this for red-headed Scotsmen. Their tempers were mighty things when stirred up.

"So what bit o' 'don't lift that card' did ye' no' understand? Lucky for me—for you too!—you sent it to the wrong bloke because if you had sent it to my faither, I woulda, I woulda..."

The angry accent thing. Most of it shouted. Our house was an end terrace. How much of this could our neighbours hear? His face clashed with his hair, scarlet competing with auburn glints, dark eyes glittering and that tic on his jaw threatening to explode.

The doorbell sounded and Stewart knocked on the window, holding up T-shirts. Jack glared at him. I shook my head. *Go away, go away!*

I put down my gin, sobriety hitting me full face on. Whoops times ten. Most of the time Jack laughed at my impulsiveness. Asking people round to eat when we had no food in the house. Organising a huge Christmas dinner last year and inviting everyone before I told him. Stripping off naked and flashing a traumatised teen forever.

"Um... but, er... forgiveness?" Then, "Sorry, sorry, sorry spur of the moment thing, y'know, thought it would be lovely if you had more people from your side at the wedding to match all the folks who are going to come from Great Yarmouth, etcetera."

He slapped the side of his head. "D'ye think he's begged my mum for forgiveness yet, seeing as he tried to strangle her the last time he seen her a couple o' years ago when he popped up lookin' for me because he thought I was rich and famous thanks tae Kirsty's blasted non-stop pics on Instagram?"

Ah. News to me. I hadn't known about McAllan Senior's assault on his ex-wife.

Jack dropped onto one of the armchairs. "I'm used to you interfering and doin' things without asking me. But this, this..."

"Interfering?" I squeaked. "Not making plans that benefit the both of us?"

He locked eyes with me. "Proposing out of the blue and doing it in public so everyone knew, which meant Ashley was able to bully us into gettin' married in a hurry. Saying 'aye' to that job in London, then saying 'aye' again when they asked you to move there early. Gettin' involved with Kirsty. Agreeing to her stupid wedding plans and lettin' her do everything for us. I dunno what this wedding is, Gaby, but it seems I'm just the sucker who turns up on the day and says yes."

Sucker? Sucker?! My eyes prickled. That list made my insides shrivel. I'd checked everything with Jack, hadn't I? And he'd been okay about things? His little speech suggested otherwise. Truth under pressure.

"You vile, horrible, lousy, rotten..." I ran out of words, tears taking over.

I got to my feet and swung my handbag around. It caught the back of my head so everything spilled out of it, forcing me to delay the dramatic bit where I stormed up the stairs. Outside, Stewart still stood at the window. He mouthed something I didn't catch. Jack whisked the curtains shut.

I gathered my stuff together, whistled *Flower of Scotland* to get Mildred to follow me and stomped up the stairs as loudly as possible.

Mildred shot me a disappointed look when we got to the bedroom and food didn't materialise. "Soz, Millie-moo," I said, "but you are part of Team Gaby tonight. I might have Crunchie treats hidden somewhere."

And a vegan protein bar Katya had foisted on me that I could eat for dinner. Needs must. The door slammed and the minibus started up.

I threw myself on the bed, Jack's 'the sucker who turns up on the day' stuck on a loop in my head. That list... I studied the ring on my finger and scolded myself for my earlier optimism. Gaby, Gaby, Gaby... what did you say to yourself earlier today? Everything is okay! We're heading for the happy ever after thing! Jolly good!

The evening descended into a self-pitying, wallowing mess. I tried watching stuff on YouTube—oh, Cat Man Chris, you've no idea how distracting you can be!—and I even logged onto my Blissful Beauty email account to see if there was any work-related stuff I could pick up before Monday. Nothing. The minutes ticked by, each one slower than the next.

No sign of the minibus or Jack. His face swam in front of me—all the little bits of him I summed up when I missed him. The broad forehead, the sparkly dark eyes and the red hair I'd have killed for. Honestly? Wasted on a guy. Imagine yourself with dark auburn locks you allow to curl in a halo around your head. Would you spend a single night in? Not when you could be out every night, attracting guys—and girls—who slavishly stared at your hair?

But much as the bits of him dangled there, those words still reverberated. *I'm just the sucker who turns up on the day and says yes.*

I stared at the ceiling.

Hours later, I woke up, Jack beside me. Unlike Friday night, this time he didn't bother to curl around me. Mildred had resettled herself between us. She blinked at me, whiskers twitching as I turned onto my back as unobtrusively as possible. About to poke Jack into wakefulness and discussion, I changed my mind. "Way to make yourself way more unpopular than you already are, Gaby," I whispered to Mildred.

Tomorrow. We could address it—Jack's dad. Jack's true feelings about getting married. Me being an interfering person who never bothered with his opinions and left Jack the stupid sucker who... I stopped all thoughts there.

Tomorrow was another day.

As weekends go, this one had started badly, soared and plunged. A rollercoaster of a few days.

∙ ∙ ⚜ ∙ ∙

MONDAY MORNING. BY the time I woke, Jack was up. Mildred had deserted me too—even if it was stupid o'clock. I skipped the shower, shoved everything back into my rucksack and made my way downstairs. We had half an hour before Lachlan was due to pick me up and take me to Glasgow to catch the morning flight to London.

Better than travelling there by bus even if Lachlan made me a bit nervous. He was slight and wiry, always smartly dressed and mild-mannered. Beneath that though...? Jack had never confirmed what Lachlan did exactly. But one of the guy's sterling qualities was he resembled his uncle in more than just appearance. He liked peace and quiet; the perfect companion for someone who'd had a terrible night.

Jack stood in the kitchen with his back to me. When he turned to hand me a cup of tea, his expression was neutral, rather than angry.

"I'm sorry, Gaby. I shouldn't have said what I did."

'Shouldn't have said'. 'Shouldn't have said out loud what I really feel', the true meaning?

I bit my lip and fiddled with a lock of my hair. "I'm sorry I tried to ask your dad to come to our wedding."

He nodded at that and leant back against the kitchen cupboard. "I know you meant well, but I would need a tonne of proof he's changed. He broke my mum's nose years ago. And gave her a lot of bruises. I know everyone makes mistakes," heavily said, "but I..."

I touched his arm. "Very, very times one hundred sorry. Um... are you okay about everything else? Not feeling too pressurised or anything?"

The words dangled. The real question—*do you* want us to get married?

Cowardice prevented me asking it.

"Yeah. Fine. I'll call later, right?"

He pulled me to him. A hug that felt like an obligation rather than genuinely meant. I gave it back with interest, tightly squeezing love and willingness to wed into him. When his head stopped to rest briefly on mine, I closed my eyes, let out a sigh and promised Jack to keep the wedding idiocy to a minimum from now on.

Lachlan's battered old jeep drove up, the horn sounding outside. I picked up my rucksack and headed for the door, followed by Jack and Mildred. As I let myself out the door, Lachlan's eyes met mine in apology. So much for peace and quiet. Mhari sat next to him in the front seat.

As she was an on and mostly off girlfriend, I hadn't reckoned on this. Great. Her presence also meant I couldn't ask Lachlan about the messages he'd sent to Jack on Saturday night. Now they loomed again. What were the two of them up to?

Mhari opened the door and smiled widely before remembering herself and rearranging her features into something she thought resembled sympathy. Blasted Stewart must have told her about the argument he witnessed.

"Gaby! How are ye?"

"Aren't you working today?" Her job in the local pharmacy was a perfect role for a nosey person. All that access to folks' personal and medical details. How she kept her job I did not know.

"October holiday—it's traditional in Scotland. So I said to Lachlan here, ye'll need me in the car so I can offer the womanly sympathy bit. Here," she jumped out of the jeep. "You sit in the front and I'll go in the back."

I got in and fastened my seatbelt.

"So," Mhari didn't even wait until the car drove off. "You met Jack's dad and invited him to the wedding."

Beside me, Lachlan twitched. Mention of Jack's dad appeared to make him uncomfortable.

"And then you sent your message to Jack by accident and youse two had a big stand-up row. Screaming and shouting and everything!"

London might be huge, dirty and exorbitant but the anonymity was A. Brilliant. Thing.

"What about your wedding? Will this do anything to your plans? And then there's…"

Lachlan put the radio on—a heavy metal channel—and whacked the volume up to ear-splitting. He caught my eye in the mirror and winked.

We got to Glasgow two hours later, Lachlan's driving of the hair-rising variety. Still the speed he took so many of those corners made Mhari carsick as she complained vociferously from the back seat. It stopped her trying to shout questions over the top of the music.

As I thanked him and got out of the car, I heard further complaints. Along the lines of "You're so dumped, Lachlan Forrester! Forever!" He turned to look at her. "I hope that's a promise and no' a threat this time, Mhari."

"Gaby," he called as I headed out of the drop-off car park for the terminal building.

"Jack's father's a waster. And he did his ma a lot of damage. You cannae blame him for being angry about it. Give him time. He'll recover."

I nodded, but the smile I gave him was half-hearted.

Departure gate identified, I popped into one of the coffee shops to find something to eat—preferably a sandwich or wrap that cost less than five pounds and didn't look as if it had been in the fridge for a week beforehand. Brie and cranberry bagel paid for, I checked my phone one last time before switching it off. There might be a message from Jack. *Love of my life—forgive me for shouting at you. It's agony when we're apart.*

As. If.

Instead, one from Hyun-Ki.

"Gaby, please get back to the office as soon as you can. The bosses are here and they want to see you urgently."

My appetite vanished. 'Bosses', 'urgently' and 'see you' were never words in a sentence that signalled good news. What the heck had I done?

CHAPTER 16

Hyun-Ki's message made it a terrible flight. Honestly, bad turbulence would have improved it no end. Then, I might have been able to concentrate on fighting terror that the plane might crash, wiping out my life before I managed to achieve anything of significance. There wasn't even a screaming baby or a nervous passenger nearby to serve as a distraction. My mind battled worries about Jack and the fear I was about to be sacked.

"Get to the office as soon as you can…"

What could a designer do wrong? Do jobs for other people on the side while using your official work iMac. Guilty in the past, yes, but working for Blissful Beauty meant I had no time to do anything *but* work for Blissful Beauty. Give away product secrets/launch details? Again, no. All I did was work my butt off. All those skin-creams, potions and powders blended into one. I had no idea what was for sale and what was about to be launched. Steal things? I hadn't so much as helped myself to a notepad. Look at dodgy NSFW websites while at work? No time and no inclination.

By the time I got to Blissful Beauty's office, the sweat was pouring off me. I'd battled through a huge queue for the Stansted Express and spent my Tube journey pressed too close to other people's armpits. If only I had made more effort with my clothes. The designer 'uniform' of hoodie tops and leggings was fine for everyday comfort. But if I was to be hauled before boss-type people I'd prefer to do it in a suit, and be showered and fragrant.

The receptionist pursed her lips when she saw me, eyes widening behind oversized specs. "That way," she pointed, gesturing to the boardroom. The blinds were down. Eeks. Golden rule of offices—blinds up the meeting is above board, normal and okay for passers-by to glimpse in. Blinds down, the opposite. A nasty, shouty dressing-down awaits. I pushed open the door, my hands shaking.

Dexter, Hyun-Ki and two others sat inside. The former two smiled at me, the gesture hard to work out. A 'this is not that bad' signal, or pity? Person three I recognised. The woman worked in personnel and she'd handled my original recruitment. Now, she'd lost that hyper American friendliness. And despite the ever-present London heat she wore a crisply tailored suit, high heels and flawless make-up. Presumably, the strong perfume I could detect was hers. At least it might cover the sweat coming off me.

Person four I didn't know, but he seemed to be in charge. Ice-blue eyes fixed on me. I blinked a couple of times. He didn't.

"Gabrielle Richardson?" he asked, standing up. "I'm Lawson Kramer. I'm responsible for the European operation."

Not even the UK office—the European one. Argh, double argh.

"Take a seat," he said, pointing at the end of the table so the four of them faced me. No-one offered me water.

"It has come to our attention that you have flouted one of the conditions set out in your contract of employment. The terms and conditions we list at the end of the document?"

Flouted what? And also, who read the terms and conditions? I honed in on the pay and holidays and zoned out of everything else. Didn't everyone?

Marcia, the personnel woman, slid a sheet of paper down the table to me. She'd highlighted the condition and underlined it in red in case I missed it.

Bullet point 10a. *"Blissful Beauty employees must not publicly endorse any other make-up or skincare brands."*

I reread it none the wiser.

"Usually, that's aimed at our celebrity ambassadors," Lawson explained. "The people we pay hundreds of thousands of dollars every year to appear in our ads. But we keep it in for all employees. Everyone can be a star these days, right? Thanks to YouTube."

Oh. Enlightenment dawned. Ruddy Kirsty and her make-up video where she filmed me in that salon and kept plugging the super-expensive skin-cream, highlighter, primer and foundation she plastered on me. At the end of the film, a discount code popped up where you could get fifteen percent off everything, which meant they'd cost you an arm and a leg, instead of both arms and legs. They must have sponsored her. And I might have got away with it had that video not been so popular.

"Sorry," I said, "very, very, very, very sorry. I hadn't realised and I didn't see the final video."

Hyun-Ki cleared his throat. "I filmed Gaby and Kirsty. I didn't realise either."

He looked as if he might burst into tears. Poor Hyun-Ki. If his parents didn't rate becoming head designer for the Korean Blissful Beauty operation at the age of twenty-two, what would they do if he was sacked? Disown him?

But never mind Hyun-Ki being sacked, what about me? The clock in the room ticked, every sound far too loud for the space and all its occupants too silent. If I got onto my knees and begged, said "sorry" a million more times then would they keep me on? How many people my age could afford to be unemployed, their previous employer not willing to forward references to the next one?

I moved my chair back. As Katya would tell you, humiliation and I weren't strangers. The blinds in the room were closed so only four people would see. I dropped to my knees and put my hands on the floor in front of me about to prostrate myself.

"What are you doing?" "I've got an idea."

Lawson and Hyun-Ki spoke at once. I scrabbled back to my feet and sat down again, muttering something about having dropped my pen.

Hyun-Ki outlined his idea. If the company and Kirsty were in agreement, why not try this...?

Lawson Kramer's face gave little away, but Dexter's took on a fevered look.

"That's amazing! And the best timing ever. Caitlin's getting married next year so this will work brilliantly."

It seemed I was off the hook.

·· ❦ ··

"BUT THIS IS MARVELLOUS, Gaby? Can't you see the opportunity here?"

"No?"

Kirsty's eyes shone. I'd arranged to meet her in the Staffordshire Hotel where we'd filmed the original video for her dumb wedding planner business to fill her in on what happened when I returned from Lochalshie.

As I'd predicted to myself, Kirsty loved the idea. She was late for our meeting—half an hour like I had nothing better to do than wait for her—wafting in on a cloud of sickly sweet perfume and a skirt that skimmed her bottom. When she saw Dexter and Hyun-Ki next to me, she fluttered her eyelashes in Dexter's direction and slid into the booth directly opposite him.

"Kirsty," I said, gritting my teeth. "Meet Dexter, Blissful Beauty's marketing manager and the loved-up significant other of Katya, my best friend. Totes in love."

When Dexter told her what they wanted, I thought she might explode with excitement. Hyun-Ki had suggested we continue with the wedding prep videos. But we'd replace the expensive range Kirsty plugged with Blissful Beauty's make-up and skincare. (Slightly) more affordable and perfect for the bride to be.

"And Caitlin's getting married too!" Kirsty said, swivelling around so she could bat her eyelids all the more at Dexter. "Do you think..."

She'll appear in one of my videos and make me so famous they'll beg me to go on Love Island next year?

My guess at how her mind worked. She was mentally picking out her bikini wardrobe already. Three a day plus the odd sarong to drape around her hips and a pair of high-heeled sandals even if they were the least practical choice for the beach.

Dexter murmured something non-committal and the two of them ran through make-up choices for the bride-to-be. Glow serum, bronzer that sculpted your cheekbones—"brilliant for you, Gaby, so you lose that hamster look ha ha only kidding!"—mascara that made your lashes look like falsies and fake tan.

"No way," I said. "Weddings involve white dresses generally, remember? My dress will end up covered in nasty brown stains." I thought of the beautiful dress I'd tried on and banished the vision from my head. Forget. It. Gaby. Not. Gonna. Happen.

Dexter waved a hand and promised the Blissful Beauty fake tan guaranteed stain-free clothing. A miracle product then. Every fake tan I'd ever used left marks everywhere.

They agreed a plan for 'going forward', and Dexter pushed a ten-page contract at Kirsty to sign where she agreed exclusivity and a fat fee for promoting the Blissful Beauty products. When I'd seen it earlier, I'd wondered aloud about my own fee. Marcia flashed me a glacial smile and told me to consider myself lucky I still had a job. I was in my probationary period, remember?

Kirsty signed the contract, her signature an exaggerated sprawl that took up too much room. As I reached out for my glass of water she spotted my left hand and the ring, dropping her pen and grabbing my hand.

"Gosh. I didn't have you and Jack pegged as so old-fashioned."

Hyun-Ki's thigh nudged mine under the table. "But vintage is such a great look," he said, eyes wide and earnest. "Caitlin's already asked Gaby where she got her ring."

Dexter smiled. "Yeah, she sure envies that ring."

"Vintage rocks!" Volte face from Kirsty. "That gives me ideas for your wedding dress, Gaby. I've got plenty of retro fashion contacts I can approach to find you an awesome dress you can borrow."

Another cost to strike off the list. Much as she did my head in, the image of me in a gorgeous 1930s inspired free dress was appealing. I forced my lips upwards and let her arrange dates for further filming, agreeing to every daft idea and promising I couldn't wait to do the lipstick video.

She sailed out of the place, eyes glued to her phone. I gave it ten seconds before an update appeared somewhere. *So excited to share with you that I'm going to be doing the official make-up videos for Blissful Beauty. Isn't that amaze-balls?* Where did that leave her virtual wedding planner plans? Not quite so high on the priority list?

I said goodbye to Hyun-Ki, thanked him for saving my bacon and then had to explain what that meant as it was a British-ism he'd not heard before. He noted it on the memo app on his Samsung.

Dexter and I headed back to the flat.

"A good day at the office, right?"

Mondays, as a rule, were rubbish. This one had outdone itself for ghastliness. I nodded anyway.

But Katya took one look at my face when we came in and whisked me into my bedroom. "Are you okay?" she asked as I collapsed onto the bed. She lay next to me, the two of us watching the fan above circulating the too-warm London air. Even in October, the city sweltered.

I started with the Blissful Beauty story—that one easier to discuss.

"I dunno why you let Kirsty talk you into that stupid plan in the first place."

"Jack and I do not have enough money to invite everyone who expects to come to our wedding," I said. "And Kirsty promised me all these freebies. Harpists, toastmasters, cute favours and rose petals on the bed."

"Rose petals on the bed?! Are you bonkers? What do you need them for?"

"Oh... er, I thought they were standard?"

Duh, Gaby. Of course not. And where did you get them in December?

"Anything else bothering you...?"

She clasped my hand. Ah. Katya knew already. The Lochalshie WhatsApp group would have discussed it in detail. Me thinking it was a brilliant idea to invite Jack's estranged father to the wedding and the row we had afterwards.

I told her my version of the events. How we'd had such a nice weekend up until the point I decided to play happy families and attempt to reunite Jack and his father. How sincere he'd seemed. A man who'd changed and wanted to make amends. Imagine what might have happened if I *had* sent the text to Jack senior... Still engaged? Unlikely. Even, even... The thought made me shudder.

"And now I've got to do these stupid wedding make-up videos if I want to keep my job. And the thing is... the thing is..."

Some people cry beautifully. Not me. It's the full-blown snotty thing, piggy eyes and a bright red face for me. Katya found tissues from somewhere and handed them over. I blew my nose, snorting so loudly the sound reverberated around the bedroom.

"What if Jack doesn't want to marry me at all, Katya?"

My best friend tightened her grip on my hand. "That's not true, Gaby. I've seen the way he looks at you. Adoration, pure and simple. He'll come round. Promise."

Speaking of which, I'd not checked my phone for ages. One message. I pressed the phone to my chest, too scared to read it.

Katya took the phone from me. "I take it you've heard from Jack. Do you want me to read the message for you?"

"Not yet."

Dexter knocked on the door. "Katya, Gaby? I've made us some food. A butternut squash curry and naan bread. Ready in ten minutes?"

Katya prodded my stomach. "Bet you haven't eaten much today either."

True. Dexter excelled at spicy food and he made his own bread. Katya got up and stuck her thumb up as she opened and closed my bedroom door. I unlocked my phone and read the message.

"Hope you got to London safely. Got a jam-packed week ahead with my last tour of the season. Phone you Weds/Thurs? Jack x."

T'uh. Well, that was a fat lot of nothing. I fired off hugs, kisses and every single emoji I could think of. Smiley face, kiss-y face, sorry face and the aubergine one. (Just because.)

My phone bleeped again. This time, a message from Hyun-Ki. "Gaby! Your saviour of bacon here!" Not quite the original meaning, but sweet anyway.

"Hope you are okay?"

Tears threatened once more. Kindness did that to me. A pig of a day. Forgive the extension of the pork analogy. I tapped out a quick reply. "Yes. No. Will be glad to say goodbye to Monday."

"Things can only get better two hundred and second-best designer in the world. How about the BEST designer in the world takes you out on Friday night to London's most awesome venue? XXXXXXXXXX."

A lot of kisses. I was a kiss-person who sent them out willy-nilly but Hyun-Ki's ten thrilled me. Especially when I compared them to my fiancé's lousy one. Friday couldn't come round soon enough.

CHAPTER 17

By the time Friday arrived, I'd spent so much time in front of my computer at work my eyeballs itched furiously and a thumpity-thump noise had taken up permanent residence in my head.

How Hyun-Ki did this day in day out was a mystery. Perhaps his age gave him the advantage. Him being five years younger than me made him better suited to hours in front of a screen, his brain still able to come up with fresh ideas when it was all I could manage by now was changing a font or colour.

When I came in early on Tuesday, I'd wanted to be at my desk for a quarter to seven. Gaby the super-conscientious employee. But I didn't beat him. There he was, empty coffee cup next to him and a cheery 'hello!'.

"Gabs."

Ooh, nickname. Once upon a time, I read daft dating advice that said men who gave their female acquaintances nicknames only thought of them as 'sister' territory, i.e. not fanciable. I disagreed. If Hyun-Ki had his nickname for me—just as I called him Hunky in my head—was it a worrying sign of an inappropriate mutual crush?

"There's a push on for Blissful Beauty's spring make-up line. Pages and social media graphics to be ready for the end of the month."

I stared at him in disbelief. "That's..."

"Ten days away. I know. But hey, at least you'll get to check through the product lines and find your perfect wedding lipstick. We can tie it in with that video we do with Kirsty."

That nickname was the highlight of the week. The rest of it was sheer hell. I worked seven till nine most days, muttering about the European Working Time Directive every time Marcia sailed past my desk pretending not to hear me. And my phone calls to Jack hadn't cheered me up. He veered from snappy to apologetic and back again. I said nothing wedding-y. Neither did he.

Halfway through Friday afternoon, Hyun-Ki stretched his arms above his head. His T-shirt rode up a little too far, exposing Pilates-tautened abs and the bottom of a prominent rib cage. "Shall we use the playroom, Gaby? I'm out of ideas."

Mine had run out Tuesday afternoon. I doubted I'd ever have one again but I nodded. Despite the space hoppers and table tennis, I'd yet to see any employees in the playroom. No-one at Blissful Beauty had time to spare for a pee, never mind creative play where we came up with pretty pictures, slogans or ten more brilliant ways to flog a foundation.

I followed him into the room.

"Table tennis or space hopper?"

The space hoppers felt like less work so I opted for that. The two of us faced each other and bounced lightly. Hyun-Ki was better at it than me—bounces with more boing. I gripped the handles tightly, pushed my feet down and let them spring up. The space hopper moved much farther than I'd anticipated. Another bounce and the ball caught the side of Hyun-Ki's space hopper, sending the two of us tumbling over. He recovered quickly, uprighting himself while I landed in an undignified heap on the floor.

"Sorry about that," I said, turning over. Safer to stay where I was rather than risk the space hopper again. That table tennis table had sharp edges. "I dunno what to do with that lipstick, though."

Hyun-Ki bounced alongside. He'd given me the lipstick pages to work on, asking me to come up with suggestions that made the lipsticks look so fabulous, every girl in South Korea would rush to order one. He had overestimated my talents. Every idea I came up with was no different from lipstick product pages on any of Blissful Beauty's rival brands' website pages.

And if I ever saw another lipstick again in my lifetime, it would be too soon. Kirsty had called me earlier that day too, breathy-voiced as ever.

"Gaby! When will we do our film on bridal lipstick? It's crucial, don't you think?"

No.

"So important to choose the right one! You want your lips to look as kissable as possible and that means a barely there lipstick. Dark, bold colours frighten men off."

Gosh. The poor delicate flowers.

I mentioned this to Hyun-Ki now. "Does bright lipstick scare you?" He bounced thoughtfully. "No. You suit every shade of lipstick, Gaby."

Everyone in the office—guys included—had spent half an hour earlier in the day trying out the new range. Hyun-Ki suited the dark plum one, while Dexter rocked the gloss with gold flecks. But there were so many shades to choose from I lost count after a while. One peach-plum blended into the next peachier plum or plummier peach.

"There's an idea though." The bounces slowed. "What about we upload the Kirsty lipstick video, get her to try out every single lipstick on you, put it on the South Korean Blissful Beauty Instagram account and ask people to vote for the one they like the best."

I got back on my space hopper and bounced hard enough to propel me across the room. "No, no, a thousand times no. And don't tell Dexter. He'll get ideas."

Hyun-Ki bounced closer. "Please, Gaby! It'll be awesome. Imagine the interaction we'll get."

"You ARE doing Dexter's job for him. And come on. It will take hours to film. There are fifty different lipstick shades in that range."

We'd only do ten, he said, and run promotions for them all. Set up hashtags. Encourage people to upload their own pictures or films of them wearing the particular lipstick shade. Get the colour on the product page to change according to which lipstick people voted the most popular.

"... and to pay you back, I'll take you to London's most amazing place now. We won't stay at work any longer."

I stopped bouncing and raised an eyebrow. "Yeah?"

"Oh yeah. Let's go now."

· · ⚜ · ·

THE MOST AMAZING PLACE in London was a bold claim, but Hyun-Ki managed it. We left the office, giggling like naughty schoolchildren sneaking out of class early. Hyun-Ki refused to tell me where we were going, shaking his head and smiling mysteriously every time I asked as we changed Tube lines.

I liked him when he was in silly mode. A smile transformed his features, turning him from male model to something much more human and...

Gaby! Behave yourself.

We got off at Shoreditch High Street, spilling out of the overheated station onto a busy concourse packed with double deckers. Hyun-Ki pointed to the high street, its building a mix of ultra-modern high-rises and old style brick buildings.

"Here!" he said, stopping in front of a shopfront in one of the brick buildings. The window was draped in velvet, cushions nestled on shelving at different heights. Eyes regarded me. Fondly, I hoped. "Best place in London, right?"

I clapped my hands in glee. "Yes! It's perfect."

We were outside Caley's Cat Cafe, a tea shop for stressed-out city dudes unable to keep cats where they lived (Hyun-Ki) or who missed their own pet (me). I'd heard of such places—and Hyun-Ki said there were eleven of them in Seoul—but had never been to one before.

The door was bolted shut and the entry system tightly controlled. The outer door opened, you handed over the entry fee, and then an inner door swung open. The woman at the door gave us a five-minute lecture on the do's and don'ts—mainly don'ts. Don't feed the cats, don't pick them up and above all, don't try to smuggle one out when you leave. To ensure that didn't happen, she took our rucksacks off us.

The inner sanctum was something else. Tables and chairs featured, but every kind of cat tree ever made dotted the place. Multi-level ones, ones with beds and scratchers, tunnels and hammocks. Walkways connected them all. A fair few cats had positioned themselves well out of the way at the top of the trees, though some of them wandered the floor space, pausing to be petted at the tables. I counted twenty-eight cats altogether, and silently congratulated the owners for managing to keep the place smelling neutral. Where were all those cats 'doing their business' as my nanna would say?

"I'll get us something to eat. Would you like afternoon kitt-tea?"

Yes, the cat cafe offered teas, scones, cream and jam and sandwiches. As I'd foregone lunch (again), I nodded. We were joined by a ginger and white cat who reminded me of Mildred, albeit not quite as 'big-boned'. She jumped on my lap and purred, proof, Hyun-Ki said, of my innate attraction to pussies.

He slapped his hand to his mouth. "How rude!"

I giggled. "Now we need to try to squeeze in as many pussy jokes as we can. Winner gets both bits of chocolate cake?"

A waitress had placed a three-tier cake stand on our table, the bottom section loaded with smoked salmon and cucumber sandwiches, the middle scones, cream and jam, and the top Victoria sponge and chocolate brownies. The cat on my knee sniffed the air and looked at me hopefully. Mildred went wild for smoked salmon, as did this one by the looks of things.

"You're on," he said, "So what's the difference between pussy and pizza? Nothing. Because I'll eat—"

I kept my face straight. "Hyun-Ki. That is *totes* inappropriate."

He flushed, dismay flooding his features. "Gosh, sorry. Um, that's not funny at all. You can have both bits of the cake."

I burst out laughing. "Got ya! I'm not offended. And you've won the cake fair and square."

Cats wandered over to see us as we worked our way through the sandwiches and scones, saving the best bit till last. Checking no-one was looking, I sneaked the ginger and white one a bit of smoked salmon which she wolfed in record time teeth grazing my fingers. We decided a long-haired tortoise-shell was the prettiest cat—the brown-black and gingery fur soft and fluffy.

"That's the one I'd steal if only they'd let us keep our rucksacks," I said. "I bet she'd love a flat all to herself."

Hyun-Ki took hundreds of pictures, managing to capture the cat at her cutest.

I ate the last mouthful of scone and my nose tingled, an all-too familiar feeling. I sneezed, half-digested food flying out of my mouth straight onto Hyun-Ki's chest.

"Oh hell! I'm so sorry," I said. "How embarr—"

Another sneeze. And then another again. When I'd first moved to Lochalshie to look after Mena, I'd discovered I was badly allergic to cats. Not ideal in a cat-sitting situation. Dr McLatchie had prescribed strong antihistamines. And after a while, my own immune system kicked in and the allergic reaction stopped. But I'd been living in a cat-less flat for weeks now. And Caley's Cat Cafe had so many of them. The allergic reaction picked its perfect moment to return.

My sneezes drew attention. The same waitress who'd presented us with our kitt-teas hurried over. "Are you allergic to cats? There's, like, tonnes of signs on the door coming in saying people with allergies shouldn't enter. Like, duh?"

"Not us—a-choo!—lly. Just so—a-choo!—many of them in—a-choo!—one place."

I stood up. My eyes were streaming and I needed to get out before it got any worse. I'd scared most of the cats away—the sudden noise and the flying droplets too hideous for them. They watched me from the top of the cats trees and walkways. Everyone else in the cat cafe had pulled their seats back, obviously worried I might spray them with snot.

The possibility growing more likelier by the minute, I stumbled to the inner sanctum door, yanking it open.

"Wait!" The screech behind me came too late. The inner/outer door system was tightly controlled. Only one could open at a time. It just so happened three overexcited Japanese girls stood at the barrier waving their £5 entry fees—the door behind them wide open to the big, bad world outside.

My smoked salmon fed ginger and white chum made her bid for freedom, slipping through the barriers and bolting out, the cafe staff's screams behind her. I watched in horror as she tore up the street heading goodness knows where. When I turned, the waitress and an older woman who must be the manager were behind me.

"If we don't get Lily back, we'll sue," the older one said. "It's in the T&Cs—cafe attendees must adhere to the rules at all times."

Another set of T&Cs I hadn't read. The vibes radiating from these two felt like the fallout from a nuclear explosion. Hyun-Ki moved forward and gripped my elbow. "We'll find her," he said, steering me to the door.

Outside, there was no sign of poor little Lily. Red double-deckers thundered up and down the street and my hand flew to my mouth. What if the poor little thing tried to run across the road...? Having lived through one flattened cat experience, I had no wish to go through it again.

"There!" Hyun-Ki pointed at a row of ash trees planted near the older buildings, their foliage not yet impressive enough to take up much space. I spotted a flash of ginger and white—the proverbial cat stuck in a tree. Would we need the fire brigade? By the time we got to the tree, three other people had gathered there, holding their hands up and calling, "Here, kitty, kitty!"

Lily viewed them disdainfully. Perched in a perfect view point, I doubted she was coming down any time soon. "What are we going to do?" I asked Hyun-Ki. At least Lily had the good sense to steer clear of the main road and its lumbering double-deckers.

Hyun-Ki handed me his phone and wallet. "Hold these. I'm going in!"

And with that, he shinned his way up the tree and along the branch to Lily. The people around us began to cheer, and he put his finger in front of his mouth.

"Yes, shush," I said, "we've got to be really quiet." Everyone around me shut up, eyes fixed on Hyun-Ki sat astride the branch where Lily perched. I edged closer, a piece of smoked salmon I'd earmarked for her earlier still in the tissue in my pocket. I passed it to Hyun-Ki.

He held it out and Lily's nose moved; a cat's superior sense of smell able to detect food instantly. She moved along the branch, took the smoked salmon from Hyun-Ki's fingers and he grabbed her. Lily was not best pleased. She yowled furiously as we ran back to the cafe, Hyun-Ki clutching her to his chest, her tail swishing furiously.

Inside, he handed her over and she bolted for the nearest cat-tree, stopping once she got to the platform at the top to glare at us.

I sent her telepathic messages—*It's for your own good, little Lily! You wouldn't survive Shoreditch High Street.* She narrowed her eyes. The manager didn't seem that appeased. "We'll need to take poor Lily to the vet," she snapped. "She's an indoor cat. God knows what nasty things she's picked up out there. I'll charge you for that."

My sneezing started up again, punctuating the end of her sentence with a loud a-choo.

"Re—a-choo!—ally?" I said. In between several more explosive sneezes, I pointed out that the Cats Protection League didn't sanction cat cafes, and certainly not the number of cats in Caley's place. Did she want a visit from them any time soon?

That got our exit from the cat cafe toot suite without any further threats of suing or vet's bills. I gave Lily a quick apologetic wave as I left, hoping her experience hadn't proved too traumatic.

Outside, we headed for the Tube station. "If anyone filmed you," I said, "it's so going viral. Plus, the girls will be lining up to date you. Look at all the adoring comments Cat Man Chris gets."

Outside the station, Hyun-Ki stopped. It was then I noticed his hands and forearms. Lily had ripped into them and angry red marks covered the surface of his skin, blood beading all along the lines.

"Oh. Does that hurt?"

"No. Yes."

He pulled up his T-shirt. Hyun-Ki's hands weren't the only thing Lily had gone for with her claws. Livid lines marked his chest too, and they stood out against his smooth olive skin. I gazed at the damage far too long, distracted by the muscles emphasised by the scratches.

When he dropped his shirt, I hugged him. "You're my hero! The best boss ever—apart from your slave-driving tendencies—and the rescuer of poor little cats!"

His arms encircled me and I inhaled the musky, woody scent of him. Goodness me. Up this close it was... stimulating. The hands on my back burned through my top as they rested above—and only just—my bottom. His heart pounded against my chest, so when he bent his head to mine what else could I do?

I raised my lips to meet his.

CHAPTER 18

A kiss can be many things—comforting, soothing or passionate. Hyun-Ki's kiss ticked none of those boxes. Our lips didn't so much meet as clash, the bump of them clumsy and awkward. It reminded me of the first time I'd kissed someone as a thirteen-year-old. Neither of us knew what we were doing; modelling our kiss on what we'd seen on screen, the open mouth and tongue thing shocking.

Hyun-Ki and I sprung apart. "God, sorry, sorry!" Both at the same time. I fiddled with my engagement ring, a conscious reminder of why this was wrong on every level.

Hyun-Ki ran a hand through his hair, flushing once more. "I thought...do you think this counts as sexual harassment because I'm your boss? I'm very sorry. I didn't mean..."

"Not at all," I said, pink cheeks matching his. "I'm an about-to-be married woman. Who shouldn't be doing such things. But I guess it's good to know we can stop fancying each other? No offence, but that kiss just didn't work."

He nodded, face colour returning to normal and eyes sparky. "Yeah. Weird, huh? It felt like kissing my sister. We have no chemistry at all."

I threaded my arm through his, congratulating myself on my goodness. *Yes, Jack*, the conversation in my head went, *I did snog a guy but it's okay because we had no chemistry!*

Hmm.

At least it meant work on Monday wouldn't be awkward—neither of us worried we'd done something wrong or me

154

fretting because he felt more strongly about the kiss than I did. I stifled my conscience and we headed for the Tube home. Nevertheless, when I got back to the flat and entertained Katya and Dexter with my sneeze explosion/cat rescue story—Dexter laughed till the tears poured down his cheeks—I kept what happened at the end of the evening quiet. Best friend and all, but Katya had a thing about complete honesty. She'd urge me to confess all to Jack.

And I didn't want to hand him a ready-made, convenient excuse to say once and for all: we are not ready to marry.

•• ⚜ ••

THE FOLLOWING WEEK was as busy as the one preceding it, which left no time to linger on silly snogging episodes. Hyun-Ki greeted me the same as always on Monday—a cup of coffee and a quick YouTube cat video diversion before he cracked his whip.

If I'd expected excitement when I moved to London, I got that completely wrong. The irony, right? Here I was in one of the world's biggest cities, its attractions 24/7, and yet I had far more fun in Lochalshie. At least there, I had the weekly pub quiz, Jolene's Body Pump classes, walks around the loch, car journeys to beautiful scenery and above all Jack to entertain me. Here? Nothing.

On the plus side, I'd been forgiven for the Jack's Father Incident. Jack called me on the Saturday. I'd answered the phone super cheerily, determined to tell Jack about the Hyun-Ki snog. Honesty, as my nanna liked to say because she and Katya shared a belief system, is the best policy.

"Hey!!!"

"Hi—are you okay? You sound manic."

"Busy, busy at work. We've a big push on for a new range of make-up for the South Korean market."

I idled with small talk. Was Jack relieved the tourist season was over; it having been such a busy year? And had he started painting Alfie the ancient greyhound yet?

Tell him, Gaby! No chemistry, remember? Rubbish kiss but we did it at the height of the moment—all that excitement because of the cat escape, etc.. Mildred wandered over Jack's laptop, obscuring the screen. She looked a lot thinner.

Jack came back into view. He'd lost the knackered look of the past few months. I guessed he'd been making up for missed sleep. He cleared his throat.

"Gaby, I'm sorry I said what I did the other week. I didn't mean it."

Oh! I smiled and blew him a kiss he pretended to catch.

"Are you sure? You're not the sucker who just turns up on the day?"

"Nope. And it was kind of you to want to invite my dad. You're a much nicer person than I am."

I apologised once more. Jack McAllan Senior had no right to attend—even if he was now a non-drinker and sorry for everything he'd done. Jack rubbed the bridge of his nose. He might suggest to his father they meet up after the wedding—taking the recovery of their relationship, if such a thing was possible, slowly.

Maybe I ought to take up a career in counselling and family mediation, bringing love and peace to the land, after all.

"But best he's no' at the wedding anyway," Jack added, "if he sees Lachlan he might—"

"Might what?"

"Nothing. Forget it."

Oh well. We blew each other kisses once more. The doorbell sounded and Katya came into the room, sketching a wave at Jack. "Kirsty's here," she said, "wants to discuss your hen night."

Jack screwed up his face. "Right, well I'm off. It's my unofficial stag party tonight."

"What?"

He leaned back from the screen. "I had to do something. Stewart went on and on about Blackpool. And Lachlan kept saying we should go to Edinburgh for the weekend. An old contact of his could sneak us into a club. I put my foot down and said we would do the pub quiz at the Lochside Welcome, order some pizzas and then come back here afterwards."

He gestured at the living room behind him. Now that I looked closely, I could see he'd set up as temporary bar in the corner with a selection of whiskies and gins. No doubt, the fridge bulged with lagers.

"Don't let any of them annoy Mildred," I said. Mildred was okay with company—she'd got used to it living with us—but woe betide the unwitting person who sat on her favourite spot on the couch.

"I won't. Enjoy your evening. If you can."

And with that, he hung up and I closed my laptop, wondering what outrageous suggestions Kirsty had for the hen night. It was bound to involve a make-up video where I road-tested Blissful Beauty's more outlandish items—the silver sparkle stars you stuck on your cheeks or the temporary tattoos.

Kirsty had timed her arrival well. Dexter had ordered yet more Thai takeaway. But luckily for the three of us, Kirsty waved the offer away. She followed a rigid detox diet, she told us—no wheat, no dairy, no red meat, no sugar, no caffeine, no alcohol and no foods beginning with b, c, d, f and z. Or something. Being a YouTube/Instagram star was, she said, a full-time job. One had to look one's best at all times. I got her a glass of water.

"I've spoken with the harpist," she said, taking a seat opposite me as I helped myself to Tom Yum soup and a generous portion of chicken in satay sauce. "And she's free on December 21."

"Excellent."

"The rose petals are arranged and you can tick off the chair covers on your to-do list."

What to-do list? Beside me, Katya stifled giggles.

"I checked with the venue, and they have plenty of chairs. Do you know your numbers yet?"

I shook my head. Jack and I were only just back on speaking terms. Imagine what navigating the choppy waters of guests might involve. My mum was already muttering about my Norfolk cousins—the ones I saw once a year. If that.

"And the food's arranged—you're going to adore it. A brilliant new chef who loves experimenting with food to challenge and excite the palate. I've eaten his stuff. It's out of this world!"

I wrinkled my brow. When had Ashley brought in a new guy? He did most of the cooking himself, with a bit of help from his barmaid. And when had Kirsty been back to Lochalshie to taste this man's food?

"I didn't know you'd been to Loch—"

"So, next up. Your Bachelorette Party?" Kirsty butted in.

Katya and I stared at her, nonplussed.

"The bride-to-be's party with her female guests? Just before she gets married?"

Katya grinned at her. "I hadn't realised we were American, Kirsty. Do you mean Gaby's hen party?"

Kirsty sipped her water and tinkly-laughed, fluttering a hand at us. "I've got such an international following I forget other people get kinda parochial. Bachelorette's a much better word, right?"

"Wrong."

She and Kirsty exchanged one of those smiles that only work for the bottom half of your face. I shovelled in more chicken satay and hoped it wouldn't get awkward. I might have to step in with small talk.

"I've researched some ideas," Kirsty said, breaking the impasse. She bent down and took a folder from her bag, placing it on the table.

"Here."

She handed me print-outs for various organised hen parties. In one, the bridal party watched their own private viewing of *Fifty Shades of Grey* and then spent the evening learning how to pole dance. The eye-watering price included professional videos of your attempts for uploading onto Instagram and Facebook. In another billed as the Spiritual Hen Party, a professional psychic read everyone's fortunes before we embarked on two hours of yoga and an evening of meditation. I made a note to myself to tell Caroline about that one. The hen party market must be ripe for plucking. As she made it up as she went along, no-one would need to worry about hearing bad news.

"No." I put the papers down. Katya helped herself to them too, glancing up to meet my eyes. Here, we were united. "They all sound hideous."

"But I can get discounts on all of them!" Kirsty burst out. "When I dropped my name into the conversation they got very excited. Imagine how fabulous those pole dancing videos would be!"

Dexter, a forkful of noodles half-way to his mouth, paused. "What do women do with that pole-dancing knowledge once they've got it?"

Kirsty blinked. "Isn't it obvious? Gaby performs a pole dance for Jack at the wedding. Much more thrilling than a first dance. And your girlfriend," she batted her eyelashes his way, "does her own personalised version for you later in the evening."

I choked on my chicken. "No. Three hundred and fifty million times no."

Dexter swallowed noodles. And possibly disappointment as that private pole dance was snatched from him. Katya, out of Kirsty's sight line, tapped her middle finger to her head and mouthed 'screw loose!' to me.

"What about this one then," Kirsty found another bit of paper and shoved it across the table. "It's an army assault course where we—"

"No!" I cut that one off before Katya got any ideas. "Can't everyone just come here for a few drinks and a chat?"

"Gaby!" Tinkly laugh. "Your friends are coming from Scotland and Norfolk. They do not want a few drinks and a chat."

Katya tapped a chopstick on the table. "I've got an idea. Your hen party doesn't have to be on a specific date, does it Gaby?"

I shook my head.

"Caitlin's book launch is on November 23 and yours truly is a special guest so long as she doesn't reveal just how much Caitlin wrote of her book," she flashed Kirsty a look, puzzling the latter. No, Kirsty didn't remember that a long time ago Katya was supposed to write her terrible self-help dating guide. Which would have been presented as all Kirsty's own work—just as Caitlin's book was about to be.

"It's going to be held at the Crowley Townhouse where we went for that wedding fair the other week—champagne, canapés, speeches, wall-to-wall celebrities. The works. Why don't we smuggle Gaby's hen party in?"

"Yes!" Kirsty jumped in ahead of me. Tricky to judge what she liked best—Caitlin or wall-to-wall celebrities. And too easy to predict what would happen. She would leave us all to it as she muscled her way into as many high-profile circles as she could manage. I could see the hundred or so selfies with Caitlin already.

Dexter, noodles finished, nodded slowly. "Hey, that would work. You two could grab a quick five minutes with her too and we'd film it for YouTube—Caitlin makes her personal recommendations for wedding make-up?"

Dexter. Always on. Kirsty's excitement, already at border-line fever pitch, ramped up another level. "Oh yes, yes, yes, yes!" Her expression changed to alarm all of a sudden. "How many weeks is it until the twenty-third?"

I checked the calendar on my phone. "Just over three."

She scraped back her chair and jumped to her feet. "Thanks you, guys. This has been amazing. I've gotta go. I'll need to book in for as many sessions as I can with my personal trainer and up the ante on the detox diet. That video will be seen by millions. Bye!"

And with that, she hurried out the flat.

.. ⚜ ..

MY PHONE RANG AT ONE in the morning. Jack. And a very drunk Jack at that.

"Hey, beautiful, I love you!"

"I love you too. Has everyone gone?"

Unlikely. In the background, I heard music and chat. I made out Stewart talking about—guess what?—porridge and the role it played in the making of babies, Tamar proof positive of this. Urgh. And Jamal in conversation with Lachlan about the best rivers to illegally fish from nearby. Ranald might have been there. Impossible to tell.

"No. Everyone's sh'here. Schtill. No-one's shat—sat, I mean sat!—on Mildred yet. Have 'oo seen schtupid pict..."

There followed more words, most of them unintelligible but I caught 'WhatsApp' and checked my phone. There, on the Lochalshie WhatsApp group was a picture of my beloved. One arm wrapped around a woman who had made 'If you've got it, flaunt it' her motto. Long dark blonde hair, its tips much lighter, fell to her waist and tanned mounds of flesh spilled out of a low-cut top, nipples standing to attention. She flashed a dazzling white smile, teeth showing through bright red lips at the camera.

Responses on the WhatsApp group ranged from 'Go on, my son!' to 'I hope Gaby doesn't see this!'. A neat comment, seeing as I was part of the group.

"Goodness. What a friendly girl. Don't tell me. She thought you were Jamie Fraser and wanted to discuss the intricate plot details of the latest series of Outlander with you?"

A long explanation followed, made tres tricky thanks to Jack forgetting most of what he said and repeating himself several times. That, and slurring his words. Gina was nothing whatsoever for me to worry about, I gathered eventually. She was Lachlan's sister and back in Lochalshie to say hello to her mum and dad, and beloved brother.

"She's a sister to me as well," Jack said, making me squint at that picture again. Did brothers ogle their sisters' chests?

The words reminded me of Hyun-Ki and what had happened at the cat cafe. The perfect opportunity to confess. Made even better because there was a fair chance my beloved would have forgotten everything by the time tomorrow morning came round. That way, my conscience would be clear.

"Did you snog her? Tell me the truth. I can handle it and I'm okay with it," I said.

"No! Absolutely not. Infidelity is the pits—and I would never do that to you, Gaby."

I paraphrased the last. It took him three attempts and a lot of me saying 'what?' to understand his meaning. When I did, my blood ran cold. Ah. In Jack's world snogging someone else was a no-no. As it should be. I stared at the ceiling hoping the universe might give me a sign. No such luck. *Do it, do it, do it, 'fess up to the Hyun-Ki thing, Gaby. Imagine how much better you will feel once you have told the truth...*

It took me a few seconds to realise Jack had started speaking again. And a few more to work out what he was saying. The gist was now that he'd taken his last group of tourists to the hills, lochs and castles of the Highlands he had plenty more free time. Enough to finally visit me in London. What did I think of that?

"Brilliant," I said. "Next weekend then?"

Arrangements made—I had better send him a reminder in the morning—I hung up. Much better to make any confession when you were face to face with someone.

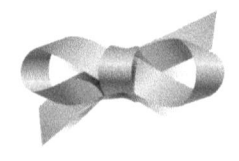

CHAPTER 19

Katya and Dexter kindly agreed to vacate the flat for Jack's visit. Katya had persuaded her workaholic other half they should jump on the Eurostar at St Pancras and head for Paris.

I spent Thursday evening sprucing up the flat. The lease included a weekly cleaning service so there wasn't much to do. Jack hated flying so he'd opted to get the train and it got in just after six o'clock, which gave me plenty of time to hotfoot it from the office and meet him at Kings Cross.

The best-laid plans of mice and men, right? All week I'd worked until eight o'clock at night to make up for the fact I'd be leaving the office at—shock horror—five o'clock on Friday. Marcia knew. Hyun-Ki was fine with it. My other office colleagues asked if Jack would be wearing his kilt when I went to meet him at Kings Cross, and if so was it true what they said about the true Scotsman and what he wore underneath one...

No comment.

But at three o'clock in the afternoon, an emergency crashed its way onto our desks. A new batch of Blissful Beauty's glow serum—the company's most popular product—had caused severe allergic reactions in some customers. Who'd all blogged/photoed/commented online about it. In the office, we squinted at the images. Women with angry red rashes and raised dots all over their faces. As beauty emergencies went, this one went to the top of the list.

"What are we going to do?" I asked Hyun-Ki. Neither of us had anything to do with Blissful Beauty's productions and I eyed the clock, its hands suddenly moving too quickly towards five o'clock.

"They've hired a crisis consultant," Hyun-Ki said. "She's due here any minute and we've all got to go to the meeting."

'Due here any minute' wasn't a statement you could use with confidence in London thanks to the traffic and sure enough, her minute turned into an hour. By this point, my foot tapped out a furious rhythm under my desk. I still didn't know what we as designers had to do with any of this. Did they expect us to put on white coats, hurry to the lab and recreate the serum from scratch ourselves?

The black-suited and stern-faced Donna Ingram of Crisis Communications swept in just after four o'clock and we gathered in the boardroom to hear her pronouncements, me checking the time every few minutes. The firm's own PR person—a lovely woman called Carrie—looked as cowed as the rest of us. Most of her job involved writing press releases about new products and hob-nobbing with beauty journalists. Angry red rashes were beyond her expertise level.

"Here is what we are going to do," Donna said, rattling out a set of instructions so comprehensive and detailed, I lost the will to live after ten minutes. But I'd clocked that yes, in a crisis such as this, every single person in the company had to do something. Hyun-Ki and I needed to go off and design cute-sy messages posts for Blissful Beauty's website and social media feeds—ones that reassured people rogue samples of product had turned up. Blissful Beauty was doing its utmost to recall them, and no if you used the serum from now on you wouldn't end up looking like a plague victim.

I typed out a quick message to Jack. "Work emergency. Soz. Be there about seven-ish?"

Half six came round and we still hadn't been given the sign off on the designs we'd created. I sent another apologetic message. There were lots of shops around Kings Cross. Could Jack entertain himself there or grab a coffee somewhere? By the time eight o'clock arrived,

I suggested he make his way to the flat and sent him the directions adding the word 'sorry' two hundred or so times.

I made my escape at nine o'clock. Outside, I called Jack. The phone went straight to voicemail. He must be on the Underground. I tried again three or four times, finally getting through to him ten minutes later.

"Where are you?"

When he named the station, I groaned. He'd got on the wrong line and was now miles away. And very grumpy. Safe to say Jack was a not a city person, and the hours spent jostling with crowds on the Underground had confirmed every bias he felt about London, Londoners and Transport for London. As for the prices—daylight robbery on every corner. He'd already blown most of the budget for the weekend.

I met him at Piccadilly Circus station. Jack had been wearing his waxed biker jacket; the one with a glove-like fit that made strangers stare at him in awe. He'd slung it across his shoulders, the thin T-shirt garnered him admiring looks from men and women alike. I hugged him, heat and frustration thanks to the past few hours radiating off him in equal measures.

"We've got the flat to ourselves," I said brightly. "And tomorrow is going to be such a lovely day. We'll get up late and then do some tourist-y stuff. The free bits."

I'd need to Google it. Apart from walking, was there anything in London where you didn't hand over your life savings to do?

"Have you had anything to eat?"

Mistake of a question. It triggered another rant about London prices and how you got overcharged for everything. He'd eaten a burger earlier which could have doubled up as shoe leather and the pint he'd drank in one of the pubs was weak, far too warm and at least three times the price of one back in the Lochside Welcome.

"Brilliant little cake shop there!" I said, pointing at the all-night Patisserie Valerie on my right, doing my best to highlight London's charms. "Would you like a cream slice?"

Jack peered at them, inspected the price and said absolutely not. No way was he letting me spend that amount of money on a wee dod o' pastry and cream.

"Not far now!" I announced. Once he was in the flat, cold drink in hand and the big bad world locked out, the mood might improve. I turned the corner onto Warwick Street and the Blissful Beauty shop, the usual queue snaking its way metres back from the front door. Friday night the shop opened till midnight because yes, people wanted to buy skincare and make-up at that time.

The bouncer, a nice chap called Eddie I'd gotten to know pretty well over the past few weeks, winked at me as we passed before opening the door to let one lot of customers out and another lot in.

I spotted her a nanosecond before Jack did, and gulped. This would do nothing for Jack's mood.

Kirsty. And delighted to see us.

"Gaby! Jack! So fabulous to see you both!"

As ever, Kirsty's appearance outshone everyone around her. She'd picked a gold metallic dress, the perfect foil for her ash-blonde hair and marble white skin. High heels put her at the same height as Jack and showed off spindly ankles. She put a hand on her hip angling herself. Strangers might think she was Jack's girlfriend rather than me.

Some of those queuing to get into Blissful Beauty recognised her. She blew them kisses and took out her phone.

"I'd better get a pic with you, Jack darling, so our fans don't think Gaby is making her boyfriend up. No-one's seen him yet and we don't want people thinking she's really a sad single, rather than a blissed-up bride-to-be!"

Before Jack could object, she cosied up to him and held her phone high above.

"Be so funny if my fans see this on Instagram and think we're back together, right, Jack?"

Jack's expression changed from dismay to horror.

Kirsty continued, oblivious. "Such a great opportunity! I've picked up some more of my freebies and we can film the both of you. I can offer skincare advice for guys!"

"Soap and water," came the growl from Jack, who was yet to embrace metrosexuality. "And no chance."

Kirsty weaved an arm through his, swinging him around so they faced the queue, all watching with interest. "You guys! What do you think? Should I do a video about male skincare for the groom-to-be with this gorgeous guy?"

"Yes!" "Too right!" "I'll powder his nose anytime!"

"There! You have to do it now. Shall I come round tomorrow and we can film it in the flat?"

Dear oh dear. We were in an explosive situation. I took hold of Jack's other arm. A brief tug of war took part before Jack wrenched his arm from Kirsty's, and I pulled him away hurriedly.

"Of course!" I said. "Phone us before you pop round!" Out of the corner of my mouth, I promised Jack my phone would be off all day and we'd answer the door to no-one. Even the world's most persistent bell ringer.

Inside the flat, Jack stared out the window at the crowds below. "Do you ever get used to the noise?"

"The advantage of my new job is," I said, taking his rucksack from him and turning the TV on for background noise, "I'm so knackered most of the time I could sleep through a hurricane."

Katya had left the remains of her latest raid on an upmarket vegan deli in the fridge and I dished it out. Ordering a takeaway or going out for something was too risky. Kirsty might still lurk below, waiting to pounce on us with her phone and insisting on selfies and films for YouTube or Instagram.

Food finished and the outside noise levels dying down, I cleared our plates and took them into the kitchen. I perked up as I rinsed them off. Friday night—oh all right, almost Saturday morning—and here we were all alone in a flat. Time for us to try out that big bed made for two in my room seeing as I'd been rattling around it all on my lonesome for weeks now. About to suggest it, I headed back to the living room, removing my top to make it that bit more enticing.

"Ta-da!"

The best-laid plans... my fiancé had stretched out on the couch, the fine lines around his eyes and on his forehead ironed out.

Ever present London noise or no, he was fast asleep.

· · ⚜ · ·

THE UNIVERSE WEIGHED up my Friday and decided in terms of karma I deserved much, much more... I awoke late morning to the smell of freshly made bread and coffee.

"Morning!" Jack appeared at the bedroom door, fully dressed and red hair still sleep tousled. A moment of disappointment at that. "To make up for being a grumpy git, I went out and found us breakfast. I thought we could eat, get our energy levels up and then..." Eyebrows raised, lashes opened and closed slowly on a lascivious wink.

Ooh! Goodbye disappointment.

The rest of Saturday flew by. We didn't leave the flat—ahem—until four o'clock, my phone switched off to avoid any accidental Kirsty calls where she invited herself over or, horrors, suggested a double date with whatever bad boy billionaire she was seeing. She got through a lot of them. The latest guy owned a multimedia company and was forever pictured on gossip websites and magazines in dark glasses with his arm slung over identikit tall, skinny blonde women.

I'd dug out a free guide to London's sights so we walked through the capital, Jack managing to keep his complaints about the crowds to a minimum. When we wandered around Leicester Square, he drew a few stares—doubtless people wondering if they'd just spotted Sam Heughan, the actor who played Jamie Fraser in Outlander.

He even played along when two Americans approached and asked if they could get a selfie with them. I took the pic and told them I was his publicist. He was in London for talks about the next series. Bet they couldn't wait to see what happened...

By the time it got to Sunday afternoon, we'd successfully dodged Kirsty, seen the obligatory bits of London (from the outside) and had enough fun to get me through two more weeks without him. Jack's train was due to leave early evening in time to get him back to Lochalshie before midnight. About to suggest we end our weekend with a celebratory Indian takeaway, I switched my phone on to order through Just Eat.

Goodness. What a lot of messages. Where to start? The Lochalshie WhatsApp group wasn't worth checking. If you switched off the notifications or your phone for even a day, a three-figure number of messages greeted you when you looked again. But someone had also phoned me a few times. Voicemail told me I had six missed calls.

"Gaby. Phone me back, aye?" Ashley.

"Gaby, I need to speak to you URGENTLY."

"Gaby—I've tried Jack too. Where are you?"

"Gaby. What the FU—"

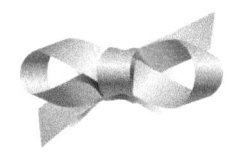

CHAPTER 20

Blimey. I held the phone away from my ear, Ashley having chosen to shout his last message left half an hour ago. Jack glanced up, having turned his phone on at the same time and listened to one or two choice messages himself. "What's the matter with Ashley? He doesn't sound best pleased."

An understatement. The second two messages he left on my answerphone were even more graphic. I wasn't sure what he suggested I do with my body was physically possible.

"Um, did he tell you what he's angry about?"

Jack, shook his head, his face creasing in puzzlement. Reluctant as I was to break the good vibe of our weekend, phoning him back while Jack was with me made the prospect (slightly) less scary. And given how many messages he'd left, he was only going to call again.

I put the phone on the coffee table, dialled the Lochside Welcome and put it on speaker.

"Gaby."

"Hi, Ashley! Great to hear from you? Is anything wrong?" Sunny cheeriness might disarm him.

There followed a long string of swear words, sunny cheeriness disregarded. "The whole point of youse two getting married was to gie the Royal George a ruddy great ya boo sucks to you, no' endorse their soddin' wedding package!"

Eh? And, er, our marriage wasn't *solely* aimed at sticking it to the Royal George. Jack took the phone from me, switched it off speaker mode and spoke to Ashley himself. Nods, plenty of 'I sees and 'We'll fix its' followed. I heard snatches of what Ashley said, but it still made no sense. What had I done?

Jack hung up and rubbed the bridge of his nose sighing.

"Well?" I asked.

"Your wedding planner."

Mine? Ours, surely.

"Did you ever discuss with Kirsty whereabouts in Lochalshie you wanted to get married?"

"Of course I did!"

But the sudden tight and uncomfortable gripe in my stomach made me pause. I'd just said 'Lochalshie', never specifying the Lochside Welcome. Ashley's cousin's best friend's husband and a part-time DJ, Jack explained, had been booked for a 'top-secret' event at the Royal George on December 21. Laney, Ashley's cousin, said to the guy, "Oh aye? Is that the official launch of the hotel? We know all about that."

"No," the husband said, "some London wedding planning company has booked me. Fancy new chef doing the catering an' all."

At that, the gripe tightened. I thought back to Kirsty's words when we'd made the plans for my hen night.

"And the food's arranged for the wedding—you're going to adore it. A brilliant new chef who loves experimenting with food to challenge and excite the palate. I've eaten his stuff. It's out of this world!"

A brilliant new chef. Ashley hadn't taken on anyone, but Zac had returned to the Royal George having honed his skills in Hammerstone Hotels all around the UK. Kirsty knew him well. She must have tasted his food before, weird detox diet allowing. And she was linked to the Hammerstone Hotels operation already. Her dating boot camps took place in the group's London boutique hotels. Easy enough for her to organise something free with them and kudos for the hotel—brilliant pictures, masses of coverage thanks to Kirsty's eager eye for publicity and self-promotion.

I stabbed my finger on her name on my phone contacts. Straight to voicemail. Ironic, hmm? The woman I'd switched my phone off to avoid all weekend now doing the same. Because someone must have got word to her and she'd taken on a low profile.

I corrected myself. *If you didn't tell her, Gaby, how was she supposed to know? And in Kirsty's world this is a huge favour. Posh, super-fancy hotel offers facilities—and food, unlike the Lochside Welcome—for free.*

Jack paced the floor, muttering about tomorrow morning and what was going to happen when he dared leave his house. Would he be spat at in the street? He stopped in front of me.

"I warned you, didn't I, how devious Kirsty is. But no, you, Gaby, knew better. A free wedding. Soddin' rose petals on the bed. It's just that we'll hae tae leave Lochalshie afterwards because all our family and friends will hate us. And no-one, no-one, Gaby, will come tae the wedding in the first place!"

The wise woman kept her mouth shut. The one whose flashes of temper sometimes matched her husband-to-be's snapped. "My side won't care."

The response was none too polite—a resurfacing of the feeling he was only the sucker who turned up on the day. Though, mark him, he wouldn't be going anywhere near the Royal George. I admired the affection, mark me. Straight from Bonnie Prince Charlie's words to Jamie Fraser in Series 2 of Outlander. Unfortunately, that made me stress-giggle, which drew the barked response, "I dunno what you think is so funny."

"I'll fix it," I snapped at him. "And smooth Ashley's ruffled feathers."

"They're a lot more than ruffled. He's planned the menu, ordered the food and organised extra catering staff."

"Fine. As I said. I. Will. Fix. It."

Jack checked his phone, heaving his rucksack over one shoulder. "I need to go. My train's in forty minutes."

We stood opposite each other, resentment shimmering between us. I'd meant to take him to Kings Cross where we would exchange hugs, kisses and fond farewells. I held my phone up. "I'd better stay here and keep trying Kirsty's number."

He nodded, leaning forward to peck me on the cheek. Dutiful, not affectionate. "Okay. Let me know how it goes."

And with that he was off. I watched him from the window, shiny red hair making him easy enough to pick out from five floors up as he walked towards the Tube station. Once he'd disappeared within—no backward glances to the flat—I tried Kirsty again. No reply, and no reply ten minutes later. I kept my messages for her answer service politer than Ashley's had been.

"Kirsty, hi! Please can you call me as soon as you get this? I need to talk to you about something, like, crucial."

Then, "Kirsty, hi! Caitlin says she can't wait to appear in one of your wedding make-up videos. Phone me back, yeah?"

Desperate times demand desperate measures. When she hadn't phoned back half an hour later, I checked her Instagram account in case she was dead. The Caitlin hook—even if it was a lie—should have made her abandon everything else and jump on her phone. Nope. On her feed, she'd posted up one of those inspirational quotes—*Look to the Stars! You're amazing, you truly are!* Next to a picture of Kirsty grinning inanely and staring at dark skies. 1,262 likes and 832 comments.

"Gaby! How did your weekend with Jack go?"

Katya and Dexter back from their Eurostar jaunt to Paris. I stirred myself and wandered out into the hall, stifling back envy. Here were two people who'd just enjoyed a fantastic weekend. Katya's blonde hair looked even more sun-kissed than usual even if it was late autumn, and she must have picked up that stylish navy blue shift dress that hugged her curves while she was over there.

Dexter had his arm draped around her, and their luggage included several cardboard bags from iconic Parisian stores.

"Fine... not really. It started badly, perked up and then went rapidly downhill."

What happened?" she said, following me into the living room and kicking off her heels.

"Little misunderstanding over the wedding location," I said, filling her and Dexter in about what had happened.

"Oh dear," Katya said. "But fixable, right?"

"Right. Once I get hold of Kirsty who is not answering her phone." To prove the point, I rang her number again, holding my phone up so Katya could hear it ping straight to the answer service.

"Well, it's easy enough to sort out. You can phone the Royal George, explain Kirsty acted without your say-so and you wish to cancel any ideas they have for weddings on the twenty-first of December."

I nodded. Dexter, catching the tail end of what Katya had suggested, said that sounded sensible. And Ashley would recover.

"You got me to book out his whole hotel once, didn't you, Gaby? Ashley charged far more than it was worth..."

Ah. I'd always wondered if Dexter knew how much Ashley had diddled him. Still, he didn't seem to bear a grudge and it had been Blissful Beauty's money. Good point too. Ashley might hate me now but residual feelings from that once-upon-a-time insanely expensive hotel booking must still be there.

I stared at my phone and took several fortifying deep breaths, trying to sum up forceful Gaby. She hid behind more usual 'I hate confrontation Gaby' shaking like a leaf.

"Do you want me to do it?"

"Would you?" I beamed at my best friend. "Blame Kirsty for everything."

Katya found the number online and called. She hadn't put the phone to speaker, but her higher-spec model made it audible anyway. We exchanged astonished stares at the voice that answered.

"Good evening. The Royal George. How may I help you?"

Silky smooth vowels and a plummy accent. I knew he was the chef, but the receptionist too?

"Zac. Hello."

Dexter, his attention on the piles of fliers we had for local takeaways, looked up sharply. The dreadful Zac, murderer of cats, teller of lies and once-upon-a-time love interest of Katya. I'd always wondered how much she told Dexter about what happened between them. The incident at Monaghan's fish and chip shop, for instance...

"Katya!" The warmth came straight through. Liar he might be, but I knew how strongly Zac had felt about Katya. Maybe he thought this out-of-the-blue phone call signalled a change of opinion. She waggled her eyebrows at me and swung straight into small talk. How was he? Executive chef and manager of the hotel now? Did that mean he did everything, even answering the phone?

"No, no," he said, "I happened to be passing. Anyway, what can I do for you?"

I heard the note of wistfulness and hope there. So did Dexter. He moved closer to Katya, perching himself on the edge of her armchair.

"Well," Katya said, adding a little giggle in true Kirsty tinkly-laugh-y style. "I'm calling on Gaby's behalf. She can't come to the phone just now because she's got terrible diarrhoea."

I stifled an outraged scream. This was what you got for offloading difficult phone calls. I held both hands up, two fingers spread in perfect vees. Katya poked her tongue out.

"There's been a silly misunderstanding. Kirsty booked the Royal George for Gaby and Jack's wedding. You know how she is trying to set herself up as a wedding planner? Only she didn't ask Gaby or Jack where they wanted the wedding to be, and they're desperate to marry in the Lochside Welcome because it has so many fond memories for them."

A pause—a far too long one. When Zac's voice came back on, it was considerably less friendly.

"Plans have been put in place. Kirsty made the booking weeks ago. I've been working hard on the menu. I thought if Jack was willing to get married in the Royal George I was willing to forget about—"

Neither of us heard the rest of the sentence, Katya's phone cutting out suddenly. She stared at it. "Stupid thing's run out of charge. I was using it a lot in Paris for pics and everything."

I slid my own phone across to her. "Please would you call him again? Though if you could lay off remarks about diarrhoea, that would be much appreciated."

When she reconnected Zac's plummy home counties words were cool and clipped. Gaby and Jack, he said, should think themselves lucky that Kirsty was yet to return the contract. Otherwise, we'd both find ourselves sued to kingdom come and back for breach of contract/loss of business etc., etc. The raised voice when he said 'Gaby' told me he knew fine I was sitting nearby. Rather than on a toilet.

(Unless Katya and I were very close.)

She threw in a few more general remarks, wishing him well in his new venture and hoping life was working out for him, adding that she thought about him from time to time. Dexter raised an eyebrow at that and she shook her head furiously, mouthing, 'No, I don't! Ever.'

"That's that," Katya said, handing me my phone back. "Safe to say, he didn't take the news well. If I were you, I'd block the number from your phone. Just in case he decides to send you abusive messages."

Posh idiots with bad opinions of me aside, the relief that the news had been passed on was overwhelming. Now for the nice bit, where I called Ashley and gave him the news. Thankfully, Ashley had kept what he'd heard to himself. Otherwise, I dreaded to think what the Lochalshie WhatsApp group might have dreamt up in insults.

"Ashley! Brilliant news. I've made it clear"—Katya cleared her throat; I ignored her—"to the Royal George that there's been a terrible misunderstanding. I don't know why they thought we were going to marry in there. The very idea!"

Another loud 'humph' from my friend.

"But it's all sorted and I for one can't wait!"

Ashley surprised me. Profound apologies for ever doubting me, so sorry in fact—he gave thanks to me and Blissful Beauty every day for the Caitlin visit last year—he wanted to throw in some freebies. Did we want, for example, a cake made by his wife's cousin's husband's aunt? What that woman could do wi' sugar craft had to be seen to be believed. And then there were chair covers. When he thought about it, it seemed mean to charge for them. If we wanted rose petals on any beds, he'd source them too. A toastmaster. One glass of champagne for each guest, etc. I said 'yes' to everything.

Ashley stopped me just as I was about to hang up. "Gaby, the guest list? You've no' got long to go and you and Jack havenae even given me a rough figure. Are we talking fifty or one hundred folks? I cannae do more than one hundred. Plus, some of your guests will need to book rooms. As soon as."

"Of course, of course!" I tried adding them up in my head, losing count after thirty. "Next week. Promise."

Dexter high-fived me when I hung up. "Way to go. I said, didn't I, that he owed you? Now, can we finally get some food before I die of hunger?"

HIGHLAND WEDDING

• • ~~ • •

GIVEN THE FROSTY ENDING to our last meet-up, I figured messaging Jack rather than phoning him was the better idea. I'd present him with my success in restoring the good name of Gaby and Jack—Lochalshie wedding of the year to take place in Lochalshie venue of the year and NOT the Royal George. He could mull it over, reflect on my brilliance and phone me later declaring undying love, etc.

ME: Hi—everything A-OK, hunky-dory, 100 percent on at the Lochside Welcome December 21. Not long to go... *Squeals*!!!!!! XX

JACK: Good.

[Me to myself—good, what? Everything is sorted or that the wedding is so close? Reminded myself that Jack was rrrrrrrrrubbish on any form of text communication and thus should be excused.]

ME: Ashley so pleased, he's thrown in TONNES of freebies. Chair covers. Stand for the cake. A toast master. A glass of champers so everyone can raise a glass to us!! We're forgiven!!!!

JACK: You're forgiven. Nothing to do with me.

[Me to myself—yes, well you made that clear enough before.]

ME: So, my hen party is coming up. Should be v exciting and glam. Caitlin, wall-to-wall celebrities etc! XX

JACK: Sounds fun.

[Me to myself—note lack of kisses as well as enthusiasm. Huh.]

ME: Lots of our friends will be there—plus you'll see all the pics. Mhari will upload loads. Will try not to get caught on camera snogging any Hyun-Ki's!!!!!!

[Me to myself—SHOOT! Slip of the finger there. My blasted auto-correct was set to change hunk to Hyun-Ki because he and I messaged each other all the time. Amend, amend, amend.]

ME: Hunks, obvs!!!! Ha ha ha!

JACK: Obvs. Enjoy. Gotta go.

ME: Bye!!! XXXXXXXXXXXXXXXXXXXXXXXX

[Me to myself—oops! Too late. He's gone. Rough figure for guest list. Still not drawn up, discussed and argued about. Still, loads of time. Will do after the hen party.]

A most unsatisfactory exchange. Still, Jack had plenty of time between now and the hen party to come round. Plus, I knew that the next time he ventured into the Lochside Welcome, Ashley would pile on free drinks and a pizza, relieved that the wedding and all its ensuing publicity was going ahead.

Message done and the doorbell chiming with the arrival of our food, I got up. My phone rang once more. Kirsty. About flipping time.

"GABY!"

Did a memo float about somewhere that said this Sunday was National Shout at Gaby day? Three times so far in less than two hours.

"What on earth have you done? The Royal George was *the* perfect venue for your wedding. Imagine the photos! I'd set everything up with them. Spent hours finding you free stuff and arranging Instagram promotions with my suppliers. You rotten, ungrateful, boyfriend stealing, cat murdering…"

CHAPTER 21

"Aye so, we're a wee bittie lost. How do you get to yours from..." A whispered consultation took place while Mhari asked if anyone knew where they were. Only eight people from Lochalshie would ever think borrowing a minibus to drive all the way to London—and that when you got there, you'd be able to park outside someone's front door—was doable. I'd tried, Jack had tried and even Katya and Dexter had got involved. No, it wasn't a good idea. Why didn't they jump on a stagecoach and come down?

Or, as I cheerfully pointed out, not bother at all? I wouldn't mind.

But no, Mhari, Jolene, Caroline, Enisa, Laney, Laney's sister, Mhari's cousin and Mhari's cousin's best friend (I was still to meet the latter three) thought it splendid larks. About to ask who was driving, I bit the question back. Better not to know—and then I'd be able to claim ignorance when Jack grilled me on who'd bashed or crashed his precious minibus.

"Birmingham!" Mhari announced triumphantly. "On some big ring road. We've been round it a few times already."

Luckily—or unluckily depending on your perspective—the hen party attendees had set out in plenty of time. This way, they'd only be two hours behind schedule instead of five if I'd told them the right time I'd expected them to arrive. Dexter found it hilarious, sticking his nose around the kitchen door where he was preparing sugar syrup so he could make us all cocktails.

"Where are they now? Birmingham?" His Texan accent stressed the 'ham' bit.

In the spirit of diversity and openness, I'd invited him and Hyun-Ki along too. Hyun-Ki, who'd never met Caitlin before, was so excited I feared he might explode. He kept popping out of the kitchen, suggesting further risqué names for cocktails and asking us what we thought of his outfit. Would Caitlin approve?

I took in check striped trousers, a black silk shirt and super-shiny polished brogues. "Yes."

Katya, painting her nails dark green, eyed me. "Which is more than can be said for you. I know you don't believe in sartorial elegance, Gaby. But we're going to the Crowley Townhouse. Please don't make the doormen mistake you for a Big Issue seller."

My mother, who'd come up last night, added her agreement.

Rude. And as it happened, I'd treated myself to a new outfit I planned to change into later. London charity shops were something else if you knew where to go. Earlier that morning, Mum and I had taken ourselves to the leafy suburbs of Harrow where people cleared out their wardrobes at the end of every season. Once I'd waded through the old lady cruise wear, the perfect bargain of a dress presented itself—turquoise silk with a wide cummerband waist band and a puff ball skirt. It clashed spectacularly with the red tights I'd bought to go with it, and as long as I didn't walk too far, the red sock boots finished my outfit off nicely.

After that, Mum insisted we hit the horror show that is Westfield Shopping Centre on a Saturday so she could find her mother-of-the-bride outfit. Mission unsuccessful after what felt like three hundred trips in and out of changing rooms. "I think I'll just go to Jarrold's, love," she said to me, naming the department store in Norwich that had been there since the dawn of time. As I'd known she would.

"I'm going to shower," I told her and Katya now, "and get changed."

Why Katya thought I'd go to my hen party while wearing trackie bottoms and a faded black hoodie top, I had no idea. Even if I had debated the possibility earlier.

I was just finishing drying my hair when the doorbell rang. OMG—had the Lochalshie contingent achieved the impossible, battled their way out of Birmingham, raced down the M1 and found themselves a parking spot in Central London?

I stuck my head around the living room door. "So amazing to see... Oh. It's you."

Katya stood beside Kirsty, arms folded. I'd passed on the details of the other week's exchange. The call ended when we hung up simultaneously, me telling her she was fired as the wedding planner and her shouting at me that she quit. Her contract for Blissful Beauty meant she had another five wedding make-up videos to do. She could find another bride-to-be to appear in them.

My best friend's expression told me I only needed me to tip her the wink and she'd launch on Kirsty and tear her from limb to limb. While I cheered.

Kirsty wore an over-the-top fancy outfit—too fancy for a casual drop-round. The velvet jumpsuit made it obvious she'd skipped her underwear, and her hair was piled on the crown of her head—delicate tendrils hanging down to frame her face.

"Gaby! You look SO beautiful. I'm delighted you've taken advantage of all my free make-up lessons."

Jeez. I hadn't put any slap on yet.

"Why are you here, Kirsty?" Katya asked, foot tapping. "We're heading out shortly."

"Are you? Where are you going?" Kirsty swung around to face her, a piece of overacting so hysterical I almost applauded.

Sod it. Kirsty had her hundreds of thousands of online chums, and yet here she was blagging an invite to the hen party of a woman she barely knew. It said a great deal about her in real life friends.

Mine, bossy, annoying, nosey and interfering as they often were, would take a bullet for me. Besides, once we got to the Crowley Townhouse I knew what would happen. Kirsty would abandon all pretence of friendship and flutter off to wheedle her way into Caitlin's inner circle. We'd only have to put up with her for an hour.

"Would you like to come to my hen party?" I asked, as Katya waved her hands and mouthed, "No, no, no!" But Kirsty's recent Instagram feed had included naff inspirational quote number 377—*Believe, believe, BELIEVE in the magic of kindness*. 6,531 likes and 469 comments and endless emojis. Inviting Kirsty to my hen night covered me for kind acts until halfway through the next decade at least.

"Gosh, I'll need to cancel a few things," Kirsty said, and I nodded along. Dexter appeared and presented her with a cocktail. This being a hen night—and his first—he'd opted for the tackiest ones he could dream up. So, we had Porn Star Martinis, Screw Drivers and one made from Bailey's topped with whipped cream and a name that made me blush. He handed it over and told Kirsty what it was called, face poker straight. She batted her eyelashes—a double row of falsies that looked so heavy it astonished me she could keep her eyes open—and drank it down, sticking out her tongue to lick the cream that rimmed her mouth. Hyun-Ki widened his eyes, mouth hanging open.

My mum was on the Prosecco. Always a mistake. She called it lady petrol. I called it the quickest way to make a twat of yourself when you are in your late forties and ought to know better.

"Any update on our Lochalshie friends?" Katya asked, and Dexter nodded. "I found them a parking place."

"What?"

"Blissful Beauty has an underground car park—not well known about for obvious reasons. I got them a space there."

Unbelievable. Yes, my Lochalshie friends would be able to find a parking spot virtually outside the front door. On cue, the doorbell rang and eight fractious people burst in.

"Aye, aye Gaby—filthy city this."

"You got cocktails on the go? I have one o' they Porn Star Martinis."

"Kirsty? What's she doing here, Gaby?"

"Can I phone Stewart? My phone's dead and he's in charge of Tamar for the weekend. I need to check he hasn't accidentally left him in the pub."

The last comment from Jolene. Stewart in sole charge of a tiny child a terrifying prospect. Jolene clearly thought so too. She exchanged fraught words with Stewart—*No, no, no he's not ready to be weaned, do NOT give him porridge*—and knocked back her Screw Driver in one.

My almost mother-in-law gave me a big hug. "I'm glad you got the Lochside Welcome sorted out, Gaby. That was a silly mistake to make, wasn't it? As if any of us would ever want tae go tae that terrible place wi' that awfy man in charge."

I put my finger to my lips, tipping my head towards Kirsty but I needn't have worried. Mhari's cousin and Mhari's cousin's best friend—still to be introduced—were busy fan-girling her, going on and on about how brilliant her YouTube channel was. When they asked her for selfies, Kirsty protested for all of two seconds. She couldn't possibly upstage Gaby's hen night. And then did anyway.

"We'd better leave soon," Katya said. "The book launch starts in an hour."

I grabbed my Oyster card and cringed at the idea of getting eight Lochalshie residents and my mother onto the Tube in one piece and out the other end without losing anyone. Katya waved her head. "I've got us valet parking at the Crowley Townhouse," she said. "Caitlin book author privileges."

Unbelievable yet again. We were going to drive to a venue in Central London and park outside. Dexter offered to drive as he hadn't touched the cocktails and he knew his way around London. In the bus, Mhari made sure she bagged the seat next to me. "Aye, so you and Jack are speaking again, are you? It's just that I've bought my wedding outfit—and it didnae come cheap—so I want tae wear it."

"Thank you, Mhari. Yes, we are speaking. We're perfectly happy."

Happy-ish. I found myself wistful for our early days and all that relaxed joyful fun we had. Perhaps that would return once we were married, and not fretting about reformed fathers, mistakes about venues and the hundred or so decisions about tiny stuff that weddings seemed to entail.

"Is your plus-one going to be Lachlan?" My turn for sly questions.

"Him! Huh. He dumped me the other week just because I said my pet name for him in the pub. Said it didnae do his image any favours."

My mind boggled but before I could explore this any further (Buunyboo? Squiggly Dumplings? Mr Softee?), Hyun-Ki took the seat in front of us, and perched up on it so he could introduce himself.

"Hello! So nice to meet you. I'm Hyun-Ki."

"Hiya, Hunky. Great name."

"Gaby told me you are JellyBabyXEX," he said, tones of awe and wonder. Mhari confirmed it—yes she was JellyBabyXEX, Scotland's greatest Candy Crush player and ranked twenty-seventh in the world. Was he a fan too...?

I left them to it, and took a seat next to Katya.

We reached the Crowley Townhouse in double quick time, Dexter knowing every sneaky side road in Central London. A uniformed valet took the keys, squinted at the bus and drove it away. We could expect to have it returned to us valeted—a job that might take longer than usual, given that the minibus had arrived in London its sides splattered in Scottish muck.

Hundreds of fans awaiting the arrival of Caitlin stood outside held back from the red carpet by thick gold rope and bouncers. They stirred when they saw the bus, obviously anticipating celebrity arrivals but hushed down again when we got out. One of them spotted Kirsty, and she nudged those around her who all took up the cry, "Christina!"

Kirsty vanished, disappearing into a sea of arms held aloft and waving cameras.

"Bye, Kirsty," Katya shouted after her, "lovely of you to come to Gaby's hen do!"

I doubt she heard.

Inside, we were directed to the garden at the back by a member of staff who appeared to glide rather than walk. Patio heaters turned the temperature to tropical and the trees around the place were draped with pink and silver bunting in the Blissful Beauty colours. At the front was a cardboard cut-out of Caitlin holding her book and grinning. *No Need to Cover Up: Caitlin Cartier's First Chapter*, the title inspired by the tag line for Blissful Beauty.

"Are you proud of yourself?" I asked the book's true author.

Katya shrugged. "Ish. I'll be better pleased when I get a book with my own name on it. Still, the money made up for it." She rubbed a thumb across two fingers. Too right the money did. When she'd first told me how much she was going to get for ghost-writing Caitlin's autobiography I fell off my seat.

Caitlin's publisher rushed over to Katya, glancing behind her worriedly.

"Goodness Katya, I hadn't expected you to bring so many..." She searched for the polite word. Hangers-on? Freeloaders?

"Don't worry CeCe," Katya waved a hand. "We've got Kirsty, aka Christina the Dating Guru, with us too. She's a 'gram star in her own right, so that makes it okay, doesn't it? And Psychic Josie," she waved her other hand in Caroline's direction, "whose advice Caitlin took so she could find true, enduring love."

My best friend had learned a trick or two over the years. She never let people with braying posh voices intimidate her.

I looked around me. The wall-to-wall celebrity thing was true. I spotted five soap stars, three Love Island finalists, two Hollywood A-listers and... GLORY BE. Sam Heughan himself. He was deep in conversation with one of the Love Islanders, who'd dressed as if she was still on a desert island in the middle of the summer.

I poked Katya. "Over there," I whispered and she smiled. "Yup, I heard he was coming. My own little surprise for you. Your challenge for the evening is to manage a conversation with him without coming across as a dork."

A tall order. The best opening line I could come up with so far was—"Hi Sam! You play Jamie Fraser in Outlander, right?" *Do not*, I told myself adding extra sternness to slam the message home, *say that to him under any circumstances.*

Mhari didn't know what the word embarrassment meant. She wandered freely among the stars, sliding up to them, asking them if they would mind her taking a selfie and snapping said pic without waiting for a reply. Hyun-Ki watched her with what I took to be admiration. I guessed he had gelled with someone else whose phone never left her hand.

Katya persuaded the circulating waiters to wander over to us first with the drinks and canapés. They were happy to do so, as we were the only ones eating them—tiny versions of fish and chips, roast beef and peas in mini Yorkshire Puddings and pieces of sushi. The joys of being normal size rather than celebrity skinny meant we got to eat most of them.

Caroline shook her head. "I need to hae a word wi' yon woman over there," she said pointing her glass in the direction of one of the

Hollywood stars. "And ask her if she's ever heard of osteoporosis. Awfy nasty, ye ken, and mair likely when you're that underweight." She headed off. 'Yon woman' looked taken aback when Caroline butted in and began her lecture on the dangers of under-eating. Perhaps when Caitlin arrived the actor would perk up and take notice as the reality star rated Psychic Josie's (fake) advice highly.

Katya, Jolene, my mum and I found a table and sat down.

"Is this your first weekend away from Tamar?" I asked Jolene who'd lost that haunted look from earlier. Hopefully, Stewart hadn't begun feeding their son porridge. Or left Scottie to babysit him while he went to the pub.

She nodded. "Yeah. I slept all the way down on the minibus—no wailing, screaming and messes to be cleaned up. And that's only Stewart. You and Jack okay, eh?"

"Fine, fine," I said. "Wedding plans proving a bit stressful, that's all."

Another nod from Jolene. "Yeah, why would anyone want to get married? All that fuss and money. And it being an—"

"—an outdated patriarchal institution no sane woman tries!"

Katya.

I helped myself to another drink. "Thank you as ever, dear friends, for your support."

They laughed and told me not to be such a grouch.

Still no sign of the tiny one. The official start time of the book launch had been an hour ago. Oh well. Not many people of my age could claim to have held their hen party in one of London's poshest venues for free. Even if Caitlin only turned up for five minutes—or not at all—it still counted as a big win.

Waiters brought out equipment—a portable hob by the looks of it, fridge, a worktop and knives—and set it up at the back of the garden. Beside me, Katya stiffened.

"Oh no! Surely not..."

A man in chef's whites began chopping vegetables, knife moving at record speed up and down onions, leeks and aubergines. When he shifted position so his face was clearly in our sight line, I groaned too.

I picked up my bag and scanned the crowd for the rest of my hen party attendees. If Katya and I—and probably all the Lochalshie crew—didn't want to be poisoned or at the very least have our food spat in, we needed to leave right now.

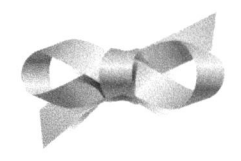

CHAPTER 22

Katya tugged my arm. "We can't let him spoil our party. We'll just eat the canapés and try to stay hidden."

Which would have been a fantastic plan if Caroline, her lecture on the perils of perpetual thinness to the Hollywood star finished, hadn't spotted him first.

"Zac Cavanagh!" she pointed at him, her voice taking on an unearthly quality as if a spirit really had channelled itself through Psychic Josie. "Why are you here?"

His head whipped up and he stared at her in disbelief. But as everyone had stopped their conversations—some of them holding their drinks midway to mouths—it looked like he needed to answer her. Mhari's face lit up. A spot of confrontation would make her night. Her fingers flew over her phone screen and sure enough, beside me Katya, Jolene and my phones beeped in unison as those who hadn't made the journey from Lochalshie got to hear all about my hen night anyway.

Zac straightened up and folded his arms. "I'm the chef for the evening. This is one of Hammerstone Hotels' properties. I'm getting some practice in before the launch of the Royal George later this year. Which will be a fantastic event."

His eyes picked out Katya. Defiance, longing or what? She returned the stare with knobs on, missing out the longing bit. You could almost see the laser beams that joined the two. Mhari's phone flashed, and Katya broke off to glare at her.

"Aye, well good luck wi' that," Caroline shouted back. "But dinnae expect any locals to attend. We'll be too busy at a wedding in the Lochside Welcome, is that no' right, Gaby?"

"Er..."

"Hunners o' people going!" Mhari said.

"And Hello! magazine is taking pics!" Laney Haggerty added.

They were?

"Stewart's done the coding for Ashley's website," Jolene joined in. "And it's so search engine friendly, it'll be at the top of any website search for Lochalshie every single time? No-one will even know the Royal George exists?" That question at the end of every sentence that thing New Zealanders do.

"Folks will see Gaby's wedding pictures." Person I didn't know. Mhari's cousin? Mhari's cousin's best friend? "And think to themselves, 'What an awesome place the Lochside Welcome is. I'll DIE if I dinnae get married there.'"

"And I've designed a VR app for Gaby's wedding! People from all over the world will be able to attend. Bet they can't do *that* at the Royal George!"

Hyun-Ki. He must think uniting with the other hens to shout insults at someone was standard British hen party practice.

Sam Heughan watched the proceedings, his expression a combination of bemusement and amusement. Maybe it was a nice change for him not to be the focus of everyone's attention.

Zac's face turned puce. He hadn't let go of that oversized kitchen knife either. Caroline was directly in front of him. All he needed to do was hurl it and... Dear oh dear.

Out of the corner of my eye I spotted CeCe gesturing frantically at Katya indicating she should get everyone to shut up. Not sure how she thought the unstoppable train that was Lochalshie people who'd taken against someone could be halted but there you go.

A flurry of yet more waiter activity at the door distracted Caroline and Zac, both of them turning to look. Five security guards flanked the doors, one of them whispered into the tiny microphone next to his mouth. Big star's arrival imminent then. Just in the nick of time too.

"Josie!!!! I'm so glad you're here!!!!!"

Caitlin, manager to one side and Dexter on the other, flew to Caroline, clasping both the doctor's hands in hers. Katya often moaned that Caitlin said everything as if she'd added ten exclamation marks to each sentence. In Katya's book few things surpassed such a crime.

"You *must* help me choose the best date for my wedding next year—the one the spirits think best."

Caroline/Josie nodded solemnly. "Aye, a wedding is a serious occasion. If your nuptials are to last, the stars must align and the elements be as one."

Beside me, Katya muttered, "Oh for heaven's sake." Quite. The stars would magically align, Jupiter find itself in Venus and earth, water, fire and air combine on a choice of five days—all of which Caitlin would have chosen anyway. Still, at least the mood had changed. The tiny one drew the crowd towards her, acolytes around the mini-goddess, the argument with Zac forgotten. At least I hoped it was. He'd taken up that knife and renewed chopping vegetables pressing down with a ferocity that made me wince.

Kirsty had magically reappeared, circling Caitlin, Caroline and those around them as she searched for a big enough gap in the circle to muscle in.

One of the hotel's staff members wheeled out a table piled high with Caitlin's books. Katya had shown me her copy earlier—a thick tome with a glossy dust jacket, Caitlin's beaming face on the front and the background a swirl of pink and silver, the spine and back illustrated with products from her range. After some hard negotiation—my friend had dropped her percentage on royalty rates for the Bulgarian translations of the book—the back cover included the line, *Edited by Katya Bukowski*.

CeCe clapped her hands. "Caitlin do you want to talk about your book?"

Caitlin took the mike from her. "Yeah, sure. I didn't write any of it. I talked to people, they recorded what I said and then Katya did the rest. She's, like, the most amazing writer in the whole world."

"True," I said to Katya who'd gone scarlet. A first. My best friend left blushing to me most of the time. From the look on CeCe's face—blind panic—I assumed Caitlin's little speech was unscripted. Dexter once told me she was impetuous. When she came to Lochalshie for the Highland Games/ launch of Blissful Beauty in the UK, she took her clothes off to open the games demonstrating Blissful Beauty's make-up and skincare was so good, you didn't need to cover up. A last-minute decision the Highland Games committee would not have sanctioned in a million billion years.

Speech made, CeCe's carefully invited journalists only had two questions for Caitlin: what she'd learned from setting up her business and becoming a 'self-made' billionaire at the age of twenty-one and how much she was in love with her new beau.

Caitlin pointed at Caroline. "I only fell in love with Donal because of Psychic Josie. She told me I needed to stop dating baseball stars and rappers, and find someone normal. Donal's the greatest, no—*the* greatest. I wake up every morning and give thanks to the Lord and Psychic Josie for leading me to him."

The religious bit was a new development. Still, it wouldn't do her reputation in the States any harm. Katya took a swig of her drink. "Check this out," she held up her phone. "Psychic Josie's website's just crashed. Three million people must be trying to book her. Your almost mother-in-law is about to become very, very rich."

The One Show. I could see it now—Caroline on the couch opposite Alex Jones and Matt Baker. Alex's dulcet Welsh tones. "So, Josie... a lot of people say astrology is nonsense and yet Caitlin Cartier credits you with helping her find love."

Caroline patted the back of her head and smiled. "Aye, well that's true. And if anybody else wants tae find love, I'm available for individual consultations at five hundred pounds an hour."

Good luck, Jack, I told him in my head. *Try reining your mother in after this.*

Katya nudged me. Sam Heughan had drifted over. Now would be the perfect opportunity to stand up, say hello and point out his similarity to my fi—

"Sam, hi!" Beaten to it by Kirsty, happy to flutter her too heavy eyelashes his way. Most of her conversations with guys were flirtatious but I'd never seen her in full-on mode. Good grief. Katya and I watched as the tinkly laugh sounded at frequent intervals, hands lightly touched him at every chance and she dropped her voice forcing him to lean in extra close to hear what she said.

"We should rescue him," Katya whispered. "Save him from a fate worse than death. Where's her latest alpha bad boy billionaire anyway?"

"You're right," I said, getting to my feet. "And I've always wanted to meet the real Jamie Fraser."

I walked up to them, holding out my hand. "Sam, hi! You play Jamie Fraser in Outlander, don't you?"

Behind me, Katya spluttered with laughter. But honestly, what would you do? Presented with a man you'd drooled over on screen for so long, stupid words were bound to come out.

Sam Heughan, bless him, nodded solemnly. "I do."

"I love the programme. And I've read all the books. Some of them three times!"

More razor-sharp wit and acute observation. More splutters of laughter behind me.

Kirsty's trademarked boyfriend hunter smile became fixed.

Sam looked behind me. "So, your friend wrote Caitlin's book? Is that why you're here?"

"Oh no," Kirsty said, "Gaby's here because this is her hen party. She's getting married in December. I'm her wedding planner and I've organised tonnes of fabulous freebies for her."

I'd sacked her. Or she'd quit—whatever happened first. Kirsty ignored my furious gesticulations, turning her back so Sam Heughan couldn't see my face either. She took her phone out and asked Sam if he would mind appearing in a selfie with her as her hundreds of thousands of fans would be super excited to see them together.

She held her camera up, Sam gamely plastering on his best 'delighted to be with this persistent fan' expression. I pulled a face, dived in front of them and photobombed it, making Sam burst out laughing. Kirsty shifted me back to the top of her most-hated list but as I'd amused Sam Heughan she had to keep her opinion to herself.

"I've got to go," he said. "Nice meeting you, ladies."

Kirsty shot me an evil look and stalked off.

Questions and answers finished, Caitlin drifted over to our table followed by her retinue, all the hangers-on and Kirsty doing her best to edge closer to the tiny one as sharp elbows either side held her back.

"Gaby, Katya—you wanna go clubbing? This party's lame."

"Er, well I've got quite a few people with—"

"Aye, all right then," Mhari jumped in, Laney Haggerty echoing her.

We skipped out of the place, Zac's food untouched and he, CeCe and the Hammerstone Hotel staff sending us dagger looks.

Outside the hotel, two stretch limos awaited—Katya, Dexter, my mum, Caroline, Mhari, Jolene, Hyun-Ki and I in the one with

Caitlin, her manager, hairdresser and personal make-up artist and the others in the second. There had been an undignified skirmish when Kirsty tried to get in the car with us but Caitlin's security staff bustled her into the second limo.

The limo had blacked-out windows, its own mini-fridge filled with small bottles of champagne and chocolate truffles and fake-fur lined seats. I surveyed it all and made myself pay attention to all the details. Chances were I'd never see the likes of this again. My mum squeezed my hand, her jaw hanging in a none too flattering way and a mini champagne bottle in hand.

"Is Caitlin going to come to your wedding, love?" she whispered, and I cringed. Mum was at the too much fizz stage where the volume control left the building. Luckily for me, Caitlin tipped her head, her expression puzzled. Mum's Norfolk accent was too strong for her to understand.

The limos pulled up outside a building in Soho, and we found ourselves whisked past queues and upstairs straight to the VIP area. I'd expected ear-splitting progressive trance, psychedelic lighting and a bar queued knee-deep serving hip cocktails. Instead...

The VIP area looked like a living room, soft lighting, velvet-padded walls, low-slung armchairs and sofas, beanbags all over the place and everyone wearing headphones, the wearers all dancing to different beats. Ah—the silent disco. Also, no bar. Only staff members who glided in and out of the doors bearing trays loaded with teas and coffees, and tables with bowls overflowing with crisps.

Caitlin sank into a beanbag next to me. "Gaby! Let's swap notes on weddings! And can you bring me a bowl of those chips?"

Chips? Ah, she meant crisps. Around me, my friends exchanged flummoxed looks. This was a club but not as they knew it.

Acceptance and then relief slowly set in. Jolene settled into one of the bean bags and fell fast asleep. Mhari and Hyun-Ki snuggled into another one, phones held in front of each other as they compared Candy Crush scores and what their respective phones could do. Laney Haggerty donned headphones and bopped to something, a beatific smile on her face. Dexter and Katya also put on headphones, their song choice the same so they could dance together. Kirsty zoned in on an attractive man dressed head-to-toe in designer gear who appeared to be on his own. My mum persuaded a waiter to bring her crisps and a glass of wine instead of tea, patting the seat on the sofa next to her beckoning Caroline to join her.

And I settled back on one of the sofas to talk to the world's most famous woman about weddings.

Caitlin grabbed my hand. "That ring," she breathed reverentially. "It's the best."

We held out hands. I agreed with her, even if her ring was a thousand times more expensive than mine. Hers a ginormous diamond and bling too far, mine a sparkling sapphire surrounded by tiny jewels.

"Tell me about Jack. Is he the greatest?"

Flattering when the world's most famous woman remembers the deets about you. "He's the best, Caitlin, the best!" I said. "And the most marvellous man ever, but..."

"What, honey?" She took my hand in hers.

It all spilled out. I couldn't blame too much drink, as I'd skipped the cocktails in the house and only had one glass of champagne in the hotel. Jack's lack of enthusiasm, the way we'd been bulldozed into marrying in the Lochside Welcome to save it from the Royal George, the mistakes, mishaps and misunderstandings along the way... and how I wished things could be simpler.

Caitlin, her head by now on my shoulder and one hand shovelling Pickled Onion Monster Munch into her mouth, smiled at that.

"The runaway train, right?"

Jack's words too. I nodded, helping myself to the Monster Munch before Caitlin snaffled the lot. "Rose petals on the bed—who needs that? And as for the guest list..."

"My mom and sisters each want a hundred of their own guests, and my agent has come up with four hundred other people I need to invite. Donal's freaking out."

No wonder. Close to a thousand guests. Weren't brides and grooms meant to talk to everyone on the day? She'd need to make the wedding last a week if they were to get around them all. Another waiter passed by, arms full of Monster Munch bags he tipped into bowls. I replaced our empty one.

"And I did this really stupid thing," those pickled onion crisps put me in confiding mood. "I snogged someone else. It was a complete mistake and I'd never do it again, but it was a spur of the moment thing."

I pointed at Hyun-Ki now in headphones and dancing with Mhari, though it looked as if they'd chosen different songs—Hyun-Ki finger tutting while Mhari waved her arms above her head.

"Girlfriend," Caitlin nodded approvingly. "He's snog-worthy for sure. I guess everyone's allowed one mistake."

Cue another mistake. Kirsty, who'd been hovering in the background, spotted an opportunity and pounced, landing on the now vacant armchair opposite our sofa. "Hey! So lovely to see you, Caitlin! Is that eyeshadow the Rust234 shade? It's amazing on you!"

Someone had done their homework. As Kirsty whipped her phone out ready for what would doubtless be three hundred or so selfies, I headed for the loos. I've been in my fair share of club toilets. These were the fanciest ones—a high ceiling, huge mirrors, hair straighteners and dryers in case you needed a quick blast, and a woman on hand to give you a fresh snowy white towel to dry your hands.

When I came out, Caitlin stood up. "I'm gonna go," she said throwing her arms around me. Kirsty tried her best to join in, missing the rude names Caitlin whispered in my ear, making me giggle. Once she'd gone, taking her retinue (and Kirsty) with her, Katya wandered over.

"What now, hen party girl?"

There was only one place I wanted to be. Failing that, seeing as I was almost five hundred miles away from Jack and the double bed in his house, the next best thing was the flat. When I made the suggestion, expecting protests from the rest of the party—it was only two am after all—everyone nodded, relieved.

Caitlin had left one of her limos for us especially, and Katya promised we'd be okay leaving the minibus at the hotel overnight. The Lochalshie party had booked rooms at the Hotel Ibis near to the flat and we dropped them off there, my mum and Hyun-Ki coming back to the flat with us. The latter, thanks to him being younger than the rest of us, wanted to finish off the cocktails and play drinking games. I took one of the more lurid coloured concoctions from him, while Katya and Dexter apologised and said they needed to go to bed. My mum, having downed far too much champagne, hugged me, told me I was her favourite child (ha! Wait till I told Dylan that!) and stumbled off in the direction of my bedroom.

"Can I come to your wedding too?" Hyun-Ki asked once we were alone.

"Of course, oh best boss in the world."

Crap. Yet another guest on the list I'd yet to write. Still, those cocktails made everything about the wedding seem suddenly doable. Guests? We should have tonnes. Lochalshie deserved a ginormous celebration! Jolene wasn't planning to marry Stewart any time soon, so the next wedding was probably decades off. Jack, the too-often reluctant groom? Not at all, not at all—he adored me. He couldn't wait till the moment he got to call me Mrs McAllan...

I squinted at my glass, alarmed to see I'd finished it off so soon after the first one. The walls of the room began to wobble and the ceiling appeared to lower and raise itself. Hyun-Ki's voice drifted over me, the words too unclear to make out. Dear oh dear—never trust a man who's never made cocktails before to know how much or rather how little spirits you should put in them. I shuffled closer to the sofa, its squishy depths too comforting to resist. I closed my eyes, wondered if we should also have Pickled Onion Monster Munch crisps instead of canapés (much cheaper, right?) and blacked out.

"WHAT THE HECK IS GOING ON?"

Mhari—her face and body backlit by sunshine that streamed in the living room window. How had she gotten in? More importantly, where was I, who was I and who... who was the man cuddled up behind me, one arm slung over my waist and wearing just his boxers? And was that...

No prizes for guessing whoever he was, he wasn't Jack.

CHAPTER 23

The minibus had to stop three times on the way back to Lochalshie for one occupant to stumble from it and throw up. Me.

Still, it felt as if I deserved the punishment. Even though nothing had happened. The night before, Katya had handed Mhari the spare keys to the flat. "Let yourself in whenever!" she'd said. "Dexter will make breakfast for us all!" He only looked taken aback for a few seconds. "Yeah, or I'll order us something in." Like many Americans, Dexter thought nothing of ordering in any meal—not just dinner.

Mhari, the fearful noise of London traffic keeping her awake most of the night ('How do youse ever sleep?') decided 10am was the perfect time for a spot of breakfast. She'd let herself into the flat, wandered into the living room and screamed her head off when she spotted Hyun-Ki and I curled up asleep on the sofa.

The end of the evening—or rather earlier that morning—was hazy. I remembered feeling woozy thanks to those too-potent cocktails and collapsing on the sofa. Hyun-Ki tried to call an Uber but couldn't make his fingers work properly. As the heating in the flat had accidentally been left on overnight, he stripped off to cool down. And then sat on the end of the sofa and tipped to the side behind me.

Mhari's shrieks brought Katya, Dexter and my mum rushing through—their expressions matching hers. Horrified disapproval. I jumped up, brushing bits of Pickled Onion Monster Munch off my top. At least that accounted for the disgusting vinegary taste in my mouth.

"Nothing happened!" I said. "I fell asleep drunk because I'd had too many cocktails. Hyun-Ki's my boss, for heaven's sake!"

Hyun-Ki's lean muscularity—and a strategically positioned cushion—made him appear impossibly tempting. Mhari clearly thought so, her eyes flickering first to me then to him, her mouth tightly pursed.

"Jack's an awfy good friend of mine," she said, hands on hips. "And he doesnae deserve this!"

"I expected better of you, Gabrielle Amelia Richardson." My mother, that ticking-off tone and words the ones I so often used on myself.

I flapped my hands. "Oh, for..."

Katya's mouth twitched. I knew she knew no shenanigans had taken place. I also knew she wouldn't bother sticking up for me just yet—my peculiar brand of Gaby chaos far too entertaining. I scowled. She shrugged.

"I'm fully dressed! And if I was going to cheat on Jack, I'd hardly do it in a flat full of people, would I?"

The logic convinced my mum, who nodded sagely and offered to make everyone teas and coffees. She turned to Hyun-Ki before she went. "Do you want to get dressed, love? It's awfully cold in here."

Poor Hyun-Ki. I laid my hand on his arm. He'd grabbed his shirt and held it in front of him like a shield. "Sorry about all this." He picked up his shoes and trousers and disappeared into the bathroom.

Mhari shut the living room door. "But you snogged him, didn't you? Kirsty told me."

Whhaatt??? I thought back to last night and Kirsty barging her way into the conversation I'd had with Caitlin. Blasted woman must have overheard us and saved the info up to pass on. Cow.

Katya's expression altered from amused observer to dismayed friend. No, I hadn't got round to telling her about the post cat rescue snog event. You know—the one where Hyun-Ki and I decided we had no chemistry so IT DIDN'T MATTER. But put it together with this morning's scenario and it took on a different meaning.

Damage limitation. A lot of. To do now.

"Once," I said. "It didn't mean anything."

Katya aligned herself with Mhari, the two of them united as judges. Dexter looked as if he'd rather be anywhere else. Or perhaps he was too busy worrying about the implications for Blissful Beauty. Head designer snogs not so head designer. After I got into trouble publicly endorsing another make-up range, I read the employment terms and conditions in full. They included a clause that Blissful Beauty employees were not allowed to date each other. So, who to sack—the vastly talented head designer or me?

"It did not."

Mhari reached for her pocket. I flew across the room and went for it too, doing my best to wrench the phone from her hand. An undignified tussle took place as she thrust it back into her coat pocket and I yanked the front of her jacket towards me. A rip sounded and the material came away in my grasp.

"I'll buy you a new one," I said, staring aghast at the material I held. I'd just ripped apart a waxed jacket, so a) expensive to replace and b) where had I found the strength? Wanting to stop someone updating the Lochalshie WhatsApp group must give you superhuman powers.

"You better."

Mum and a fully dressed Hyun-Ki returned bearing steaming mugs of tea and coffee. They took in the sight—me with my bit of ripped jacket and Mhari's outraged expression. The doorbell sounded. Great. The rest of the Lochalshie party. Mhari would fill them in with the news and they'd turn on me too. Particularly Caroline, a tiger mom when it came to Jack.

"Don't say anything," I begged as Dexter let them in. This was all deeply unfair. A girl has one small, misjudged snog with her admittedly super-attractive boss, and then ends up curled up with him because they both drank too many cocktails and everyone turns against her.

In the end, it was Dexter who came up with a solution. Of sorts.

Jolene, Laney, Caroline and the others were all in good spirits, particularly Jolene.

"I had the best, greatest, most fantastic night's sleep I've had in a long time," she told us, taking a cup of coffee from my mum. "And when I called Stewart to ask about Tamar, he hadn't abandoned him in the pub, got Scottie to babysit or fed him porridge. Result."

No-one noticed that Mhari and I weren't on speaking terms, and Dexter's breakfast takeaway kept everyone occupied while they wondered at the marvel of Deliveroo riders working all hours to keep Londoners fed and watered.

"Gaby," Dexter said, as I forced down a couple of mouthfuls of cream cheese and smoked salmon bagel before giving up. "Hyun-Ki and I have been talking about how hard you've been working. You could take some time off. Go up to Lochalshie on the minibus and surprise Jack?"

I refrained from hugging him too worried I might burst into tears. Yes, a surprise visit was perfect. The girlfriend with the non-guilty conscience visits her beloved, tells him what happened—snog and all—explains it meant nothing, nothing. And we all live happily ever after.

Katya, Jolene and Caroline thought it a splendid idea too. Mhari tutted, but didn't disagree. I'd achieved some kind of miracle as she had not yet opened her mouth. Plan made, Dexter offered to fetch the minibus back from the hotel and told us all to be ready to leave in an hour.

Katya wandered into my bedroom as I hastily flung clothes into my rucksack. "Nothing happened, did it?" she asked, filling my toiletries bag for me.

"Of course it didn't. Don't be disloyal."

Her eyes met mine in the mirror. "It's just... your whole wedding thing. It's been bonkers, hasn't it? And you have been so stressed. I don't blame you for looking at someone else. And wondering about alternatives."

I swallowed hard. Time and again, I came back to the same feeling. Back in August, everything felt simple and right. A small, cosy wedding. Done in six months' time. Since then, mistake after mishap happened. I thought of Caitlin and her runaway train. She and I were on it together, hurtling farther away from our fiancés every second.

She hugged me. "Go up there and tell him the truth. Tell him exactly what you feel."

"Everything?"

I felt rather than heard the 'yes' in response. "And also have a shower before you go. You stink."

A night on the sofa in yesterday's clothes and too many bags of Pickled Onion Monster Munch on top of cocktails did that to a girl. In the shower, I picked the hottest setting and stood there for five minutes summing up my favourite memories of Jack—the first time he kissed me, when I'd moved in with him and he lifted me in his arms to carry me over the threshold, how kind he'd been to me when Zac ran over and killed Mena...

By the time the minibus was ready to leave—Caroline insistent on driving seeing as Laney had done most of it on the way down, I couldn't wait to get on it. Part of it was a longing to return to Lochalshie. Funny, I'd spent most of my life in Great Yarmouth and yet a tiny, remote Scottish village felt more like my home. But I desperately needed to talk to Jack, and well before Mhari did.

After the bus had stopped for the third time for me to throw up—all those Monster Munch and wretched cocktails coming back to haunt me—she stopped sulking, patting the seat beside her when I came back in.

"You shouldnae have eaten all those canapés," Caroline said, taking the handbrake off the minibus. "That ruddy man put something in them to make you ill out of spite."

Nice of her to offer me an excuse but everyone else had scoffed plenty of them with no ill effects. "Nothing dodgy happened with you and that Hunky guy, then?" Mhari asked, one eye on her phone. When I glimpsed at it, I saw his name. They were messaging each other her thumbs moving at lightning speed over the screen. Hmm.

"Not a thing," I said, and then mercifully fell asleep on her shoulder so the rest of the journey was puke-free.

It was dark by the time we got to Lochalshie—late November making sunset that bit earlier in the north-west of the UK. Nevertheless, when the minibus headlights picked out the 'Welcome to Lochalshie' sign, my spirits lifted. Even if the nerves set in too. What kind of welcome awaited me? And how was I going to explain the whole Hyun-Ki thing?

I'd rehearsed the words a lot.

"Jack! I was desperate to see you! You'll never guess what! Last night, me and Hyun-Ki slept together and he was almost naked but NOTHING happened!"

Or:

"Jack! Surprise! So, there's something I need to get off my chest. I snogged my boss but it's okay because we then found out we don't fancy each other at all. Fab, eh?"

Caroline insisted on dropping everyone off at their front doors, so I was the last off the bus. She drove away asking me to tell Jack she'd bring the minibus back the next day. Our little house glowed in the darkness, the curtains shut but glimmers of light poking through. Mildred sat in the window. I liked to think she spotted me and mewed in recognition. More likely, I'd ruined her view of the loch or some bit of random wildlife she'd been eyeing up.

I knocked on the front door, too nervous to use my key to let myself in.

"Aye, alright, Mum I said you could—Gaby!"

My beloved, heart-breakingly handsome fiancé in a thick jumper over a lumberjack shirt, old jeans and bare feet. Hair in need of a wash, dark eyes wary. He blinked and then widened his gaze, a slow smile spreading itself across the lower part of his face. Did the smile reach his eyes?

"This is a surprise." He pulled me to him, burying his face in my hair. Mildred had come to meet me too, yowling loudly in unmistakeable 'feed me!' fashion.

"I'm off for a few days," I said, my voice muffled by none-too-clean either jumper. "And I've got something to tell you."

A pause and a tight squeeze.

"Me too."

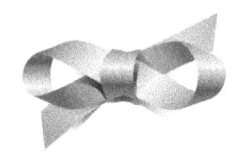

CHAPTER 24

The nerves intensified. When I'd been heaving up Monster Munch, canapés and cocktails earlier, I'd thought it wasn't possible to feel worse. Turns out that was only the warm-up.

'Me too' easily translated, right? *I do not want to marry you...* Perhaps Mhari hadn't kept her word and told the Lochalshie WhatsApp group. As my phone had died at Carlisle, I wouldn't know. More likely, he'd felt like that all along, too swept up in the chaos to object loudly enough and now he needed to stop it all before I ended up on my own in the Lochside Welcome waiting for a groom who'd fled the country.

How humiliating.

Jack took my rucksack from me. The house was warm inside, a contrast to outside. Winter came earlier and harder to the north of Scotland than it did to London and I shivered. Several new paintings took up space on the wall, though the picture of Oban harbour had gone—the one Jack had used in exchange for my engagement ring. Did he regret it?

He vanished into the kitchen, returning rubbing a hand through his hair. "I wasn't expecting anyone so I've not got any food in. Do you want to go to the pub for something to eat?"

"Yes!" I pounced on the suggestion. If he was going to tell me he didn't want to marry me, why would he do that in a busy pub? My spirits dragged themselves off the floor. And then plummeted once more.

Because you won't make such a fuss in a public place.

"Okay! I'll just get changed and put a bit of make-up on!" I fled upstairs and into our bedroom, flinging myself onto the bed to try to slow my pounding heart. Mildred followed me, jumping onto the bed and clambering onto my chest. She settled down there, purring her head off and needling me lightly with her paws. "Shall we stay here, Mildred?" I whispered, "and hide from the world?"

In deference to the colder weather, Jack had covered his bed with two of those thick fleece blankets he used in the minibus for tourists shocked by Highland summers—in that the temperature barely rose above 15 degrees most days. I turned my face and breathed them in. The smell—Jack to a tee—made me want to cry. Something I wouldn't experience for much longer?

I put Mildred to one side, swearing when she scratched me in response. In the bathroom, I looked hard at myself in the mirror. *Well, Gabrielle Amelia Richardson, if you are going to be dumped in a public place, do not look as if you deserve it.*

I got out my make-up and did the opposite of all Kirsty's daft wedding make-up rules—slathered on foundation and powder to cover up the greyness, gave my eyelashes four coats of Blissful Beauty's So Good They Look Fake Mascara, and found my reddest, glossiest lipstick and plastered it on. In the wardrobe, I picked out what Katya called The Hooker Dress. Dark red, bodycon, three-quarter length sleeves and—the best bit—a zip at the front that went from top to bottom. I'd never worn it here and as I wriggled into it, it felt a lot looser than the last time I'd put it on. That was something, I supposed.

Jack did a double take when I came down. "Er, we are just going to the Lochside Welcome?"

"Yes. I felt like dressing up."

He reached out a hand, cupping the side of my face. "Okay."

Then he proved Kirsty's rule—the one about dark lipstick sending men screaming in the opposite direction—wrong. One arm wrapped around me, the other tilted my head back and his lips landed on mine, hard, urgent, front teeth grazing the top of my mouth before the tip of his tongue escaped and traced its way around the opening of my mouth. I closed my eyes and when I opened them, his were fixed on me, the intensity boring into mine. Nerves jangled, heat rushed to my face, my chest, my groin... The zip at the top of the dress dug into my skin. One yank and the whole thing would descend to the floor and we could—

Jack's phone rang, the vibration in his front pocket startling both of us.

"Leave it," I whispered, but he murmured about needing to check just in case his mother had crashed the minibus into one of Ranald's stone dykes. We broke apart, the sight of him made me laugh. Glossy red lipstick smeared his lips, cheeks and chin. He looked like a vampire with a messy eating habit.

He studied his phone screen, face darkening.

"Anything wrong?"

Black-brown eyes back on mine. Expression still wary. Me confused. Hadn't the kiss just proved something? Today had been a roller coaster as far as my poor ol' emotions were concerned. Down, up, up and down, soars and plummets one after the other. That Chinese curse—May you live in interesting times. I'd settle for ordinariness right now. Me, Jack, Mildred and our little house, this tiny village and a few friends. Quite enough for me.

"Let's go out. You need to clean your face up."

"So do you."

Outside the wind set in in earnest, trees rustling and the waves on the loch lifting and crashing on the shores. I huddled close to Jack, who'd wrapped his arm around me. A good sign, I decided. And once we'd eaten, we could pick up where we left off.

Ashley spotted us as soon as we came in, the pub quieter than usual because of the time of year.

"You two!" he said, hurrying over, stopping suddenly as he took in my make-up and what I was wearing. "Aye, aye, Gaby. Are you auditioning for a part in the Lady Boys of Bangkok?"

Cheek.

"So, how many folks are coming to the wedding? I need to know by the end of next week, latest. Can you at least gie me a rough idea?"

"Five hundred and fifty," Jack deadpanned, and Ashley swallowed hard. "Aye, well I s'pose you're both awfy popular, and if we set up a marquee oot the back, we might be—"

"He's kidding," I jumped in before the poor man gave himself a heart attack. "Not that many. I promise we'll get back to you by Friday."

He took my hand. "Do you swear?"

"Yes! On my mother's life, Jack's life and Mildred's too."

He dropped it when I said Mildred's, and shuffled off to make pizzas.

Stewart, occupying his usual place at the bar, gave us a wave. "Jack, I've got my best man speech ready. It's awfy funny. You're gonnae love it, Gaby."

"Not that you'll ever hear it," Jack whispered, "seeing as Lachlan's my best man not him."

I smiled, relief flooding me. Confirmation that Jack was one hundred percent onboard with getting married if he'd finally made a decision about his best man. All I needed now was a big pizza—it was a long time since that half-eaten bagel—the rest of the evening in bed with Jack and all would be tickety-boo in my world.

Not quite. My conscience jolted me. The Hyun-Ki confession, remember? Two voices took up room in my head. *Look, it was nothing*, said one. *No need to tell him about nothing and spoil the mood, right? Oh no, you don't*, said the other. *Lady, you don't get away with it that easily. Do not start off married life with secrets and lies.*

Voice number one knew number two was right. I gulped down a fortifying mouthful of soda and lime and sat up straight. "Jack, I need to tell you something."

He stiffened, fingers fiddling with a beer mat stopping. "What, Gaby?"

I closed my eyes briefly. "So, my boss Hyun-Ki. After the rescue of that cat that escaped from the cat cafe that I told you about, you know the time Hyun-Ki shinned up a tree and captured the poor little thing before she got run over and flattened by a double-decker on Shoreditch High Street, and I'd have felt guilty for ever more and hardly been able to live with myself waking up every night and reliving the nightmare where the cat dies and the cat cafe sued me for thousands of pounds for the loss of the cat and emotional trauma and—"

"You snogged him."

Neutral voice, fingers fiddling with the beer mat once more.

"Er, yes. Yes,. I did."

This was what happened when you told the man you love you'd snogged someone else? Or rather he worked it out. No bolts of fury, no curses, no threats to rip Hyun-Ki (or me) to shreds and stamp on the remains. I kept talking. Felt nothing for Hyun-Ki at all, no, no not a thing. A spur of the moment kiss that we'd both decided afterwards proved we didn't fancy each other in the least. Not in the least, Jack!

He took my hand, thumb pressed hard onto my palm. "Gaby, we're all allowed a mistake."

Now for the accidentally sleeping next to a mostly naked man bit. "True, true but also—oh, it's gone quiet."

The Lochside Welcome's jukebox permanently set to 90s Britpop as per Ashley's tastes had stopped. Murmurings from the other punters drifted around us, words not clear enough to make out.

Jack had stilled, his jaw tight and his eyes flinty. I turned to see what he was looking at—two police officers talking to Ashley at the bar who pointed at our table, mouthing "sorry" to me.

"Jack McAllan?" Officer one, a pimply lad who didn't look old enough to shave, let alone be a police officer, asked.

Jack nodded stiffly.

"You're under arrest for the..."

Whatever it was, I didn't hear—the rest of the sentence drowned out in a chorus of catcalls and boos.

CHAPTER 25

"What?" I asked, getting to my feet and standing in front of them. "You can't be serious! My fiancé is the finest, most law-abiding man in the Highlands, if not Scotland!"

Officer two, an older woman whose frown looked permanent, rolled her eyes. "They all say that, love."

"Mr McAllan?" She grasped me by the arms and thrust me aside. I wanted to kick her but decided it might be unwise. Besides, her shins were probably carved from steel.

Her colleague brandished handcuffs. I stared at them in disbelief. "But what's he done? Jack, they've got this wrong. This is stupid."

Jack turned his head to look at me and my heart sank. His expression told me the police were right. I wondered at the possibilities. Drunk driving? No, Jack wouldn't threaten his livelihood that way. Speeding or reckless driving? Same.

"Did you rob a bank to pay for this blasted wedding?" I burst out. He'd been worried how pricey this whole ruddy business was. And since I'd ditched most of Kirsty's freebies, we now had far more expenses to worry about. All that secret stuff with Lachlan. Perhaps he'd been driven to desperate lengths.

Despite it all, my bank remark made him smile. The officers struggled to rearrange their expressions too; smirks battling sternness.

"Aye, right enough," officer one said. "I'm getting married next year and my about-to-be missus wants owls to deliver our wedding rings. Ye've no idea how much that costs!" Officer two hissed something at him and he returned to steely-faced, telling Jack to hold his hands out so they could cuff him. I snapped that they'd better be gentle. Any marks on his wrists tomorrow and I'd complain about police brutality. They ignored me.

"No, Gaby. I haven't robbed a bank. Lachlan will tell you everything." He looked over his shoulder and I spotted the man in question walk in, his face grim. He and Jack exchanged a look I couldn't work out.

"But where are you taking him?" I wailed, as the two police officers marched Jack out. Our audience—far too many Lochalshie locals—gawped, hands reaching for mobiles and fingers moving over screens. My newly recharged phone bleeped. The first of no doubt hundreds of WhatsApp updates. Mhari rushed to my side. I hadn't even spotted her in the pub when we'd come in. The charitable person might think she rushed to me to offer support. The experienced one knew it was to get a ringside seat and gauge my reaction so she could report back to the Lochalshie WhatsApp group.

Outside, officer one opened the car door and pushed Jack into the back seat, climbing in beside him. "Oban, love," officer two told me. "That's the nearest station with processing facilities."

Processing facilities? Ah, she meant prison cells. Not sure of the etiquette—did you wave cheerily as a police car drove your beloved away?—I watched the car head off, and then stamped my feet in frustration. So much for our grand reunion weekend about to end with spectacular sex. And, er, more importantly, what on earth had Jack done?

Lachlan and Stewart joined me, Scottie sniffing my legs and wagging his tail. I thought dogs were meant to pick up on your mood and reflect it. "Aye, well," Stewart said, "Ah did tell him it wasnae worth it."

He shook his head and wandered back indoors, stopping just as he went in to ask me to tell Jack most people could make Blackpool next weekend for the proper stag night. Or what about Edinburgh as Lachlan had suggested if the polis took away Jack's passport?

"You don't need a passport to travel to England," I said, and then wondered if that was true of a person accused of a crime. Perhaps they were going to put an electronic tag on him and it would alert the cops whenever he drove more than five miles... What would that do to his business and us? Forced to stay in Lochalshie and its immediate surrounds for ever more...

"Lachlan," I whimpered, "what's Jack done?"

"I'll take you back to the house," Lachlan said, laying a hand on my shoulder, "and tell you everything."

Cue Mhari. "I better come too in case Gaby needs a wee shoulder to cry on. You're rubbish at the touchy-feely stuff, Lachlan. And I'm wonderin' why you never told me what crime Jack committed!"

As Lachlan's on-off girlfriend, Mhari reckoned she could boss him around.

"No, Mhari."

"But—"

"No."

We headed back to the house in silence. I let us in and Lachlan made a fuss of Mildred—yikes, weren't otherwise cold-hearted villains meant to love cats?!—while I put the kettle on to boil. Lachlan's phone rang.

"Auntie Caroline! You better come round too."

He took the cup of coffee I held out. "Is that okay, Gaby? I thought Jack's mum better hear it from me rather than the Lochalshie WhatsApp group."

I nodded, longing suddenly for Dr McLatchie/Psychic Josie and all the nonsense she'd talk about the illnesses and infections a person might contract from a prison cell.

We didn't have long to wait anyway—the doorbell sounded three minutes later. Wherever Caroline had been, it wasn't the farm where she lived, a good fifteen minutes away. I opened the door and she swept in, a flurry of velvet skirts and cashmere shawls, clinking beads and the smell of incense. She must have been dropped the bus off and gone out to forecast someone's fortune.

Behind her stood Ranald, his face thunderous. Lachlan blanched. I'd never seen him look anything less than assured.

Caroline hugged me. "Gaby, Gaby are you okay my wee pet? Interesting outfit, by the way. Reminds me o' something I saw RuPaul wearing once."

Huh.

"An awfy shock for ye, though. For me too," she muttered darkly. "Lachlan, this had better be good."

In the living room, I closed the curtains. It might have been my imagination, but I'd spotted a face outside and suspected Mhari had sneaked along the road, determined to overhear what went on. I sat next to Caroline, who patted my knee and said she was sure there was a rational explanation for whatever this was.

"Some weeks ago," Lachlan began, "Jack gave me a lift back from Oban. He'd dropped tourists off at the Whisky Vaults for the night and I was there anyway."

Ranald, his fingers drumming out an impatient tattoo on the armchair, harrumphed. Whatever Lachlan had been doing in Oban, it was bound to be something he didn't want to draw attention to. I tried to remember what I'd been doing a month ago—oh, hadn't that been the week before I came up to Lochalshie and we went engagement ring shopping? The weekend had ended in a spectacular row over Jack's dad. Hang on, hadn't…

Lachlan's story continued. Whatever I was trying to remember could wait.

"We got back here at eleven o'clock, and there was something going on in the George. We heard raised voices—one of them was Angus."

That made me sit up. Angus, part-time fisherman, rugby player and bouncer for the Lochside Welcome when it got too busy in the summer months. Built like the proverbial brick house.

Jack and Lachlan followed the noise. Inside the grounds of the Royal George, they spotted the mobile van—the one the hotel used so its guests could sit outside and enjoy fresh seafood and burgers by the loch side. Also run by one Zac Cavanagh, the cat killer, when he wasn't doing things for Hammerstone Hotels in London.

"Angus was a bitty drunk," Lachlan said, "the Lochalshie Rugby team had won their first match of the season and they'd been celebrating in the Lochside Welcome."

When Angus clocked the van parked up in the George and how many people it had attracted, he was outraged. Stealing all that custom from his favourite pub. He stumbled in and started yelling, screaming at the guests and Zac. Called him a few choice names.

Zac had come out of the van and tried to exercise his public school charm, wittering on about how the George was no threat to the Lochside Welcome and the businesses could co-exist. Offered him a free cheeseburger too.

"We thought it best if we could persuade Angus to come back with us before he got into trouble. Which would have been fine if another guest hadn't made that comment— talking about how Angus embodied the Scottish stereotype. Drunk, violent and determined to blame everyone else for their problems."

Ouch.

"So Jack replied he lived up to the perfect southerner stereotype—posh, braying and an utter wanker who he'd happily dunk in the loch."

Double ouch.

"Which made Zac angry. He said we had no right to be there and no right to treat the hotel guests that way. Jack shouted at him where he could stick his rights. Zac told him to eff off—excuse my French, ladies—and Jack saw red. Punched him twice. Once for what he'd just said and the second time for what he did to your cat, Gaby."

"I think he broke his nose. We didn't stick around to find out."

"Why didn't he tell me?" I burst out, horrified.

Lachlan sighed, chewing his bottom lip. "Ah. I think we thought we'd got away with it. That Zac wouldn't do anything. And Jack was awfy ashamed of himself. One of my mates at the cop shop let me know earlier this evening the police were looking for Jack. I tried to warn him."

Lachlan's dodgy operations included friends in useful places.

"I've no idea why Zac changed his mind and went to the police," Lachlan added.

Ah. "I think it might be to do with my wedding planner and last night."

I told him and Ranald what had happened at the hotel-—how we'd humiliated Zac so thoroughly. And that thanks to Kirsty, Zac had thought Jack and I were getting married in the Royal George. The news we weren't hadn't gone down well. Last night must have been the last straw. As a chef, he'd appreciate the saying, revenge is a dish best served cold, mulling over the punch and the insults all night and calling the police the following day.

Ranald, his face not quite as red now, curled his hand around Caroline's. "I'll call my solicitor, Caroline. Get her to go down to Oban as soon as."

He vanished into the kitchen.

"Aye, well," Caroline said, rubbing the back of her neck, two spots of high colour in her cheeks. "I'm no' excusing him but that Zac isnae nice. All those lies he telt us!"

She was referring to last year when Zac had arrived in the village promising all he wanted to do was set up supply lines for upmarket restaurants in Edinburgh and Glasgow. I nodded, but I wasn't sure I felt the same. Jack had punched someone weeks ago. He hadn't told me. Then there was what a criminal record might do to him. Did you go to prison for an assault?

My future appeared—me lining up with all the other women as we visited our orange-suited boyfriends and husbands in a grey building, its outside walls topped with barbed wire, and coping with the indignity of being strip-searched as we went in. My prison life knowledge was based on *Prison Break* and *Orange is the New Black*. Perhaps conditions were even worse in British jails.

Ranald let himself back into the living room. "Sorted," he said.

Lachlan stood up. "I'd better go."

Ranald shot him a flinty stare. "Don't even think about getting in touch with Zac, Lachlan. Do you hear me?"

"Yes Uncle Ranald." Meekly said. Perhaps he even meant it.

I counted them up. Tonight, Ranald had said twenty-nine words. A record.

He wasn't finished. "I mean it. Do not go after him the way you did with Jack's father, dragging Jack into that too."

"What?" Caroline and I said the word at the same time.

Ranald clamped his mouth shut.

Caroline stood up. "What happened then?" Ranald looked at his feet. Lachlan shifted uncomfortably, muttering about needing to go.

"Aye, so," Caroline said, beady eyed. "My ex-husband was badly assaulted by two men who the police never managed tae question. Are you sayin' they were Lachlan and Jack?"

I closed my eyes. Not one violent assault but two. When Jack's father had spoken to us in Oban, he'd said something about the last time they'd seen each other and that he didn't blame him. At the time, I assumed he meant he didn't blame Jack for snubbing him. Not so?

"He tried to strangle you, Auntie Caroline."

"You," she stabbed her finger into his chest, "are no' Clint Eastwood. And my son should hae known better."

She turned to me, touching my arm gently. "That's no' how I brought my son up, Gaby."

Lachlan repeated his assertion he needed to go, promising Ranald once more he wouldn't go anywhere near Zac, and left.

Caroline went into the kitchen and poured me a glass of water. "Here," she said, handing it over. "You're awfy peaky, Gaby. And you're far too thin. I noticed that yesterday. All that unhealthy air in London isnae good for you. I hope you don't drink the water either. It goes through twenty other people before it gets to you."

I saw her and Ranald to the door, closing it in relief. I wanted to be on my own to process everything I'd just heard. Mildred yowled, happy at least that another meal opportunity presented itself. I headed upstairs ten minutes later, too aware that the promise of earlier had slipped away.

My chances of sleeping now I was back in silent night territory where traffic noise and electric lights were at a minimum. One in ten. Scrap that. Minus one in twenty.

CHAPTER 26

I hadn't closed the curtains upstairs so the light woke me just after eight o'clock. That and the door creaking open and Mildred yowling a welcome at the man who let himself in. Assault-y guys didn't bother her so long as they tickled her under the chin and dispensed food. In the kitchen, biscuits rattled into a dish. Crunch sounds followed.

I threw back the duvet and sighed, getting out of bed and wrapping one of Jack's old fleeces around me. I longed to see him. I couldn't face seeing him. Time to do it anyway. I wandered out onto the landing. Me at the top of the stairs, him at the bottom.

"Hey, I brought you breakfast. A nice one." Jack lifted the blue plastic bag and shook it. The smell of fresh-baked bread drifted up, reminding me I hadn't eaten since... forever.

What did a 'nice' breakfast look like? More specifically, what did you rustle up for your girlfriend to compensate for being a lousy, violent, lying git? Downstairs, curiosity piqued by the plastic bag, Mildred sneezed. I guessed she didn't know either.

Lobster on toast? Edible gold-flecked scrambled egg topped with caviar? Chocolate ice-cream on waffles?

I folded my arms and tapped my foot. "I've eaten." Pity my stomach chose to betray me with a loud gurgle. "Okay, I haven't, but one breakfast doesn't make up for everything else."

After Ranald and Caroline left and I went to bed. Katya phoned me. She'd seen the 'news' on the Lochalshie WhatsApp group. "Heavens, what happened, Gaby?" she breathed. "Is Jack okay?"

"Never mind Jack," I said, biting back tears. "What about me? Not what you expect when you go home for the weekend. What am I going to say to my nanna?"

Nanna Cooper did not like men who got into fights. They were up there with people who said the royal family were parasites and we should live in a republic, and people who drank tea from mugs rather than bone china. I did both—think Britain should ditch the royal family and regularly knocked back big mugs of tea, but I was with her on the fighting front.

"You are not going to tell her," Katya announced crisply. "Because hopefully you won't need to. Zac will drop the charges."

"Don't say that," I wailed. "Ranald's already warned Lachlan he mustn't go to see Zac for a 'friendly' chat."

Even if I half-wanted Lachlan to dig us out of this hole.

"I don't want him to be a jailbird. What if he gets locked up before the wedding? For that matter..."

I stopped myself. The doubt too terrible to say aloud.

Katya started listing things. Always her fail-safe method for any crisis. Jack, she said, lovely man. Emphasis on the lovely. At times she even thought him top of her pros and cons list, ahead of Dexter. Dropped her voice there so the love of her life didn't hear. "Sorry to say, Gaby, and it doesn't mean I'd ever make a play for him."

The fight was a one-off. She'd talk to her friends at Norfolk CID. Once upon a time, Katya wrote a lot of brochures for recruits to the CID and had a thorough understanding of interrogating suspects. She promised she'd find out what was normal procedure for someone accused of assault who had no previous criminal record.

"He'll be fined, Gaby," she said. "Or made to do community service. Picking up litter around the loch or cleaning up graffiti. Promise."

"It wasn't a one-off," I said, explaining what had happened to Jack's father. Two seconds of silence from Katya before she rushed in with further soothing noises—a two-off not that much worse than a one-off. And the police didn't know about the first assault, did they?

I hung up and toyed with leaving my phone on. What if Jack called? No, I was too angry with him. And if I left the phone on, Mhari would call.

My dreams turned nasty. I found myself wrapped in a plaid shawl in the grounds of a fort. Men in redcoats brought out Jack and tied each hand to a wooden stake so a sadist could whip him, the leather tails carving out bloody stripes on his back.

I woke up sweating, cursing Jack and my too vivid imagination that had placed me in the middle of Outlander, and the scene where Black Jack Randall flogs Jamie Fraser almost to death. After that, every time I started to doze off, a random thought would shake me back into wakefulness.

Would the Lochside Welcome survive without our wedding going ahead on December 21?

What was prison food like?

Would—gulp—Jack make it through the showers in prison? He was awfully pretty.

And the last dreadful one; words I batted down every time they swam into consciousness. *No, no, no, Gabrielle Amelia Richardson, we are NOT going there.*

"Please, Gaby—can I make you breakfast?"

I shook myself back to the present where people didn't get whipped almost to death and made my way downstairs. In the hallway, we faced each other. If I'd expected a night in prison to have tainted him, I was wrong. Sunlight, weak as it was, backlit him so his hair gleamed, and the lumberjack shirt by now grubby and sweaty in places, clung to his arms and pecs.

The sun had only just surfaced. It being late November, sunrise took place just after eight am. I watched the light dapple the table and my fiancé's face, grey-white under the freckles that dusted his nose and cheeks. The dark eyes that didn't meet mine.

"The best breakfast in the world starts with an explanation. A long one," I said, marching past him into the kitchen where I put on the kettle. And fed Mildred again. Might as well cultivate her favour, seeing as she'd been missing out on the feed on demand schedule she preferred.

"Well?" Kettle boiled, I made myself coffee. Amir Khan, or whoever Jack fancied himself as, could make his own.

"A one-off, Gaby," he said, putting the bag down on the kitchen counter.

"You didn't tell me!"

The bag thumped onto the table, making me jump. Jack closed his eyes briefly and blew out air.

"I wish I hadn't hit Zac. Losing my temper like that won't happen again. And I'm sorry I never told you when it happened."

All well and good. Nanna Cooper wagged her finger. *"Actions speak louder than words, Gaby!"* The assault on his father. Losing my temper like that won't happen again. Did he tell himself that when he and Lachlan beat the man up?

What I'd been trying to remember last night came back to me. Jack saying he had something to tell me before I came up to Lochalshie the first time. And last night. When I'd wanted to confess about Hyun-Ki and I waking up together. Jack said, 'me too' when I told him I had something to say.

Jack turned towards me. Maybe this was the bit where I flew into his arms and demanded to know how he was. Said I forgave him and all that. Another random thought popped up. Hyun-Ki wouldn't have beaten someone up, or made me worry so much. I told my brain to be quiet.

"I'm sorry."

Simple, heartfelt. And still my mind jangled and my stomach churned. Maybe it would be better when I had food in me.

"This breakfast then," I pointed at the plastic bag.

He moved towards me, arm extended for a cuddle.

"Don't touch me!"

We leapt apart. Where had that come from? It didn't help that Mildred chose that moment to weave her way around my legs, I tripped over her as I backed away, arms flailing. I grabbed for something—anything—and caught the handle to the bag. Down it came with me, landing on the flag stone flooring with a crash. A box of eggs in the bag then.

Mildred scuttled over my legs, poking her face in the bag and emerging with egg yolk on her nose. Jack picked up the bag before she could eat any more.

He peered into the bag. "I was going to make scrambled eggs anyway—cheesy ones."

My favourite form of eggs. Jack added extra whites to scrambled eggs to make them fluffy, finished them off with cream and added cheese and chives. Anytime he made them for me, I inhaled rather than ate them.

He blinked. "Gaby, you know I would never..."

Now I didn't, though. Jack's father, a man I hardly knew at all, even if I had stupidly tried to invite him to the wedding. Was Jack's assault on Zac—and his dad for that matter—those faulty genes coming through?

Who was I marrying? Caroline feared it too. I'd seen it on her face last night.

Jack blinked again and I wondered if tears made his eyes seem glassy. He was sheet-white anyway.

I got to my feet. "What happens now?"

"I appear in court on Tuesday morning and enter a plea," he said, moving the bag to the side and filling a coffee cup. "Ranald's solicitor suggests I say 'guilty'. There won't need to be a trial and I'll be released until the case is heard, all the mitigating circumstances taken account of etcetera."

"Will... will you go to prison?"

He shook his head. "Regan—Ranald's solicitor—says no. Not for a first offence."

Mildred jumped up on the kitchen counter and butted her head against Jack's hand, purring her heart out. Much quicker to forgive than I was. I took him in, my magnificent Highlander and the man I loved. Who looked as if he needed a hug more than anything at the moment.

I swallowed and pressed myself against him, the smell unfamiliar. A night in a yucky prison cell had left him stale, smoky and musty.

He clung to me, him whispering "sorry, sorry, sorry" into my hair.

The scrambled eggs were brilliant—and I never let a little cat interference spoil my enjoyment of food—but they turned out to be the highlight of the day. If I could have gone back to London that night, I would have done. But when I checked the flights they were so expensive, I couldn't justify the cost and the effort to get there was overwhelming.

Neither of us wanted to leave the house. Too many people would sidle up to us and want to know what was going on. As it was, Mhari popped around at lunchtime. The two of us slid down the sofa. We'd left the lights in the living room off. If she stared in the window trying to work out if anyone was in or not, hopefully she'd think we were out.

The letterbox on the front door rattled. "Jack? Gaby? Are ye in? I'm awfy worried and I wanted tae know if you're all right?"

And the rest... At least that made the two of us smile at each other. Mhari, middle names Persistence Personified, stayed there for ten minutes begging us to let her in.

"I'm gonnae start a petition—people who think Zac should drop the charges. Everybody will sign it."

Or, "Ashley says he can start rumours if you eat at the Royal George you end up wi' food poisoning so bad you spew your guts for days on end. That'll teach the flashy git a lesson."

Finally, "There's an awfy lot of stories flying around. I thought youse would want to get your side across."

Lochalshie's resident journalist—far tougher and hard-nosed than any seasoned hack.

When she left, we ended up watching TV. I flicked too hurriedly past *Don't Tell the Bride*. No need for any wedding reminders and we didn't bother with dinner. Later, I listened to him breathing next to me in bed and knew he was as awake as I was. When the alarm went off at six on the Tuesday morning, it was a huge relief. I bolted for the bathroom, showering in record quick time.

Jack joined me in the kitchen half an hour later. He wore a suit, something I didn't usually see him in as he preferred kilts for formal wear. He looked uncomfortable, plucking at the collar and the tie around his neck. Beautiful suit though, the jacket emphasising his broad shoulders and the trousers cropped just above his ankles. The dark blue with its thin pin stripe contrasted perfectly with his red hair. I'd offered to cut it the night before, reasoning short hair might impress an old-fashioned judge rather than longer red locks. Jack said no, which may or may not have had something to do with the last time I'd trimmed Mildred's coat to get rid of the matted clumps. She ended up bald on one side.

Once again, Lachlan had offered to take me to Glasgow airport, seeing as he needed to be in the city anyway. His battered jeep drew up outside. I drank the rest of my coffee, heaved my rucksack over my shoulder and told Mildred I loved her. She wandered off, leaving Jack and I alone.

"Good luck today. Let me know how it goes, right?"

He nodded.

I pecked him on the cheek, unable to do anything else even when I saw how hurt he looked. When I let myself out of the house, I didn't look back even though I sensed his gaze following me.

Lachlan pushed the door open and I climbed in, checking the back seat for any rogue on-off girlfriends. None, thankfully. We drove off, Lachlan putting the radio on. He must have been able to tell I didn't want to talk. Thanks to the drop-off racket at Glasgow airport—they charged vehicles just to stop for a few seconds and let people out—Lachlan didn't have time to say much to me before I left either. Didn't stop him trying.

"Gaby," he began as I reached for the door handle. "Jack is nothing like his father. Nothing."

I didn't reply.

"I've known him since he was seven years old. Over the years I've tried to persuade him to partner up wi' me in some of the stuff I do... you know, the dodgy stuff. He's never said yes."

He placed his hand on top of mine. "And he loves you so much."

"Thanks, Lachlan," my reply was automatic. Great speech, but did it change anything? I walked into the terminal and checked in, heading for WH Smith's where I might find a book diverting enough to take my mind off everything. The top ten choices were romcoms or real-life crime and I wasn't in the mood for either. I settled on a psychological thriller and hoped it was good as the reviewers claimed.

Back in London, no-one was in the flat. I cleaned the place from top to bottom even though we had a cleaner, scrubbing the sideboards and polishing the windows. When Katya returned in the evening, I burst out crying as soon as I saw her. "Thank goodness you're back."

Katya dumped her laptop bag on the floor and hugged me. "Do you want me to make you something to eat?"

A kind offer, but it was bound to involve vegan or raw food. She must have spotted my reserve, plucking a large bar of chocolate and a tub of cookie dough ice-cream from her bag.

"Thought you might need cheering up."

Armed with teaspoons, we put the tub between us on the sofa and dug in.

"I spoke to DI Wilding at Norfolk CID," she said, spooning herself up a bit of cookie dough. I raised my eyebrows. My friend's copywriting activities with Norfolk Constabulary included a brief fling with one Detective Inspector Jerome Wilding. Dumped for being too into handcuffs. "I mean," Katya announced loftily at the time, "if anyone is to be chained to a headboard begging for mercy, it ought to be him and not me!"

"He says Scots law is different, but as Jack's a one-time offender he doubts the court will give him more than a fine or community service."

"The violence thing," I said, breaking the chocolate bar in two and awarding the larger part to Katya. Noble of me. "I ca... ca... can't get over it."

Tears once more. Katya got up, returning seconds later with tissues from the bathroom. I blew my nose and my phone vibrated. An answer machine message from Jack. The court thing must be over. Katya told me to call him and left the room, shutting the door behind her.

Alone in the room, I listened to Jack's message doing my best goldfish mouth opening and shutting in disbelief impression. I stabbed the screen, aiming for the return call button.

"Hey." His voice sounded flat and weary.

"A trial? But Ranald's solicitor told you to plead guilty. Didn't you do that?"

"Yes. Guilty of assault," Jack said. "Not guilty of a racially aggravated attack."

"What?!"

"Zac claims the attack was racially motivated because I called him and his guest 'English wankers.'"

"But it's true!"

A laugh—a short one. "That's what everyone else says too. Gaby, I..."

Gabrielle Amelia Richardson! My nanna's voice—who by now had decided she was firmly on Jack's side even if she knew nothing about any of this—started up. *Your poor boyfriend (who is a most handsome fellow if you ask me) needs your love and support. Snap out of it, you silly goose!*

"I know, I know," I said hurriedly. "A one-off. Everyone also reckons Zac got what was coming to him. As do I. Yes, me too. Got. What. He. Deserved."

Oof, dial back the vehemence, Gaby. You're overdoing it.

"Such a busy day. First opportunity I've had to check my phone or I would have phoned earlier. Much, much earlier but busy, so busy, so many things to do, getting ready for going back to work when the slave driver boss wants me to come up with brilliant ideas for miracle lip gloss plumpers..."

"The boss you snogged? Although it didn't mean anything."

"Too right it didn't mean anything!" I snapped. "And at least I didn't break anyone's nose."

A deep sigh the other end.

"The trial," Jack interrupted, his voice catching. Would I be attending dressed in black and sending dagger looks to the witness for the prosecution or worse? They sent him down and I wailed, "Jack, Jack!" as he was cuffed and led away to a life of hard labour breaking up rocks with a pick axe.

[Again, not one hundred percent sure of how trials or prisons work.]

He muttered something and I had to get him to repeat it.

The trial date? December 20.

One day before our wedding was due to take place.

•• ⚜ ••

POST TRIAL REVELATION, I drifted back into the kitchen. Dexter had ordered yet more Thai, and he dished out equal helpings of flame-grilled tofu with peanut sauce, Tom Yum soup and Panang curry. I shoved huge forkfuls in my mouth, hunger triumphing over worry and anxiety.

"Racially motivated attack?" Dexter said when I explained about the trial. "Like, wow."

Katya's response was nowhere near as polite. When she'd first moved to Lochalshie, Zac had chased after her, lying about why he was there and what he planned to do. This, she said, was typical of someone so untrustworthy and probably part of Hammerstone Hotels' dirty tactics. If Jack was imprisoned for a racially aggravated attack, our wedding couldn't go ahead. And thus the Lochside Welcome could not interfere with the official launch of the Royal George.

"If I could get my hands on him," she said, stabbing at the tofu with a chopstick, "he'd think Jack's assault was nothing. Nothing!"

"Katya," I said through a mouthful of rice, "we're supposed to be against violence."

"We are. Unjustified violence against defenceless people with a strong moral code."

But when I crawled to bed later that evening, the thought I kept returning to shouted loud and clear.

I can't do this.

Not go ahead with wedding plans when the groom might not be there. It wasn't fair on Ashley or me. There were the ongoing rows to think about too. In the year Jack and I had been together, we'd bickered a bit but never argued the way we'd done continuously since my proposal. (Felt like.)

I can't do any of this.

I got under the duvet and called Jack. He answered on the second ring.

"Gaby."

"I'm so... so... sorry." The blubbing started in earnest. "But we have to call it off."

Another of those heartfelt sighs.

"You're right," he said. "We'll get married next year. When this is all out of the way."

I pressed the phone to my chest and shut my eyes. Best to say it quickly.

"No, I can't marry you. And... and I think we need time apart."

"No, Gaby, I... okay, you're right."

There. Done. Only token disagreement on Jack's part. He must feel it too. I wrenched my engagement ring off and settled in for a sleepless night.

CHAPTER 27

Small mercies happen. The Lochalshie WhatsApp group knew about the trial—and Zac's ears must have turned blue from the names they called him—but Jack hadn't yet told anyone the wedding was off. As was our relationship.

Katya knocked on my door first thing, took one look at the engagement ring lying on the table beside my bed and got under the duvet next to me.

"What happened?"

I told her about the phone call. Small mercies once more. She didn't say, "Are you sure?" or repeat the statement about people being allowed one mistake. I couldn't have handled that.

"You're off today? Okay, I'll take the day off too. Do you want me to cancel stuff for you?"

I nodded gratefully. My best friend, the fabbest one a girl could have. Wide awake at three am, I'd attempted a list of everything that needed doing. I lost it somewhere around the 'phone Ashley's cousin and cancel her journalism-style photography package' mark. And when I got to Mildred—would I ever see my poor little cat again?—I cried so hard I started to choke.

Katya picked my phone up. "It might be wise to take yourself off the WhatsApp group," she said, looking to me for approval. I blew out a big sigh. "Better not. Everyone will notice. Just turn off the notifications and make sure the app's not on my home screen, will you?"

Telling people in person or at least by phone was what the mature person did. The cowardly one muted WhatsApp groups and blocked people on her phone as I was about to do to Mhari. Heck, what about Caroline? She'd be so upset. Sod it. Jack's mum was his responsibility. He could tell her.

Katya got out of bed. "Stay here," she said, "and watch cat videos on YouTube. I'll do everything."

Miraculously, by lunchtime it was all done. Thank goodness for disorganisation. After I chucked Kirsty and her plans, I hadn't bothered sorted out anything myself. Katya had little to do. I steeled myself to ask what Ashley had said when she told him Jack and I would not need the venue.

"He was fine," she flapped a hand. "Said it was perfectly understandable given the trial date. Though I let him think you're going to get married in his pub next year. You should tell him yourself that you won't be."

She was right. I'd be feeling stronger by then. Up to having difficult conversations.

My mum called, crying herself when I told her. "But Jack's amazing," she said. "Are you sure, love?"

Yes, no, yes.

Ironic, wasn't it, that the thing that took me to Lochalshie in the first place would be the thing that took me away too. I'd fled up there when I'd broken up with Ryan, having worked out our engagement was a ginormous mistake. Now, I'd be leaving Lochalshie because my engagement to Jack had proved the same.

Was it? Oh, blasted yes, no, yes again.

Maybe I wasn't the marrying kind.

I composed endless messages to Jack, writing and deleting every one. He sent me something late the next night, the contents too garbled for me to understand. Drunk, mind warped or both.

By keeping my phone switched off, I managed to avoid any further troublesome phone calls or messages. Switching it back on the next day revealed eight missed calls, five messages on my answer machine and numerous other attempts by people to contact me on WhatsApp, Instagram, text and email.

Sure enough, Mhari had tried to get in touch every way possible. Jolene had sent me a message, a pic of her and Tamar waving at the camera and asking if I was okay. Caroline urged me to call her as soon as I could and my nanna sounded angry.

"Gabrielle Amelia Richardson—oh, I hate these stupid answer thingies! You ring me back this instant, young lady and explain yourself!"

My mother must have told her.

I made myself a couple of bits of toast, took them to bed and phoned my nanna. Nanna Cooper lived two doors down from my mum. My grandfather died young and she'd single-handedly brought up four kids on a tiny income. She knew how to skin a rabbit and fish for trout with her bare hands. "Your nanna," Katya was fond of telling me, "should run the country. I'm sure she'd be able to sort out Brexit at the very least."

Maybe she could sort out me. "Nanna," I said when she answered her phone. A newbie to the smartphone, she always dropped her voice when she answered, convinced MI5 were listening in. Still, if anyone could give a whisper the impact of a shout, my nanna nailed it.

"Gabrielle Amelia Richardson! I've bought my ruddy dress. Me and your mum spent last Monday traipsing round Jarrolds all flamin' day. Sixty-five pounds it cost me and I'm a pensioner. Hang your head in shame, young lady!"

Nanna's Norfolk accent was stronger than my mum's. The r's went on forever, spat out from the side of her mouth. Jarrrrrrold's. Rrrrruddy.

"But Nanna," I wailed. "He punched someone and broke their nose. His dad used to beat up his mum. What if he loses his temper and starts hitting me?"

"Has he hit you before now? No?" More hissed whispering. "Well, then. Such a decent chap. Much better than that dust-bag you used to go out with. What was his name? Rory? Rodney?"

Bless her. Nanna tried to get on with modern slang and Katya did her best to teach her, but dust-bag wasn't quite douche bag even though it sort of worked. Bless her too, for pretending to forget the name of the man I spent (wasted) ten years with.

I told Nanna I hadn't made my decision lightly and everything hurt—my head, my heart, my stomach, even my blasted feet. Yes, my toes protested all day even though I'd chosen cashmere socks today and slipped them into Skechers.

"Your feet?!" Nanna pounced. "That explains everything! All the blood's left your brain. Go and put your feet up so they are higher than your head. Gor, no wonder they call you millenniums snowflakes!"

The flat's front door opened—Katya and Dexter. Katya stuck her head around the door, mouthing 'who?' to me. When I mouthed back, 'my nanna', she nodded approvingly, sticking her hand out for the phone. I threw it to her. Katya was welcome to Nanna's hiss whispering. I left them to it and joined Dexter in the kitchen. Was it my imagination or did he look shifty as soon as he saw me?

"Gaby, hey!" He pocketed his phone quickly. "How's it goin'?"

Men. Jeez. *Fine, Dexter. I've broken up with my boyfriend/fiancé, do not know where I'm going to live from now on and there's custody of an old grumpy ginger and white cat to worry about. My nanna hates me, as does the whole of Lochalshie. How it's goin' is tickety-boo.*

Not.

"We were thinking," Dexter added, handing me a cup of tea. He'd acclimatised so well to Britishness, he now saw tea as the solution to everything. "You need distraction stuff, right?"

Katya came back in, handing me my phone. "Too right. Distraction by the bucketload."

"So we've booked a spa weekend—yoga, mindfulness, massages everything! Whadda you say?"

That sounds so ghastly it makes me want to be a bit sick in my mouth? Not a grateful response. Maybe they were right. Along with Nanna and her orders to put my feet up above my head and let them stay there for a long time.

"Thank you. That sounds nice."

CHAPTER 28

By the time Monday arrived I was thankful—the first time I've ever woken up on a Monday and thought the idea of work sounded wonderful. Hyun-Ki could make me do endless cut-outs of every single product in the Blissful Beauty range—a job so tedious it was usually left to the most junior designer. As it required total concentration but little in the way of creative skill, it would suit me perfectly.

I beat him to the office too. When he came in at five to seven, he did a double-take.

"Gaby, hi! You didn't need to come in so early."

Hyun-Ki was now a member of the Lochalshie WhatsApp group. If breaking up with my boyfriend qualified as things I never saw coming this time last week part one, Hyun-Ki and Mhari, the world's most unlikely couple, were part two. Hyun-Ki claimed they weren't a couple in the conventional sense. Both of them liked their lives just so, therefore making time for each other, compromises and being in the same country, let alone city, was out of the question.

But yes, he and Mhari were now in a relationship doing it the Gen Y way. This meant a lot of screen time—perfect for both of them as their phones appeared surgically attached to their hands—and tagging each other all the time on social media. Mhari had made him a member of the WhatsApp group where he could happily offer opinions on things he knew nothing about, which made him the perfect fit. They knew the wedding was off—and again the air around Zac Cavanagh must be blue given the imaginative insults they came up with for him—but nothing else.

As the office was empty, I filled Hyun-Ki in, blowing my nose the whole time.

"But he deserved it!" Hyun-Ki burst out when I explained the broken nose. Poor Zac. Tough that everyone, even strangers, hated him. "And Jack's a nice guy."

"You've never met him!"

"Mhari told me."

Oh well then. Speaking of which...

"Hyun-Ki, please don't tell her anything, will you? We haven't yet told anyone we're... taking a break. Only that the wedding's off. Mhari will ask you millions of questions because she'll be suspicious but..."

"I won't say anything."

"And nothing to the WhatsApp group either?"

He mimed zipping his mouth shut. Fingers crossed he managed it.

"You're not too suicidal, are you?" he asked, shooting worried glances at the window. We were only three floors up. If you want guaranteed results, it might be better to aim for an office higher up.

"I'm fine," I said, activating my fancy desk to sit mode, too exhausted to face standing after a weekend of non-stop crying interspersed with people poking and prodding me at the spa. "Or I will be once I've had my first coffee."

And worked out what to do with the rest of my life. Homeless, boyfriend-less and cat-less—the future looked bleak. Katya, having spent most of the weekend with her arms wrapped around me said the only way to cope was to 'take it one day at a time'. Do not focus on the future and live in the now, as the mindfulness coach at the spa day kept banging on about. Easier said than done.

Still, she and Dexter hadn't left me alone for a minute. On Saturday morning, they knocked on my door at eight o'clock and frogmarched me to the hotel after breakfast. The first session was a

Tae Kwon Do class, the moves so complicated, I couldn't think about anything else. Katya managed to keep her face straight even though I kept mucking up and facing the opposite way to everyone else.

In the afternoon, we went to a lecture on focusing the mind on the moment and then a massage. Thanks to the lack of sleep, I zonked out on the table.

"Right," Katya said once it was over. "I've picked out lots of things we can binge watch tonight and tomorrow."

"Er..." My usual picks were romcoms and Outlander. Neither would suit my present state of mind and the latter would remind me far too much of Jack.

"Thrillers and horrors," Katya announced. "The horror film is perfect for heartache because no matter how ghastly your life feels, it's unlikely to be as terrible as the person running around an abandoned building being chased by something unspeakable."

True.

A black coffee appeared on my desk and I summoned up my underworked smiling muscles.

Hyun-Ki swung his screen around to face me. "Cat Man Chris has uploaded this amazing new video. Five kittens taken from a feral colony and found new homes."

I shook my head. "No. It'll make me cry and I'll go into a full-scale meltdown. Can you give me some tedious things to do instead?"

He rested a hand on my shoulder. "Yeah, no worries. You can update all the product pages for the skin brightening range."

Marvellous. Product pages—a graphic designer's least creative but most fiddly and time-consuming job. Perfect for the suddenly single woman who needs to stop her mind repeating 'what if I hadn't' questions. And it worked a treat. I managed to concentrate on those pages for a minute at a time before memories of Jack and me appeared—the two of us in the Lochside Welcome, at home with

Mildred or that first, glorious time we got together when he kissed me beside the loch as the rain started up in earnest. A minute was a vast improvement on yesterday when I'd only managed ten seconds.

I'd worked my way through twenty different pages when I noticed the noise. Three months into my London stay, I was a pro. The ever-present traffic and sirens didn't register, but now the clamour was overwhelming. Had someone opened all the windows in our office?

Two of the women sat opposite us—Kelly Anne and Charlene who worked for Dexter—jumped up and bolted to the window that looked out onto the main road.

"She's here!"

Everyone else downed tools and rushed over.

"What's going on?" I asked Hyun-Ki as we made our way across the room.

"A special surprise to cheer you up, Gaby," he said. "Guess who's dropping by her London HQ as she finishes off her book launch promotional tour?"

Outside, crowds gathered. The Blissful Beauty London shop wasn't big, so there was always a queue of people that snaked around the block waiting to get in. Now, they gathered in their hundreds blocking the pavement as far as I could see. Photographers joined the crowds too, big fancy cameras competing with mobile phones raised high in the air.

A pink and silver limo drew up and its door swung open.

The noise amplified. "Caitlin, Caitlin!"

Out came the tiny one. All I could see was the top of her (shiny-haired) head. She paused for selfies with a chosen few before being swept into the building and upstairs.

Everyone in the office looked at each other. What was the form for greeting the big (tiny) boss? Did we spring to our feet and perform deep curtseys/bows? Or should we sit at our desks typing furiously while staring at our screens so we looked super-busy?

Too late to decide. The doors opened and she bounced in, catching us all rubber-necking at the window where a scuffle had broken out down below between two people and Caitlin's security guards.

"You guys!!!!!!" Caitlin beamed at us all. She was her usual immaculate self in what must be her version of leisure wear. Cycling shorts cut off mid thigh worn with wedge heels are a bold choice for any woman, especially in December. Caitlin was about the only person who could carry them off, her sweatshirt loosely knotted around her shoulders over a lacy camisole top.

"Gaby!" she exclaimed, catching sight of me. "So amazing to see you again!"

She gave me a big hug, suffocating me with the sickly-sweet smell of Jewel, Blissful Beauty's newly launched perfume. "I've got this idea to run past you," she whispered in my ear. "Don't let me leave without us talking about it."

She stood back, regarding me carefully. "Are you okay, hon? You look kinda grim."

So much for the restorative powers of Saturday's massage and facial. To be fair to the therapist, she wasn't a miracle worker. "A bit wobbly," I said, and she opened her mouth to ask me something—her words cut off when the rest of the office gathered around us.

"So, Gaby can you get me a phone consultation with Psychic Josie? We didn't manage to arrange anything when we met up at my book launch. I'll pay ten times her usual fee."

Ah. I swallowed hard and told myself, You. Will. Not. Cry. I didn't know if I had any influence with Psychic Josie anymore seeing as I was no longer with her son. And I hadn't talked to her yet, despite her leaving another three messages on my phone. I was too gutless to listen to them. She might be cursing me to hell and back. Much as I didn't believe her psychic fakery, what if she commanded the spirits as she claimed? I'd need to be careful opening cupboards from now on and watching out for heavy bits of furniture flying at my head.

"So, what are you guys working on?" Caitlin asked and everyone spoke at once—the South Korean stuff and the launch of the new lip plumper scheduled for early next year.

"Cool," Caitlin said. "Does the lip plumper work?"

Who knew? Given the hefty price tag it ought to make anyone look as if they'd had fillers injected. As Caitlin had.

"Look," Hyun-Ki beckoned her to his iMac where he'd been working on an app. You uploaded your own photo and got to try out different creams and shades of make-up. He found a pic of Caitlin and let her try it out, her shrieking with laughter as they opted for the more outrageous colours.

Outside, the noise had intensified—people still screaming for Caitlin as the doors to the building opened and closed multiple times. At the door, one of Caitlin's bodyguards spoke into the tiny microphone at his mouth and vanished. The other guy cast a worried glance in our direction and disappeared too. London's notorious traffic wardens must have arrived on the scene, scribbling out a penalty charge notice to plant on the stretch limo.

"Caitlin!" The scream made us all jump and turn from Hyun-Ki's screen. In front of us stood a wild-eyed man waving a– oh dear heavens surely not...

A gun.

CHAPTER 29

The wild-eyed man waved the gun above him and everyone dropped to the floor and onto their fronts.

I was right next to Caitlin, Hyun-Ki on the other side. The three of us exchanged horrified stares. The lyrics to that blasted song—*I don't like Mondays*—started up in my head. Unhelpful; a song about someone who murdered people because they wanted to liven up a Monday.

I reached my hands out, Caitlin gripping one and Hyun-Ki the other. My heart pitched forward in my chest, thumping against the floor, its woollen fibres tickling my nose. Where were Caitlin's blasted bodyguards?

The man picked his way over the people on the floor until his feet—shod in mud-encrusted white trainers—were level with my eyeballs. He crouched down next to Caitlin.

"Caitlin, Caitlin—I've got something to ask you."

An American then. And in his fifties too, I guessed—at least thirty years older than Caitlin. Yuck. A mucky T-shirt and jeans matched the trainers. Hard to work out why Caitlin wasn't tempted.

He prised our hands apart so he could take Caitlin's in his, yanking her to her feet. As she still had hold of Hyun-Ki, he was forced up as well, so he and Caitlin bumped into each other. A novel way for them to get to know each other better. The man, his gun still trained on Caitlin, got onto one knee.

"Marry me, Caitlin—don't marry him, marry me!"

Romantic, hmm? I glanced at the door. Still no sign of those bodyguards but sirens wailed outside. Someone must have called the police. I gulped hard. What if they stormed in here, the man fired at them, or turned his gun on us and we ended up in a bloodbath situation?

"Katya" I whispered to the floor. "Pick out the most flattering pic of me for those line-ups they do of the victims. *Not* the head and shoulders one where I'm doing my best hamster impression."

You can't help the thoughts that run through your head when faced with imminent death, right? If my life flashed in front of me, it chose to do so in peculiar fashion... Next, came the lovely Jack memories. The time we went to Doune Castle together and that American woman took our photo and told us how much we looked like Jamie and Claire. Our first mad Christmas together, our families and friends crowded into the living room. Those evenings we spent in the Lochside Welcome, eating pizzas, meeting up with our friends and taking part in the pub quiz we never won.

Then, there was all the private, alone stuff—from the X-rated (Jack's naked body kept appearing in front of me) to the cuddly bits, me and him curled up on the couch. Mildred yowled piteously in the background, as if to say, 'I will *not* forgive you if you leave me with this cat-starving monster.'

Nanna's words—*has he ever hit you, you daft millennium snowflake, No? Well, then.*

Another Nanna saying—*don't regret the things you do, regret the things you don't do.*

Nanna, you might be right. What happens if I don't... I bargained with the deities, Mother Nature and the universe.

"John-Joe," Caitlin said, her voice remarkably calm. "We've gone over this. I love you, but not in that way, right?"

As I lifted my head, I saw Caitlin talking earnestly to the gunman. She no longer held Hyun-Ki's hand, and he flashed me a look I couldn't interpret. Caitlin continued her soothing chat, telling John-Joe while he might be right about them being lovers in a former life (urgh), they weren't in this one. All of a sudden Hyun-Ki drew his right arm and leg back, crouched and swung the leg round in a perfect ballerina arc, the move kicking the gun out of the man's hand. John-Joe yelled and I dived for the gun, scrambling to my feet beside Caitlin, and pointing it at her would-be suitor.

"On your knees, mother******!"

Where had that come from? My first time holding a gun too—a lot lighter than I expected, and plastic-y. If the guy called my bluff, we were in trouble seeing as I had no idea what to do with one.

"Armed police! Nobody move!"

Officers wearing thickly padded black uniforms, face masks and waving guns that looked far scarier than the one I was holding burst into the room. The real gunman was grabbed as I was, the two of us pushed face-first to the floor and arms pulled roughly around our backs. Let me tell you—that hurts. I shouted out that they must have dislocated my shoulder and was told none too gently to shut my mouth.

That, Gabrielle Amelia Richardson, will teach you to think American action movies offer lessons you should apply in real life, I told myself as we were marched out of the building. Hyun-Ki and Caitlin protested. It made no difference. The blacked-out van zipped its way through the traffic and a coat was thrust over my head as we were escorted into the police office. Still handcuffed, I was left to stew in a windowless interview room that stank of disinfectant on top of pee and vomit. I added other promises to my bargains with deities, starting with a solemn vow to leave London asap.

As I found out, if you are caught holding a gun the boys and girls in blue have a LOT of paperwork to fill in. Which makes them inclined to look at you unfavourably. Three hundred (felt like) hours later, I was allowed out following a stern lecture on misguided heroics. The firearms officer delivered his speech and sat back in his chair.

"The gun wasn't real, by the way."

No need at all for him to look so smug about it.

In the waiting room—a dispiriting beige space, its walls tacked with curling posters warning people to look out for pickpockets and moped thieves—I did a double take. One person stood out, foot tapping an agitated beat on the floor. My heart, still in hyper stress mode thanks to the gunman, moved to a frantic pitter-patter.

Thank you, thank you, thank you, oh universe.

When he saw me, he leapt to his feet.

"Hey... er, Caitlin wanted to come but she's got a busy week ahead promoting her book and that perfume of hers. Jewel, I think."

Heaven forbid an attempt on her life (fake gun notwithstanding) get in the way of a reality TV star and her promotional schedule. Jack, his red hair bright his face beautiful, shimmered in front of me. I'll say this for the deities, they stick to their promises if you plead hard enough. And now they had kept their side of the bargain, I needed to do the same. But how and where to start?

Jack gave me a half-smile. He held out his phone. "You're a viral sensation. Leanne in your office got it all on film."

The distraction gave me time to think up what I was going to say, but I took the phone warily. I'd been a one-minute wonder once before when I was filmed emerging from the loch carrying a dog I'd just rescued. Cute, yes—but the film caught me red-faced, hair plastered to my skull and in the midst of a wardrobe malfunction, nipples clearly visible through my top because of the cold.

Leanne's film showed Hyun-Ki's astonishing roundhouse kick and my best impression of an American gunslinger. It looked far, far worse than I'd imagined in my head. Why, why, why had I put on an American accent? America via Mumbai and a detour past Dublin, more like. My phone, finally returned to me post questioning, beeped repeatedly. No prizes for guessing which WhatsApp group was trying to get in touch.

I slipped the phone back in my pocket. A handy distraction before the tricky bit. Out of the corner of my eye, a man wearing a neck brace nudged the guy with him, both of them staring at us. I took a tentative step forward and Jack did the same. Sometimes space is weird—the tiny bits of ground growing so much they might as well be miles.

Jack's eyes met mine, a question there. I gave the tiniest of nods and he opened his arms. I flew into them and the all-too familiar comforting warmth. Fresh air, salty skin and the aftershave he wore—I inhaled it all and let it wipe out the stink of that cell.

"An eventful day at the office, Gaby-sketch," he said, voice muffled by my hair. Jack, master of the understatement.

"How, how, how…?"

"All right, break it up," the custody sergeant moved out from behind her desk and stood beside us, hands on hips. "Much as the Met likes nothing better than helping along love's young dream." Her colleagues tittered behind her. "We prefer it when you have your joyful reunions elsewhere."

Too right.

Outside, Jack suggested a nearby coffee shop. I burned with questions and the things I wanted to tell him but I waited until we were sat inside. Jack fetched me a cappuccino and a cheese and pickle sandwich made with two thick slabs of bread. Turns out life-threatening experiences made me ravenous.

"I'd better let people know I'm okay," I told Jack, who nodded.

MUM: I know you warned me London was hotbed of evil and a city where crime lurked around every corner ready to leap out on innocent maidens like me, but the gun was fake. I'm one hundred percent fine. And very sorry about the MF word.

KATYA: OMG!!!!!!!!!!!!!!!! Exclamation marks justified. Jack's here too... Don't bother watching the YouTube video.

LOCHALSHIE WHATSAPP GROUP: There was nothing WRONG with my accent. Stop taking the mick. I single-handedly saved Caitlin.

(If you discounted Hyun-Ki's move and the armed police's eventual arrival.)

Jack watched me, waiting until I'd finished half the sandwich until he spoke.

"I flew down this morning," he said, hand fiddling with teaspoons and the sugar bowl. Nervous then. "After speaking to Katya and Dexter."

The sneaky beasts! My outrage lasted two seconds before I thanked them in my head.

"I was going to try to talk to you at lunchtime. Beg you to reconsider. Promise you I am not—and never will be—my father."

Of course he wasn't. In all the time I'd been with him, he'd been loving, kind and gentle—impatient sometimes. Grumpy too. But a hot-head who used his fists too readily? No, not the man I loved.

"I know... I know. And I, um, don't blame you for beating up your dad that time. You just wanted to protect your mum."

Jack screwed his face up, puzzled. Then, his expression cleared.

"Ah. Not guilty. Lachlan took that job upon himself. Or rather contracted it out. He's awfy protective of his own. When I found out about it, I didn't speak to him for a month."

"But Ranald thought..."

The wrong thing. Just as I had. Jack murmured something about phoning Ranald to clear his name.

The heaviness that had sat on my shoulders for far too long floated away. Joy oh joy oh joy.

More fiddling with the teaspoons. He put them down and fixed his eyes on my face. "But more than that punch, I'm ashamed of how bad-tempered I've been, Gaby. I can blame working too hard but I know I haven't been easy to be with these past few months."

That didn't strike me as fair. "Okay then, but I made so many mistakes. Proposing in public, moving to London, agreeing to Kirsty's wedding planning ideas, trying to invite your dad to the wedding. You said runaway train—it was, wasn't it?"

He took my hand, the grip fierce.

"Gaby, when I fell in love with you, I fell in love with the whole package. You're a spur of the moment type and you brought tonnes of fun and laughter to my life. Still do."

He winked. I melted. Jack's winks are killer—a slow sweep of eyelashes over a cheekbone and a move that manages to be sweet and utterly filthy at the same time.

"Jack, when my life flashed in front of my eyes—"

A tiny upturn of the mouth there. A reaction to the Gaby tendency for overdramatics.

"And Nanna Cooper's voice started up in my head."

Alarm. Jack had heard his fair share of Nanna Cooper sayings in the time we'd been together.

"She said, 'don't regret the things you do, regret the things you don't.' If I don't marry you it will be the worst mistake of my life!"

The last came out a lot louder than I intended. Four people nearby cheered, ramping up the volume even louder when Jack got out of his seat, hauled me to my feet and snogged the living daylights out of me.

Luckily for us, the cafe manager liked nothing better than helping along love's young dream, especially if people took pics, hashtagged them with the shop's name #CoffeeBeanz and #love, and loaded them on Instagram as they did with us.

Jack's hand in mine, I took a bow and our coffee shop audience clapped and cheered once more.

"People get Londoners wrong," I said as I sat down. "Perfectly friendly folks."

More cheers, but disagreement too as they called out their home cities and countries, none of them London.

Something struck me. I might have forgiven Jack but what about that court case?

"I'll stick by you, you know that, and we can get married whenever. Five years' time, if needs be. I'll visit you in prison. I'm not going to smuggle things in stuffed up my doo-dah but I'm—"

He held up a hand to stop me. "You've not heard then? Zac's dropped all charges."

"What?"

"Your best friend paid him a visit."

Oh. Ranald made Lachlan promise he wouldn't drop by Zac and use his own unique form of persuasion. He warned the wrong person, my mind flashing back to Katya stabbing tofu with her chopstick.

Jack shook his head, smiling. "She appealed to his better side. Maybe flirted a bit. Zac worshipped the ground Katya walked on, remember? Anyway, it worked. The procurator fiscal's office has no case against me if the man I'm meant to have assaulted says he's not willing to take the stand. Helps too, that he's remembered I said 'southerner' rather than English so it's no longer racist."

I clapped my hands. And then put them down again. When I fired Kirsty, I did next to nothing to arrange wedding things myself and then Katya had cancelled what little I'd done anyway. And now we had less than two weeks until this thing was supposed to take place. Never mind the rose petals on the bed, there was no venue, no minister, no invites sent out, no dress, no nothing.

"The Lochside Welcome!" I wailed. "Ashley was depending on us to ruin the Royal George's official launch. What are we going to do?"

Jack reached over, taking hold of my hand. "I've got something I want to run past you. How would you like…"

CHAPTER 30

"Lovely day for a wedding!" Jack yanks the curtains open.
"Isn't it?" I say, and burst out laughing.

He joins in. It's a terrible day for a wedding. Winter has begun in earnest. The skies are slate grey and the rain has only just stopped. You can tell it won't stay away for long as a dirty great cloud hangs over Maggie Broon's Boobs. The loch is murky brown and the wind ripples through the bare branches of the trees either side.

"Doesn't matter, though, does it?" He takes a flying leap and lands on top of me. I protest half-heartedly—he's heavy. But when a tall, muscular red-head gets on top of you, you welcome the weight. I wriggle down a bit so we align in all the right places and giggle some more.

I seem to have laughed non-stop for the past few days.

Mildred wanders in. She woke me at six am to feed her. I did so, but as it's now eight thirty, Mildred's tummy is empty once more. And I'm the softer touch. I get up, promising Jack I'll be right back and wander past two plastic-bag covered outfits hanging at the front of the wardrobe.

The formal wear.

The ceremony is at 11am—an early kick off in deference to the time of year. Hope was expressed re afternoon possibilities. Perhaps there was the chance of photos outside the Lochside Welcome, loch in the background and the happy couple beaming with delight. I glance out the window once more. The BBC weather app reckoned on a seventy-five percent chance of rain, apart from 12pm when the figure reduces to sixty-seven percent for an hour.

Oh well.

Back in bed, we start the day the best way. Afterwards, I lie in Jack's arms, Mildred purring her head off on my chest. Jack strokes my hair and murmurs the odd endearment. Scotsmen aren't known for their verbosity when it comes to expressing their feelings chat, but Jack has decided to be a bit more fluent in it. And I practise upfront honesty and discussing ideas and plans with him rather than hurtling full tilt at everything.

He stretches. "Would the love of my life and the thrill of my heart like breakfast? A big one to keep her energy levels up?"

"Yes please," I say, "and can I have it in bed?"

"You once told me you'd kick me out of bed for leaving crumbs in there," Jack says, getting up. I wonder if I'll ever get sick of the sight of him. Muscular abs, pecs and biceps developed thanks to all the champion caber tossing and dark red hair which turns up in interesting places...

"... but that I wouldn't kick you out for farting," I tell him back, "so I think you can put up with some crumbs."

As it happens, the breakfast in bed doesn't materialise. Well, the breakfast does but our doorbell goes at nine thirty just as the smell of toast and grilled bacon has drifted upstairs. I groan and plant my hand on my head, and then smile to myself anyway.

I'm back in Lochalshie on what might be one of the biggest days in the village's history—if you don't count 13 October 1745 when Bonnie Prince Charlie visited and tried to round up support for his campaign. (Two villagers joined him. The rest were sensible fellows and didn't fancy the odds.) So, it is unrealistic of me to expect Lochalshie's residents to leave us alone for much of today.

The door opens and I hear Jack greet Mhari and Lachlan. More voices. Stewart and Jolene and Hyun-Ki too? We haven't worked out if Mhari is with Hyun-Ki or Lachlan. I don't think they know either.

I pull on an old Dalmatian-style onesie and venture downstairs. Mhari, Lachlan, Hyun-Ki Stewart, Jolene and Tamar are in the living room, Jack having made them cups of tea. Stewart shouts through a few words of breakfast-making encouragement—along the lines of bacon sandwiches are all well and good, but porridge is just the thing on a wedding day. If a man's to stop sowing his wild oats, he might as well eat them.

They're all changed and ready. Lachlan and Stewart are in their kilts—one tartan red and black, the other green and gold. Hyun-Ki is hipster trendy in drain-pipe chinos with a butterfly embellishment up one leg. Mhari's tonged her hair and wears a flower-printed too tight dress and Jolene's in a maxi with a floaty wrap over the top of it. Even little Tamar looks smart—a tiny kilt over his nappy and a little fake jacket and shirt top on.

Mhari takes me in and looks at the time on her phone.

"Aye, aye Gaby—cutting it fine, aren't ye?"

I flap my hand. "I've got loads of time. It never takes me that long to get ready."

"That's obvious," she says, "though I'd have thought you'd put a bittie more effort in today."

I flick two fingers at her and blow her a raspberry. Doesn't matter anyway. Nothing touches me at the moment.

Thankfully, none of our guests want breakfast, though Mhari mooches a slice of toast lavishly covered in Nutella. I work my way through two sandwiches, tomato sauce dripping down my chin. The doorbell goes again.

"Gaby! You've got tomato sauce on your cheeks. I once had a patient who wouldnae eat anything unless it was covered in tomato sauce. D'ye know how much sugar's in that stuff? It rots your teeth and does awfy things to your tummy."

Caroline steps back. "Shouldn't you be washed and changed by now?"

I repeat the 'it won't take me long line' and she shakes her head. "Well, I just need to drop this off and then I'd better get to the Lochside Welcome. Dinnae be late, will ye?"

She hands me a bag, kisses me on the cheek and leaves. I look in the bag—four things. I've no idea what they are supposed to be for. It must be some weird Psychic Josie nonsense. Perhaps Jack will know what they mean.

Our guests decide they've had enough of our hospitality. "See you at the Lochside Welcome in an hour, then?" Jolene says. "Gonna be a great day." As she leaves, she looks back over her shoulder at the Royal George. Its car park is full and a huge green-gold sign out the front announces the official launch day. She sticks up a hand, pulling down her forefinger with her thumb so the middle fingers sticks straight up and winks at me. I laugh when everyone else turns to do the same.

I've a feeling the Royal George's official launch event—a tasting dinner with brilliant new chef Zac Cavanagh, £550 a head, which includes bed and breakfast, and a murder mystery event in the evening led by a top crime author—is about to be eclipsed. Spectacularly.

Jack's in the shower when I return. "Can I join you?" I call out and I get an enthusiastic 'yes' back. The trouble with warm water, soap and naked bodies is that the shower tends to last five times as long as it should. By the time we finish, I'm pink-cheeked and Jack's panting hard once more. And I've got twenty-five minutes to get dressed, made-up and along to the Lochside Welcome in time.

I shake Caroline's bag out onto the bed. A pair of pearl clip-on earrings, a jewelled hair slide in a packet, a blue garter and a vintage Chanel clutch bag.

"Do you know why your mum gave me these?" I ask, holding the bag up.

Jack swipes the garter, puts it between his teeth and winks at me rakishly.

"I'm supposed to remove this from your thigh with my teeth later on as everyone watches and cheers."

"Get away," I say, horrified.

He grins. "Not really. She's a bit late with it but Mum's given you something old," he picks up the earrings. "Something new." The hair slide. "Something borrowed." The bag. "And something blue." The garter.

No-one will know if I'm not wearing that garter—at least I hope they won't. I pull it on anyway. Jack and I make our own luck, but no harm in asking the universe to lend a hand. I hold my dress in front of me. It's beautiful. Not the designer one Katya originally picked out, but lovely anyway. An empire line, sleeveless maxi in a moss green silk blend material. Ever so slightly 18th century and Outlander?

Jack zips me up, standing behind me so we can inspect our reflections in the mirror.

"You're gorgeous," he says, as he drops tiny kisses on the back of my neck. "So are you," I whisper back. Lachlan and Stewart scrub up nicely in a kilt, but the man I fell in love with has always been its best model. He wears one of the older ones, its colours not as bright, all the better to show off his red-gold hair. His shirt's open at the neck.

I manage a bit of face powder and some lipstick but Kirsty's routine—primer, concealer, brightening serum, foundation, bronzer, eyelash volumiser, mascara, brow pencil and the hundred or so other products—falls by the wayside. I remind myself that she is not a bad old stick. Didn't she send me a message recently, wishing me luck? Via the medium of Instagram of course and the photo one of Caitlin and I together so it got hundred more likes and comments than had it just been me.

Jack holds out his hand. "Ready for a wedding," he says, and I squeeze his fingers. "Too right."

Outside, the rain has stayed away. The George's car park is still full, but plenty of people make their way in the opposite direction towards the Lochside Welcome. They raise their hands in "hellos" and across the street, Jamal brings in his seasonal display of welly boots, and turns the sign on the shop door to 'closed'.

Katya and Dexter are outside the Lochside Welcome, Dexter with his phone glued to his ear as he makes the last-minute arrangements. I spot my mum and Dylan with Nanna Cooper whose shiny blue sixty-five pounds dress is having its second outing. She shivers, Scotland's cold too brutal to bear. "Go inside, Nanna," I tell her. "Ashley's made a special cocktail in honour of the occasion. I think it's got brandy in it. Might warm you up."

Dylan looks me up and down and tells me my dress colour matches my complexion. Brothers, eh? I don't recommend them. He threads one arm through Nanna Cooper's, the other through my mum's and they go inside.

The Highland Tours minibus pulls up, a white ribbon pulled in a V-shape at the front. The driver—Ranald—has just picked up someone from the airfield at Oban. The door opens and the someone accompanied by her brother, Rylan, beams at us all.

"Ready?" Dexter asks, and she nods. "Uh-huh. Let's do this."

Katya, Jack and I walk into the Lochside Welcome where a sea of faces greet us—smiles, Sunday best outfits, and the clash of too many perfumes. Lochalshie folks like their scents last century and dominant. I swear someone is wearing Poison and two people have doused themselves in Obsession. Ashley has filled the pub space with chairs, an aisle down the middle and the local minister at the front tugging nervously at his dog collar. Pink and silver balloons and bunting decorate the walls.

When Jack and I take two of the reserved seats at the front and an unknown man in a tux slips to his place in front of the minister, confusion starts up. Not from everyone, but the furious whispering around us makes it impossible for me to keep a straight face. Behind me, Laney Haggerty leans forward in her seat. "Aye, all right then. What's goin' on, Gaby?" But the end of her sentence is cut off when the wedding march starts up. Ever heard it done by a piper? It's something else.

Everyone turns to the back where Dexter stands, the woman beside him veiled. I spot Ashley in his master of ceremonies suit and jaw dropped in slavish devotion as they begin their slow progression up the aisle. Whispering starts up again. Lots of "Is its" and "Can't be, can its".

The bride to be has chosen a short shift dress, an asymmetric hem and lace overlaying silk tassels from the skirt hanging behind her. It looks fabulous showing off her thin, shiny tanned legs, even if it's not the best choice for this time of year. The man who watches her walk up the aisle is awestruck and when she gets there, he lifts the veil and he and she exchange their own secret smiles before she glances over her shoulder at that sea of faces. A chorus of 'Ooh!s' sounds.

Welcome to a wedding—that of Caitlin Cartier and Donal Byrne.

·· ❧ ··

A FEW OF US WERE IN on it. Dexter and Katya, and Jack and I obviously. Ashley. The minister. My family, Jack's family and a select few friends—one of whom was told in no uncertain terms that if she breathed a word of this we would drum her out of the village.

Caitlin got the idea following our chat at my hen night. Why not marry secretly in Scotland at the place where she'd launched her Blissful Beauty range a year and a half ago, and avoid the circus her wedding would become if her agent/mother/publicist took over? She and Donal could always hold a big party in LA afterwards. Strictly speaking, paperwork for a wedding needs to be returned no later than twenty-nine days beforehand. But if you bung a substantial amount of money to a cash-strapped council and tell them to use it for social housing or further development of the tourist trade, these things can be overlooked.

The ceremony over, the official photographer moves into place to take a picture of the happy couple. Mhari holds her phone up, clicks the button and there it is—pic added to her Instagram feed, and Caitlin and the Lochside Welcome tagged in. Hyun-Ki fiddles around with the photo with the photo-editing package on his phone and adds it to the official Caitlin newsfeed. When the Lochside Welcome phone rings in reception minutes later, Ashley unplugs it.

There will be paparazzi photographers in Glasgow or Edinburgh who act as stringers for the major media outlets, but it's going to take them a while to get here. Particularly, as there's been yet another landslide at the Rest and Be Thankful blocking the main road to Lochalshie so that traffic needs to take a forty-five mile diversion.

Caroline, my mum and nanna make their way over to join Jack and I as we help ourselves to Ashley's specially created canapés. The bride and groom are chatting to Donal's mum, dad and six sisters who all came over last night.

Laney Haggerty pushes her way into our group.

"Aye, very good," she says, grabbing hold of my left hand. On it, a thin platinum bands sits under the engagement ring. "When did youse get married?"

"Yesterday," I say. "Sorry about the deception. We did it in Oban. Caitlin said she was happy to share her celebration with our one so here we are."

"I wasnae invited!" she says, huffily. I hug her and say we didn't have much money to spare so had to stick to only a few guests. It's true but a tiny, no-fuss marriage—we both wore jeans, went to Monaghan's fish and chip shop afterwards and were back in Lochalshie by five o'clock—seemed perfect in the end. Far closer to what we had originally imagined way back when I proposed and before the runaway train took over.

And now we get to join in Caitlin's more lavish celebration, even though it's miniscule compared to what would have happened had her family got their way. Her brother Rylan refuses to appear on the family show so is much more low profile. He seems taken with Stewart and Jolene, Jolene in particular. Awestruck adoration is easy to recognise.

We're among the last ones at the bar hours later. Ranald took Caitlin and Donal back to Oban where they've flown off to Ireland for their honeymoon. She must love cold, wet weather. The Irish lot are still partying hard, trying to outdo Stewart in how much booze they can put away. My mum's on the champagne and my nanna's fallen asleep in the corner.

I haven't looked at my phone that much today, but Mhari's been glued to hers. Hyun-Ki added a non-removable 'photo credit Mhari Colquhoun' line to the Instagram photos, and a watermark to the one he touched up. If any of media outlets want the official Caitlin wedding pic, they need to pay Mhari to remove it. So far, the pic has made the New York Times, the Washington Post, Sky, the BBC, CNN, the Daily Mail and numerous gossip sites.

Mhari, by now on her fourth Aperol Spritz, tells us she's thinking of quitting the pharmacy and starting up as a photographer. Her Instagram following quadrupled minutes after that pic went up, and now she can count her followers in hundreds of thousands.

Ashley presents me with my second helping of the chocolate decadence dessert he created for Caitlin when she first came to Lochalshie. I'm back to being his favourite person in the whole world. Well, second behind Caitlin.

"Fantastic day, Gaby," he tells me, a broad grin lighting up his face. "I'm now booked solid for the next three years."

He hugs me, kissing my cheek. "You tell that man of yours he'd better look after you right. Otherwise, I'll come after him."

Jack smiles. "I promise." He helps himself to a (too big) piece of my cake and asks if I want to go for a walk. I jump off my stool, find my coat and we leave. No-one notices us go.

Outside, it has stopped raining. There's a full moon too so the night's velvety-blue-blackness allows us to see Maggie Broon's Boobs in the background and the silvery tips of the waves on the loch. I breathe in lungfuls of seaweed-scented air. Jack takes my hand and we walk beside it.

"No regrets, Mrs McAllan?" he asks and I shake my head. My wedding day was perfect.

"And Blissful Beauty are okay with you not going back to London?"

Blissful Beauty will do whatever I tell them. That's what you get when you count as Caitlin's best buddy (an elite group of 750), save her from a crazed gunman and help her with a secret wedding.

"No, I'm going to work remotely and stay here with my grumpy Scotsman," I say, and smile to show I'm joking.

He blows out air. "I can't change completely but I'll try harder. When we split, I—"

His voice cracks and I shush him, determined this day is nothing but happy. He takes me in his arms and I rest my head against his shoulder, his head on top of mine. We stay there a while, the noise from the Lochside Welcome drifting over us. I am an outsider in Lochalshie and yet I am not. The wind whips around us and the deep breaths I take replant me in the sandy shores. I took up roots here a long time ago.

Jack bends his head and our mouths meet. We've exchanged plenty of kisses in our time together. This one's different. The cold air seals the two of us together, one pair of hot lips on top of another and I think of the promises we made yesterday.

Jack decided in the end against making me promise not to steal his chips, recognising it as a vow I couldn't keep. Instead he went for sweet simplicity.

"*I choose you—to stand by your side and sleep in your arms. I'll laugh with you in the good times and struggle alongside you in the bad, learn with you, grow with you even as time and life change us both...*"

Does he think of them now too? His arms tighten around me. The kiss deepens. If I open my eyes, I'll see stars and fireworks lighting up the skies—a comet that writes the words Jack + Gaby 4Ever with its tail.

We come up for air eventually.

"Home?" he asks.

"Yes," I say. "Poor old Mildred hasn't been fed since early this morning. She'll not be happy."

He slings an arm around my shoulders and we head back towards his house.

"Next chapter then, Gaby," he says, and I agree.

I can't wait.

THE END

THE GRATEFUL THANKS BIT

Oof. Another book and a tonne of people to thank... it definitely takes a community to raise a book!

This time, I was able to use three people who have creative writing qualifications as beta readers and I hope the text reflects this advantage. Sincere thanks to Emily Banks, Kristien Potgieter and Jackie Copleton whose thoughtful and considered advice did much to shape the final version of this book. I'm also grateful to Caron Allan and Kimberly on Wattpad for the supportive comments they made as I posted chapters there. Jackie also proofread the book. And is still friends with me, despite me having no idea what to hyphenate and where a comma goes... All remaining errors my own!

Thanks as always to my lovely family—my mum and sisters who are always so supportive. Sandy is my own Highlander, a far better version of Jamie Fraser, and the man who makes all this possible. Much love!

Apologies to Sam Heughan and Beatie Edney. Forgive my tongue-in-cheek borrowing of yourselves to use in this book. Acknowledgements too, to Diana Gabaldon and the Outlander series. If you haven't yet read the books, I envy you. A marvellous treat awaits.

Lochalshie is very loosely based on Arrochar in Argyll & Bute. On a sunny day, it's a gorgeous place to visit. As sunny days aren't that common in this part of the world, it's still amazing even when the clouds hang low and rain threatens.

I have a story to share... You've probably worked out how much of a cat lover I am. Earlier this month, we lost our own beloved pet, Freddie—a moggie as thoroughly spoiled as Mildred. He was knocked down on the A82. Kind strangers found him as he was spasming, moved him off the road, wrapped him in a blanket, found out where they could take him and drove him to the small animal clinic. He was dead on arrival.

The clinic vet gave me the name of the strangers—Dave and Laura Rundell. I spoke with them and the next day, they turned up on my doorstep, bunch of flowers in hand. They don't even live in my town. I will remember their act of kindness for the rest of my life.

We will find ourselves another cat, which gives me another opportunity to spread the adopt not shop message. There are thousands of cats and dogs in shelters waiting for their forever home. If you're in a position to do so, can you provide one with a home?

My other books are:

Highland Heart[1]—an absent boyfriend, a charmer nearby. Who will Katya choose?

Highland Fling[2]—a boy, a girl, a dating guru; what can possibly go wrong?!

The Night We First Met[3]—the Highland Books prequel short story

Artists Town[4]—friendship, first love and the secrets we keep

The Girl Who Swapped[5]—from 19 to 41 in one night, WTF?!

Ten Little Stars[6]—a collection of short stories

The Diabetes Diet[7]—blood sugar management via the low-carb diet

---

1. https://books2read.com/HighlandHeart
2. https://books2read.com/Highland-Fling
3. https://books2read.com/nightwemet
4. https://books2read.com/artiststown
5. https://books2read.com/tgws
6. https://books2read.com/tenlittlestars
7. https://books2read.com/diabetesdiet

You can click on the links above to view or buy them.

If you would like to join my mailing list, please email me at pinkglitterpubs@gmail.com Infrequent updates, cat chat and the guaranteed guarding of your email address with my life... My website is https://emmabaird.com[8]—musings, extracts of my writings and updates on what I am doing/writing.

Gaby, Jack and the gang will be back next year (2020) in **Highland Chances**.

Emma Baird, December 2019

---

8. https://emmabaird.com/